Smith's
MONTHLY

Every Month Original
Novels, Stories, and Articles

USA Today Bestselling Writer
Dean Wesley Smith

TABLE OF CONTENTS

Short Stories

SMITH'S MONTHLY ISSUE #45

All Contents copyright © 2021 Dean Wesley Smith
Published by WMG Publishing
Cover and interior design copyright © 2021 WMG Publishing
Cover art copyright © by Olek/DepositPhoto
ISBN-13: 978-1-56146-688-7
ISBN-10: 1-56146-688-3

The Writings and Opinions of
Dean Wesley Smith

Introduction to Issue #45
I'm Back!

The last issue, #44, was dated May 2017. I was already starting to get behind at that point, so it really didn't hit the stands until the late fall of 2017.

And that was it. Nothing since.

You see, that fall my wonderful (and very talented) wife's heath was getting worse. And I was losing my focus on the writing as we worked hard to try to figure out what was even happening. No real clue.

And other than Kris's closest friends, no one knew how bad she was getting. And Kris even hid it from our close friends for the most part.

And to make matters worse, I was spending a lot of time at WMG Publishing trying to get it through a rough patch. So putting out another issue of *Smith's Monthly* at that point seemed to just be impossible.

And honestly, it was.

With the help of a great friend, I decided Kris needed to be near some of the top hospitals in the world. And away from where we were living, where she couldn't even go out to a restaurant, let alone anything else she wanted to do.

So my friend and I, while we were down here in Las Vegas on a poker trip, found a great condo just blocks from the medical district and a month later I had Kris sort of packed and in our van headed for Las Vegas.

She started getting better almost at once. And within a couple of months she was active and getting energy back. Without a doctor's help.

It seems that Kris is one of the many, many people in the world who have a severe allergy to mold. It is a genetic thing, the scientists just figured out this last year. That's why Kris was getting sick and I was not while living in the same house.

Although, in hindsight, I did get feeling better here in the dry air and sunshine as well. So a side-point. If you have a chronic illness and are living in a damp part of the planet, you might want to look at your environment. We lived in a huge house overlooking the Pacific Ocean in Oregon. And the house leaked at times. Nothing was obvious on the surface. Nothing. But it still almost killed Kris.

After that I spent most of the next year cleaning up the mess we left on the Oregon Coast, writing some, but not finding my footing here in Las Vegas until this last summer and fall.

I didn't want to start this magazine back up again until I felt sure I could once again fill it. And that I could handle the work it takes to produce an issue and get it out.

Seems that 2020 was going to be the time. And then it wasn't for reasons everyone in the world knows.

So once again this magazine was put on the back burner until we had an idea where we were going.

It wasn't until the vaccines were introduced that I felt like I could actually look ahead again.

And that this magazine had a chance of being regular, as it had been for the first forty-four issues.

As I write this I already have four issues done and ready for formatting. I have learned InDesign again and will do all the layout of the paperback versions.

So for those of you who have waited and wondered what happened, I want to thank you. I hope over this year I can make the wait worth it.

But no matter what, it feels wonderful to be back.

—Dean Wesley Smith
January 10th, 2021

Can't Get Enough of Marble Grant?
These stories and more are available at your favorite booksellers.

Coming Next Issue in *Smith's Monthly*

HOT SPRINGS MEADOW
A Thunder Mountain Short Novel

Smith's
MONTHLY

NUMBER FORTY-SIX
FEBRUARY, 2021

*Original Stories,
Novels, and Articles*

DEAN WESLEY SMITH

HOT SPRINGS MEADOW
A Thunder Mountain Short Novel

USA *Today* Bestselling Writer

DEAN WESLEY SMITH

BLACK COFFEE

A Marble Grant Story

Ghosts Marble and Sims, with their new roommate, accounting superhero Canyon Stevens, must face a problem worse than death:

A perfect cup of coffee.

A cup of coffee so good, orgasms nearly resulted from a single sip.

Yeah, that good. And that dangerous.

Another wild day in the ghost-life of sexy Marble Grant

BLACK COFFEE
A Marble Grant Story

ONE

IT'S A RARELY KNOWN FACT that when you are dead, everything just tastes better.

And I do mean everything.

Two months before, my wonderful girlfriend Sims and I had invited Canyon Stevens to come live with us. We had started out just caring for him after a surgery because he was a superhero and we had saved his life.

It turned out that for two women ghost agents, having a real living superhero in the house had come in real handy for a lot of things.

Now granted, he was wonderful eye-candy, with muscles that sort of rippled on his very, very real and very much alive body. And he had a face that made every man and woman turn to look at him when he walked by.

Even better, he had no idea how good-looking he was and was the most down-home nice guy either of us had ever met.

But wow, just wow, was he a looker. I don't think there was a night that Sims and I didn't sigh audibly when he came out of his bedroom in his sweatpants and a T-shirt to watch some television.

And, on top of being the most handsome, funny, and smart living man I had ever met, he had been cooking for us. And that man could cook.

I mean food. Cook food.

He was a new superhero in business, but both Sims and I were convinced he should move over to work for the gods of food and fine dining.

He was making our wonderful condo in the Ogden in Las Vegas feel like a slice of heaven every day with the smells of his latest meal and tastes that often just make me close my eyes and sigh.

And since both Sims and I were dead, it might be said we did live in heaven. I loved Sims and the two of us just fit together like I had never fit with another woman, or man before. And sex with Sims was insane, so much so we often didn't go an evening in a week without making love.

And, of course, having Mr. GQ walking half naked around our wonderful place didn't hurt in firing up the engines for Sims or me. We were both healthy women who swung on the gate in both directions.

Our two-bedroom condo that Poker Boy had bought for us to live in was modern, with a wonderful, state-of-the-art kitchen where a girl could sit at the counter and look out through expansive windows at Las Vegas. And if you went out to the table on our patio, the view was of the Strip.

Both Sims and I had started making it a habit to sit at the kitchen counter for a different view. We would just sit there and talk and watch Canyon cook.

It was like a dance of beauty as far as we were concerned.

And his sense of humor kept us all laughing at the same time.

Both of us had often wondered if Canyon was interested in seeing if ghosts and superheroes could make a threesome in bed as well as in saving people in the real world.

But it was a moot point at the moment. Sims and I had a problem having sex with anyone real. We could not yet touch much of anything physical.

In fact, until Canyon moved in with us, we had a wonderful living area of soft couches and chairs with a television on the wall that we never turned on because we couldn't.

Neither one of us could even push a button on a remote. How sad was that?

Not a great deal annoyed us about being dead, but that one detail did and we worked on it all the time. Both Sims and I really needed to learn how to touch real physical things, make them move just a little. Not only would it come in handy at times when we were trying to save someone, but for real-life things like turning on a light switch or a television.

But since we had both been dead less than a year, we were told by Jewel, our mentor and a ghost agent more advanced than we were, that the touching skill was still in our future.

Now, on normal days, I was the last person awake of our little team of superheroes and ghosts. Canyon was always gone, off at work in his expensive, tailored suits, when I came staggering out of bed to get my coffee.

And Sims would have gone out on her own a few times as well. Once I got my sorry ass moving, we then worked together in the afternoon and early evening. Then we would spend time at home together with Canyon for dinner. After both Canyon and Sims were off to bed, I headed out for a late-night patrol.

As ghost agents, our job was to help people where we could. We could merge with people, read their thoughts, their problems, and give them help or direct them to help with planted suggestions or memories.

A couple times in our months together, Sims and I had run into some really nasty people, but almost all people were just normal people, with normal worries and hates and loves and such.

We also found medical problems at times, which is how we had met Canyon and discovered he was a superhero like we had been before our deaths. And we had saved his life.

This morning, expecting no one to be in the kitchen when I came staggering out, I was surprised to see both Sims and Canyon sitting at the kitchen counter sipping coffee.

And neither of them had on their happy face.

But wow did the kitchen smell wonderfully of coffee, maybe the richest smell I had had the pleasure to experience. Usually Sims just brought me a cup of coffee from a nearby coffee shop. But this morning Canyon had brewed some fresh.

I had started wearing a bathrobe to the kitchen for my pre-shower coffee after Canyon moved in, so as I poured a cup, I said, "I suppose I really shouldn't ask."

"Get your shower and your coffee," Sims said. "Then we'll talk over your breakfast and our lunches."

Canyon nodded. "We ran into a situation that will take all three of us to deal with."

I nodded and turned to head back to the bedroom with my coffee mug in my hand. As I went, I took a sip.

And damn near had an orgasm right there at the edge of the kitchen.

The coffee was rich, had a flavor I couldn't identify, but didn't mind, and just sort of went into my system like a shot of drugs.

Now I know that things taste better when you are dead, but I don't think my heart could handle coffee tasting this good every morning.

I turned and looked back at both Sims and Canyon who were still not smiling.

"What the hell is this?" I asked, pointing at my mug.

"Incredible coffee, isn't it?" Sims asked, picking up her mug.

"By far the best I have ever tasted," I said. "Where did you find it?"

Canyon frowned. And even with a frown he was still the most handsome man a girl could dream about.

"That's the problem we need to talk about," he said.

Great, just great.

The problem was the best-tasting coffee I could have ever imagined drinking. It was going to be one of those days in heaven.

TWO

I FINISHED my amazing mug of coffee and my shower in record time and was back in the kitchen with Sims and Canyon before Canyon had a sandwich made and some eggs and toast cooking for me.

Canyon was wearing his dress shirt and slacks and had his suit coat tossed over the back of a bar stool at the counter. Sims wore the same basic thing she and I wore every day. Tennis shoes, jeans, and expensive blouses. Since we were ghosts, we could see no reason to dress up for going out to work since no one could see us anyway.

Canyon made one sandwich for himself and Sims ate the ghost element of his sandwich. It didn't bother the flavor for him at all. The eggs and toast and bacon I was eating would get tossed out in the real world because all I would do would be to eat the ghost element of them.

However, Canyon said he would save the bacon for sandwiches later.

I noticed that neither Sims nor Canyon were drinking coffee when I arrived and the coffee pot was empty and turned upside down in the sink to be rinsed out later.

We all took our food to the dining room table and as we all started eating, I slowly managed to dig my brain out of the last dream I had been having when I woke up.

Finally, I asked, "What was that coffee thing all about?"

"This morning," Canyon said, "I was meeting with a young couple about a startup they were trying to put together. They wanted to expand their small coffee shop out near the old Boulder Highway into a chain of shops."

"Seems a little small-fry for the types of things you normally deal with," I said to Canyon.

Canyon nodded. "I look at all levels, usually above this sort of thing, but I was asked by a friend of theirs to look at what they were planning and see if I could maybe get them to the right level of funding."

"They have a decent plan?" Sims asked between bites of the BLT sandwich.

"They did, actually," Canyon said, nodding. "Some basic beginner issues, but their plan was solid and their income

on their small first store showed the potential."

"So what went wrong?" I asked.

"While I had them filling out some forms for me," he said, "I looked up their location and some pictures of their place. A normal small coffee shop should not be doing those sorts of income numbers. So I dug deeper and found that every picture and article showed lines of cars down the block for their drive-up and half-block lines for their walk-up window."

"I can believe it," I said, remembering that cup of coffee and how it tasted. It felt almost addictive.

"You guys have those little alarm bells in your head when something feels wrong?" Canyon asked.

"I call it my little voice," Sims said, nodding.

"Mine actually sounds like a bell on a small store door," I said, "which I have to admit is a ton better than say a Star Trek door-swoosh opening sound."

Canyon laughed and Sims smiled.

"I hear that swoosh sound every time I kiss you," Sims said to me. "I am pretty sure it's the sound of my panties falling off."

Canyon, bless his heart, blushed and I just laughed.

"So you had alarm bells go off," Sims said. "So what did you do?"

"I said to the couple that I was interested in helping them, but would need to see their place and sample their coffee."

"And that's when you sampled their coffee and brought some home for us?" I asked.

Canyon nodded. "The moment I tasted it I knew it was too good to be true. But I honestly have no experience in this sort of thing."

"We need to go find out what they are doing," I said to Sims.

"Give us the address," Sims said to Canyon as we stood and both pushed our plates in.

Canyon gave us the address. I knew exactly where it was.

"What do the young owners look like?" Sims said.

Canyon gave us a quick description and said they should either be there or at their small office in a nearby warehouse.

"We'll be right back," I said.

I sure hoped that this coffee was real and legitimate. But the little warning bell in my head was telling me it wasn't going to be.

And that we needed to be damn careful.

THREE

ONLY FOUR young college-aged kids were working in the roadside coffee shop. It was the size of a small bedroom inside and smelled so thick of coffee I bet you could almost drink the air.

All four of the college kids were efficient and friendly and had no idea about anything other than getting tips and getting as many people through the lines as they could. We checked all of them out quickly and then jumped to the office in the warehouse.

Only the young couple was there.

The office was small and stark, with a room behind the office that functioned as a supply warehouse for their one shop. There were two metal desks, a computer on each, one window beside the door, and tile on the floor. The lighting was hanging fluorescent. I felt more like I had stepped into a prison than an office.

The woman was working on an accounting program on a computer and the guy was on the phone with a supplier of some sort.

Both of them looked like any young late-twenties couple. He had short hair, she had medium black hair, and both wore dressy clothes that were not expensive, clearly still on from having their meeting with Canyon. They both wore matching wedding rings and both looked intent.

"The guy first?" I said. "Let's go in together and be careful?"

Sims nodded. "Something feels very off here and damned if I can spot it."

"Feeling the same way," I said.

I took her hand and we stepped into the guy sitting at the desk.

And it was like sinking into a black pool of ink.

No thoughts, just pure blackness.

Evil blackness.

I yanked Sims sideways and we tumbled to the ground beside the guy.

We both lay on the dirty tile of the office floor, panting, staring up at the guy as he went on with his phone call as if nothing was wrong.

Then it finally dawned on me what I was seeing.

The guy's aura was almost black. So was the woman's aura.

"No aura," I said to Sims as I tried to catch my breath.

She nodded.

When we had trained, we had learned to look at people's auras to get a sense if they needed help or not. Everyone had colorful auras and we had used the training to just sort of link in with our gut sense.

No wonder we thought something was wrong here. We didn't even notice that both of them had almost no aura. And that what they had was black.

"Back to the condo," I said.

Sims nodded and a moment later we were standing beside Canyon in our wonderful kitchen, breathing hard.

We needed help and we needed it quickly.

"Jewel, emergency."

Jewel was one of the ghost agents who had trained us. Jewel had been a medical doctor when alive and she was the one who taught us to look for heart problems in people that had then saved Canyon's life.

Jewel appeared, looking worried.

Canyon was also looking worried at our reaction.

"What does it mean when someone has nothing but a slight black aura?" Sims asked a half-second before I could.

"And inside them is pure blackness," I said. "No thoughts, nothing."

"How long were you in there?" Jewel demanded.

"A second, maybe two," I said.

She nodded. "I'm coming in."

She stepped inside me and I could feel a wave of slight heat wash through my body.

Then she stepped out and did the same for Sims.

"You are both clear," Jewel said after she stepped out of Sims. "No infections and I put up a shield just in case I missed something."

"Infection?" Sims asked before I could get the word out of my panicked brain.

Jewel nodded. "You just came in contact with pure evil. That blackness, once spread, could take you over completely."

"So that's what happened to those two people?" Canyon asked.

"You touched them?" Jewel asked, turning to Canyon.

"Shook their hands," he said.

"I'm coming in," Jewel said.

She disappeared inside of Canyon, then came back out a moment later, nodding. "You were also clear and I gave you a protection as well."

Canyon's handsome face looked white and he nodded his thanks.

"So tell us how you found these people," Jewel said, pulling out a chair at the dining room table and sitting.

I sure wished I could move a real chair like that.

Sims and I sat in our normal chairs that were already pulled out and Canyon took his normal chair.

And for the next ten minutes we carefully relayed to Jewel everything that had happened for the three of us this morning.

Including drinking the coffee.

After we were done Jewel sort of looked at something above her for a moment and then nodded. "Magic. Magic that has already gone black."

I didn't even know magic existed until that moment, let alone that it could go black.

But I sure didn't like the sounds of it in the slightest.

Sims took my hand and squeezed it. Clearly she didn't much like it either.

FOUR

JEWEL SPENT the next fifteen minutes explaining to us that what seems like magic that superheroes and gods do is actually just talents we all have. And that we practice and improve on like practicing music.

But actual magic does exist in the world and when used, almost always turns black fairly quickly and corrupts the user. There is no such thing as good magic.

"So the coffee beans are magical?" I asked. "That's why they taste so good?"

"I would bet that was the case," Jewel said. "More than likely this young couple picked up this magic skill at some point to help their business. And when magic is used for selfish purposes like that, it turns black even faster."

"What about all the people drinking it?" Sims asked. "Are they contaminated now?"

"No," Jewel said, shaking her head. "Thankfully it doesn't work that way. But we will have to check back on all of the couple's suppliers and their workers."

"I have all their records at my office," Canyon said. "They were very complete in trying to get the financing."

"Good," Jewel said.

"So what do we do now to stop this?" I asked, almost afraid of the answer. I really never wanted to get near anything that black again.

Jewel just shook her head. "Cleaning out this kind of thing is way above all of us. Now it's time to bring in the big guns. The use of magic is one of the worst crimes in all of the world. And there are entire forces of gods and superheroes who have the task of just containing and stopping the use of magic. Our job is to find it. Nothing more."

Both Sims and I nodded.

I felt relieved, more than I wanted to admit.

Jewel looked upward slightly and focused. "Laverne, we have a magic problem."

A moment later the most powerful god in all the world appeared.

Canyon scrambled to his feet and Jewel and Sims and I also stood, but a little more calmly. We had been around Laverne, Lady Luck herself, a few times already. Canyon had as well, but he had been drugged up at the time after his operation and I was sure he didn't remember.

Laverne had on a power suit that fit her trim frame perfectly. She had her dark brown hair pulled back tightly off her face that gave her a stark look.

"Magic?" Laverne asked Jewel.

"A pretty bad infestation," Jewel said, nodding. "These three found it this morning."

Laverne looked at Sims and me and then at poor Canyon who looked like he might faint at any moment. As a new superhero, you just never imagined you would ever meet the most powerful god of them all.

"You make sure they are clean?" Laverne asked.

"I did," Jewel said. "But would not hurt for you to do so as well in case I missed something."

Laverne nodded and sort of waved her hand at the three of us standing beside the table. Again I felt a wave of heat pass through me. I imagined that would be what a hot flash would feel like, but knew I would never get that personal hell since I had died and my periods stopped cold.

As I said, being dead was like living in heaven.

"They are clean," Laverne said. "Now, we need to get started cleaning out the infection."

"It is the owners of a small coffee shop down off the old Boulder Highway," Jewel said. "They did something to make their coffee taste better."

"I have all the information about who they are, their suppliers, and so on in a file at my office."

"Good job, everyone," Laverne said. "Canyon, come with me for the file and I'll get it to the right team to clean it all up."

Canyon and Laverne vanished at that moment.

"Very good job you two," Jewel said, smiling at me and Sims. "But next time, if you see a black aura, don't go near it."

"Oh, trust me, we won't," I said.

"I don't even think I'll ever drink coffee again," Sims said.

Jewel laughed. "No need to go that far."

"Oh, good," Sims said.

Jewel laughed and then vanished.

Sims and I slumped back into our chairs at the dining room table.

"We got lucky," I said.

Sims nodded. "That could have been so, so much worse."

At that moment Canyon appeared back at the dining room table and also slumped into a chair. His face was pure white and he looked like he had just had a near-death experience.

"Lady Luck thanked me and smiled at me," he said, his voice like a small child opening a wonderful gift on Christmas.

"Fantastic!" I shouted.

Sims agreed and we just kept smiling at our shaken superhero.

Finally Canyon took a deep breath and looked up. "And then Lady Luck said I needed to start practicing jumping from one place to the next if I was going to work with and try to keep up with you two."

"You can teleport?" Sims asked.

I was stunned. If he could that would be such good news.

"I think so," Canyon said, nodding.

"Into your bedroom," I said. "Now. Don't think about it. Just jump there."

He vanished and both Sims and I started applauding.

He appeared a second later, grinning from ear to ear.

"It seems Lady Luck likes the idea of our little team," I said.

"She really does," Canyon said.

"This deserves a celebration," Sims said, clapping her hands together and laughing.

"I think what I need is a drink," Canyon said. "Maybe two."

So out we went drinking and then dancing.

Lots of dancing, lots of drinking.

The three of us dancing was so much fun. I had no idea that dancing after death was so much fun.

Celebrating our team and our first really major win felt right.

And as the evening went on, only a few people looked oddly at the handsome man in the silk suit laughing and dancing alone on the dance floor.

After all, it was Vegas and things like that happened in Vegas.

Besides, we were there with him. He was far from really alone.

And we all three loved that.

~

Now Available
from all your favorite booksellers in trade paper and electronic editions.

USA TODAY BESTSELLING AUTHOR

DEAN WESLEY SMITH

THE PORTAL OF WRONG LOVE

A POKER BOY STORY

An elderly woman makes couples disappear right off the Las Vegas Strip.

Poker Boy and Patty must first stop her and then rescue the lost couples from some unknown place in time and space.

A story of aging, of love, and sanity.

And maybe just a little sex as well.

THE PORTAL OF WRONG LOVE
A Poker Boy Story

ONE

WHEN YOUR GIRLFRIEND appears and tells you that there may be a problem, any sane man perks up and pays attention.

Close attention.

I'm Poker Boy, a superhero in the poker universe, and my girlfriend, Patty Ledgerwood, aka Front Desk Girl, is also a superhero. So not only could a "problem" be in our relationship, but it could be something that meant the world was about to explode, and we had ten minutes to save everyone or die trying.

Yeah, that saving the world thing has happened a few times. Honest.

So when she appeared and said that there may be a problem, it was sort of a double "pay attention" moment.

Patty still wore her white blouse, brown slacks, and brown vest from her front desk job at the MGM Grand.

I'd just finished playing in a poker tournament down at the Golden Nugget, so I was still in my black leather coat, fedora-like hat, and jeans that; is my superhero costume for the most part.

I hadn't expected Patty to get off work for a few more hours, at least. So I'd gotten some fries and a vanilla milkshake, and was sitting in the big diner booth in my office, just eating and staring out over the city, enjoying the moment of quiet.

Superheroes don't get many moments of quiet, and, if I'd realized that, I would have also realized the moment was about to end.

"We got a problem," Patty said, appearing beside the booth and sliding in next to me and taking a fry.

I did the right thing and perked up, paid attention, focused on her, and asked, "Good problem, bad problem, world-ending problem?"

Granted, not the smartest thing for a boyfriend to say, but she had caught me by surprise.

"I don't honestly know," Patty said, munching her fry and looking worried. "Never seen anything like this before."

She took another fry and motioned for me to follow her over to the window.

My office is an invisible glass cube that floats about a thousand feet in the air over The Las Vegas Strip. A few extra chairs and the old diner booth that sits in the very center of the room are the only furniture. I had put a wooden railing all the way around the inside of the glass to kill the feeling that any moment we might fall off the black-and-white tiled floor to our deaths on the hot pavement below.

Patty pointed to a woman on the street corner near the front of the MGM Grand main entrance. From this height, the woman looked to be in high heels,

wearing a very short mini-skirt and a blouse. She had a big orange purse over her shoulder.

It was a hot September day out there, so that street corner must have been over a hundred degrees the way the sun radiated off all the concrete in this town.

A couple of our adventures had started with us looking down on the street below, but this sure didn't seem like an adventure, or even a problem. I was feeling no sense of worry or dread or anything, other than a desire to go back and finish my fries and milkshake.

We watched for a moment as a couple near the curb moved slightly to go around the woman. The couple seemed to be arguing, and not happy with each other in any fashion. The woman reached out and touched the man, sort of like she was handing him a flyer or something, but I didn't see anything in her hand.

Then, still arguing, the couple seemed to walk into an opening in the air and just—vanish.

"What the hell?" I said, blinking to see if I had actually seen what just happened.

Again, I had no sense at all of danger from the woman, no sense that any harm was coming to the people who vanished.

"So, you've never seen this before?" I asked Patty as we both watched the woman stand there, seeming to just be casually waiting, like a hooker on a street corner. Now that I looked a little closer, she sort of looked like a hooker, even though they were illegal in Las Vegas. Of course, that didn't stop them much.

"Never," Patty said. "But I'm not getting a sense of danger from any of this."

"Neither am I," I said. "But we got to figure this out. That couple had to have gone somewhere."

I glanced up at the ceiling, which I always did out of habit when calling my boss. "Stan, a little help?"

Stan, my boss and the God of Poker, arrived an instant later. Just as I always wore a black coat, a black fedora-like hat, and jeans, Stan always wore a 1960s-style button-down cardigan sweater, tan slacks, and tan loafers. His hair was cut short and he looked like he could sell insurance in 1965.

Patty pointed to the woman below. It took Stan a moment staring at the woman before he said, "Go to hell."

Then he vanished.

"God of Poker swearing is never a good sign," I said.

Patty only nodded. "Another couple is heading toward her. What should we do?"

"If we stop them, are we saving them?" I asked.

Patty shrugged. "Not a clue."

"If she's doing something nasty to them," I said, "we'll never live with ourselves if we don't stop her."

"True," Patty said. "Very true."

TWO

I TELEPORTED us to a spot in front of the couple.

They both sort of jerked back and stopped as Patty and I appeared in front of them.

"Sorry for the surprise," I said, giving them my best smile as Patty sent calming emotions toward the two. "Sidewalk is closed for repair."

The couple, clearly from a part of the country where people didn't just materialize in front of them, stepped back, then they both turned and walked damned fast away from us.

Patty and I turned to face the woman.

I was right. The woman looked like a well-worn hooker, with a tight skirt far, far too short for her older legs. She had on a very thin white blouse that left little to the imagination, and what was under the blouse was not something I had ever wanted to imagine. Or see, for that matter.

She looked like a hooker, but one right out of central casting from a "B" movie, if the cast had come from a nursing home.

"So, where did you send that last couple?" I asked.

She smiled and my bet was that if it wasn't so hot, the caked-on makeup on her face would have cracked. Her teeth looked rotted and one was missing, and her smile didn't come close to reaching her eyes, what little I could see of them through all the makeup and wrinkles.

But even with all that, I still wasn't getting a sense of danger from her in the slightest.

"Front Desk Girl," she said. "Poker Boy, it is an honor to meet you both. I have heard so much about you."

Both Patty and I stayed a good four steps away from the woman, just standing there on the hot sidewalk. "Who do we have the pleasure of talking with?" I asked.

Stan and Laverne appeared beside us on the sidewalk at that moment and took all of us out of time, freezing the traffic around us.

Laverne, Lady Luck herself, was dressed in a gray pants suit with her long brown hair pulled back tight, giving her an even more severe look than normal.

I only wished that these time bubbles would also block out the heat, but they didn't, and my leather jacket and hat were quickly becoming too much for this hot sidewalk in early September.

"Ishtar," Laverne said, stepping forward slightly, but not going near the old woman. "It has been far too long."

I did my best to place the name. Clearly an old god of some sort, but all that was coming to me was the name of a bad movie.

"Oh, my," Patty said softly beside me.

I glanced at the love of my life. Patty's eyes were huge and she was just staring in almost shock at the old hooker.

I knew at that point I was in one of those moments where my youth and lack of knowledge of all the gods was putting me at a disadvantage. And when that happened, which seemed to be more than I wanted to admit—even to myself—I always figured silence was just the smartest thing I could do.

"Good to see you again, Laverne," Ishtar said to Lady Luck.

Neither woman bowed to the other, so I figured there was bad blood somewhere in the past between the two.

"Does Gil know you have left Uruk?" Laverne asked, her voice not cold, but not warm and welcoming and friendly either.

"That impotent fool couldn't find his ass with both hands," Ishtar said. "Just sits in his chair and rocks all day, smiling at who knows what. I needed to get back to work, have an adventure."

Laverne nodded and glanced at Stan, who instantly vanished.

"So, where were you sending the couples?" Laverne asked.

Ishtar laughed. Not a nice sound, more like fingernails across a blackboard. I am sure that if we weren't inside a time bubble at the moment, that laugh would have caused car wrecks on the busy street beside us.

"Ishtar?" Laverne said, her voice sounding more insistent.

"No damn fun," the old hooker said, seeming to pout under all the makeup. "I sent them through my portal of love to bed, of course. In that towering palace."

The old woman pointed to the MGM Grand.

I wanted to laugh at the image, but I didn't. More than likely those couples ended up naked in a bed in some strange room in the MGM Grand. That might be interesting to try to explain, especially if their clothes vanished along the way.

Patty said, "I'll get it covered."

Then she vanished.

"You understand, don't you, Laverne?" Ishtar said. "Life can be very boring and I just had to get out."

"This is a very different world now from old Babylonia," Laverne said. "Or Atlantis before that."

"I know, and I find it exciting," Ishtar said. "Just the new fashions, this thing called makeup. It is wonderful to behold, don't you agree?"

A moment later Stan appeared with a stately man. He was tall with powerful shoulders and a full head of gray hair. He was dressed in a long, white robe and wore sandals. He carried a long staff that he seemed to use for balance.

"Laverne," the man said, his voice deep and powerful. He bowed slightly to Lady Luck.

"Gil," Laverne said, bowing slightly in return.

The man named Gil turned to look at Ishtar, then shook his head and made a motion with one hand toward her.

Ishtar instantly changed from looking like an old hooker to a beautiful, but aging woman with clear skin and bright silver hair and perfect white teeth. She also wore a white flowing robe and sandals.

I was surprised at the change in her, from a low-level hooker to looking like a goddess in an instant.

"What a spoilsport," Ishtar said, looking down at how she was now dressed.

At that moment Patty appeared. "No one was transported into the hotel."

Laverne glanced back at Patty, suddenly worried.

She then turned back to Ishtar. "Is the portal you used still open?"

It is," Ishtar said, laughing, this time in a way that actually conveyed amusement. She pointed at a place in the sidewalk just beyond where she stood. "My special portal of love, as I like to call it."

"How many couples did you send through the portal, dear?" the man named Gil asked, clearly used to being patient with Ishtar.

I was starting to get the idea that Ishtar wasn't well. Laverne and Gil both treated her with respect, but also almost as a child.

"Six wonderful couples," Ishtar said. "They were not happy with each other, so I sent them to their beds of love in the magnificent tower."

Again she pointed to the MGM Grand.

Patty shook her head as Laverne again glanced at her.

Now, for the first time, my warning sense was starting to activate.

And activate big time.

Those couples were in trouble.

THREE

GIL WAVED his hand at Ishtar, and she froze.

Then he turned to face Laverne and the rest of us. "In her state, there is no telling exactly where those couples ended up."

Laverne nodded. "Are her powers fading with her memory?"

"They are," Gil said. "And becoming erratic. It's tragic to watch, but I do my best to keep track of her. I'm sorry about this."

"We know you do your best for your love," Laverne said, her voice clearly sad.

Until this moment, it had never occurred to me that a god could get dementia. How horrible for anyone, human or god. Losing my mind was one of the things that scared me more than I wanted to ever admit.

I made myself take a deep breath of the hot air and glance at Patty, then back at Laverne and Gil, who were standing silently looking at each other.

"Any way to trace where that portal goes from this side?" I asked, breaking into their lost thoughts.

Both Laverne and Gil shook their heads.

"Those couples are lost somewhere," Laverne said. "There's just no telling where."

I glanced at Patty and smiled, giving her a one-eyebrow raise.

She laughed. "I was afraid you were thinking that."

I turned to Laverne and Gil and Stan. "I think you need to release Ishtar and let her send me and Patty through the portal as well."

"There is no telling," Gil said, looking very worried, "with her decreased abilities, where or when you might end up."

"When?" Patty asked, the worry clear in her voice.

Laverne nodded. "Ishtar had the ability to send lovers through time."

"We can't let those six couples be on their own," I said, forcing myself to not think about the real consequences of walking through a portal made by a woman not completely in control of her powers. "Especially if they are in the past. Remember the last time we left people from this time remain in the past? We need to return them to here and now. And the only way to find those couples is to follow them."

"I agree," Patty said.

Gil just shook his head in amusement. "Now I see how these two young superheroes got their reputation."

"I pretty much hate this idea," Stan said. "But darned if I can think of another one."

Laverne nodded and turned to Gil. "Release Ishtar and let's do this."

Gil nodded and waved his hand, and Ishtar smiled as if nothing had happened.

"We would like to go through your portal of love," I said, taking Patty's hand and stepping down the sidewalk toward her.

"Oh, wonderful," Ishtar said, her smile beaming. The portal is still open. Just walk this way."

She indicated we should walk past her.

As we walked in front of her, she reached out and touched me slightly, giving me a wonderful smile.

Then a step later, the heat and the Las Vegas Boulevard vanished.

And so did my clothes.

FOUR

PATTY AND I ended up completely naked in a vast, rolling field of what looked like wildflowers of some sort.

All the flowers were blooming in a rainbow of colors, and white clouds drifted lazily through a bright blue sky. The temperature was warm, but not hot like it had been on the street in Las Vegas.

It felt perfect.

The flowers came up above our knees and the ground underneath felt soft and inviting. You could lie down in the flowers, and no one would see you twenty feet away.

"I don't think we're in Kansas anymore," I said, smiling at the wonderful woman I was in love with, who didn't seem to mind at all that she was standing naked in the middle of a field of beautiful flowers.

Damn she looked good.

I mean really, really good.

"These aren't poppies," Patty said. Then she waved her hand and we were dressed again just as we had been in Las Vegas. She was in her MGM Grand front desk uniform and I was back in my jeans, shirt, leather jacket and hat.

"Ah, bummer," I said. "I was enjoying the view."

""I'll give you a view later," Patty said, smiling at me. "Remember why we're here. And block the love potion part of this place."

At that moment I realized my warning senses were going off big time. She was right, there was clearly something in the air here.

I blocked out and contained all feelings of love and lust and so on, and suddenly felt almost myself again.

"That was strange," I said.

Patty nodded. "Figured from the view of the god of sex and love and prostitution, where she sent us would be filled with things to help out the cause."

"I don't remember us needing much help," I said, laughing.

She laughed as well. "Now focus. We need to find those other couples."

"First," I said, "let's see if we can figure out when and where we are."

Patty nodded and I glanced up and shouted, "Stan."

A moment later Stan, Laverne, the man named Gil, and Ishtar appeared.

I was very, very happy to see them.

Gil glanced around as Ishtar just sort of danced among the flowers.

"I should have guessed," Gil said. "Elysium. She loves this place. Always did, didn't you dear?"

"My favorite place," Ishtar said, continuing to just twirl and skip and dance like a kid in the flowers.

I was stunned to say the least. I had always assumed Elysium was in the underworld.

"Where exactly are we?" I asked, almost afraid of the answer.

"Denmark," Laverne said, matter-of-factly.

At that moment, a woman squealed and some flowers rustled about fifty paces away and a woman sat up. She was naked and clearly making love to a man under her in the flowers.

"Seems we found the missing couples," Gil said, smiling. "Or at least one couple."

"The others are here," Laverne said. "Similarly occupied."

"A wonderful place," Ishtar said, dancing in circles around them through the flowers.

"We'll come back regularly," Gil said, moving over to take Ishtar's hand.

"Oh, can we?" Ishtar asked like a kid being offered a trip to get ice cream.

"We can," Gil said, smiling.

Then he nodded and bowed slightly to Laverne, and Gil and Ishtar were gone.

"How long has she been like that?" I asked.

"Most of a century," Laverne said, her voice sad.

I had no idea what to think. I had never, ever thought of the downsides of living a very, very long time. Now losing my mind scared me even more than it did before.

At that moment, the woman in the flowers let out a high-pitched sigh of pleasure, fell forward, and vanished from sight.

Laverne turned to Patty. "I'll alert your boss at the MGM Grand that six rooms are going to be needed in a few minutes, and Stan will bring the room numbers back to you and help in the transport."

"We'll wait here and then get the couples to the rooms," I said, nodding. "And we'll leave them clothes for when they surface…or run out of energy."

Laverne nodded, and she and Stan vanished.

"An amazing place," Patty said, looking around at the vast rolling fields of flowers and the wonderful blue sky. "I've always heard about this place, never thought I would actually see it. It's more beautiful than I had ever imagined."

Behind them, laughter echoed over the flowers.

I took Patty's hand and turned as a naked couple jumped up and the woman chased the man about twenty feet through the field until she caught him. Then laughing, they again vanished from sight, tumbling into the soft flowers.

"Damn that looks like fun," I said, smiling at the woman I loved beside me.

Patty laughed. "It does, doesn't it? Tell you what? Later tonight I'll chase you naked around my apartment a few times."

"Promise?" I asked.

"Promise," she said, squeezing my hand.

A sigh of pleasure echoed over the flowers from somewhere. And damned if I wasn't sure if it was me doing the sighing.

—

More WMG Writer's Guides
from all your favorite booksellers
in trade paper and electronic editions.

Now Available
from all your favorite booksellers
in trade paper and electronic editions.

USA TODAY BESTSELLING AUTHOR

DEAN WESLEY SMITH

The Magic Bakery

COPYRIGHT IN THE MODERN
WORLD OF FICTION PUBLISHING

A WMG WRITER'S GUIDE

USA TODAY BESTSELLING AUTHOR

DEAN WESLEY SMITH

STAGES OF A FICTION WRITER

KNOW WHERE YOU STAND
ON THE PATH TO WRITING

A WMG WRITER'S GUIDE

With more than a hundred published novels and more than seventeen million copies of his books in print, USA Today *bestselling author Dean Wesley Smith knows how to write fiction. And he has traversed every stage of writing along the way.*

In this WMG Writer's Guide, Dean takes you step-by-step through the stages most fiction writers go through and how not to lose hope along the way.

Want to enjoy your writing more and let your storytelling evolve in its own time? Then learn from Dean's experience and discover what to expect at each stage of a fiction writer's career.

The Stages of a Fiction Writer
A WMG Writers' Guide

INTRODUCTION

ABOUT TWENTY-FIVE YEARS AGO, I was struggling to figure out where I was on the path to becoming a fiction writer.

I had sold novels, lots of short stories, been an editor, owned a publishing company, and had readers buying my books.

But honestly, none of that mattered to me. I liked it, sure, but my goal was to be a better writer, a better storyteller, actually. And I had no idea at all where I was at on the road to that goal.

Not clue one.

For the previous twenty years, as my skills grew, I had also been studying other writers and trying to understand how they did what they did.

I was typing in other writers' work to try to learn their tricks and their craft.

I was reading every how-to-write book I could find.

But I still felt flat lost. I felt I had advanced, that I was past the basics, but what world did I have ahead of me with storytelling that I couldn't see?

I am the type that likes to look out ahead. But with storytelling, it was just a wall of mist.

So for my own use, I started to put this "Stages of a Fiction Writer" together.

I made the mistake, early on, of presenting some of this at a writer's workshop. Some of the members got very angry. And I do mean very.

I was kicked out because of my "attitude" and putting others down.

I had no intention of putting anyone down.

Seemed I had presented this wrong. But it was a work in progress.

And it wasn't until almost ten years later, about fifteen years ago now, that it all finally came together and made sense to me.

So a few years back, I did this as a lecture through WMG Publishing and put it up. It is still up as a lecture. But now I thought it might be time to get this into a book.

Knowing where I was at in learning storytelling, and where I could go if I kept practicing and learning, for me was very freeing.

Where Are You Going as a Writer?

Not a lot of writers give this much thought beyond the "I want to sell more and make a living."

Or… "I want a lot of people to read my books and be read in a hundred years."

Great hopes and dreams.

We all have those.

Nothing at all wrong with them.

But they sure don't help me in trying to figure out in general where each of us stand as a storyteller.

More WMG Writer's Guides
from all your favorite booksellers
in trade paper and electronic editions.

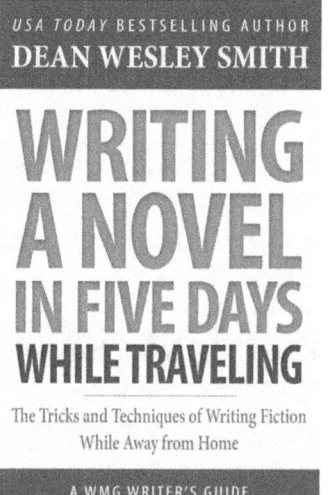

Now, there are basics in all this that I am going to state and more than likely repeat numbers of times.

First… Continued learning of craft is critical.

I can't even begin to count the hundreds, maybe thousands, of great writers who started to sell, thought they had it made, that they knew it all, and stopped learning. Now they are "Whatever Happened To" writers.

Learning can never stop. And if you have that attitude of learning is critical, then you can learn what it will take to move up stages.

Second… You can never learn it all when it comes to the craft of fiction writing.

This is sort of a shadow of the first point. The moment you think you have learned it all, that's where you freeze down. And that's where your career will remain until the craft of storytelling passes you by and no one buys your work anymore.

So where are you going as a writer?

That question assumes an end goal.

There is no end goal.

My answer is always, "Forward, to keep learning, and become a better storyteller."

My real end goal is to be challenging myself with a new story and a new way of telling it when I fall over dead.

A Poker Metaphor

In this book, I'm going to use poker playing as a metaphor to help be clear on some of the areas I am talking about. It is a very clear metaphor to how writers work.

Don't worry, I will make sure I explain poker clearly all the way. You do not need to be a professional poker player to understand this.

Or have even picked up a deck of cards. I promise to make it clear.

Why poker?

For most of my life, I played professional cards in one aspect or another. I started by playing gin rummy in the early 1970s, mostly in back rooms at golf clubs and in tournaments in Las Vegas.

I also played blackjack, and was a fan of Edward Thorp's 1966 book called *Beat the Dealer*.

Yes, I learned how to count cards.

When I went back to college in the early 1970s, I joined a blackjack team and paid my way through college completely playing on one team for a few years, then another for law school. I never told anyone I was doing that and had a couple part-time jobs to pretend I was earning money for college.

I also started playing poker in Las Vegas in the early 1970s and then off and on through the years after that; usually after the team was finished and headed home, I stayed a little longer to play some poker.

About twenty years ago, I picked up playing blackjack again at a local casino (not card counting, just playing tournaments) and then migrated to the poker room.

Then, at one point, disgusted with what was happening in traditional publishing, I basically quit writing and played professional poker to make a living. I did fine for a few years, playing mostly tournaments and writing a short story here and there along the way.

It was at a poker table about fifteen years ago in Las Vegas that I finally understood the Stages of a Fiction Writer.

And from that moment forward, I knew where I was going with my writing, what I was working toward.

Sure, book sales are great, but for me, I am happy with telling a good story. A story I feel as if I did my best with for the level of storyteller I am at the moment.

A Word of Warning

Because of the reaction to one of my first attempts at explaining this, I now understand that writers sometimes do not want to know where on the path they stand.

Mostly, of course, this is new writers who are in a hurry. Writers who get angry at this are writers who think that they should be able, with a few rewrites, to write a novel that will sell more than Stephen King and Nora Roberts combined.

And they are convinced they are better writers than those two as well as all bestsellers.

Uh, delusional, but that's the belief system.

Well, with a ton of luck, I suppose that could happen. But I always bet on skill and patience and learning.

At poker tables, when some really bad poker player was on a run of luck, and being obnoxious about it, I would say to the person, "Just hold on to those chips a little longer. They will be coming back my way shortly."

And they always did, because luck is both good and bad and evens out in the fairly short run. Skill and craft and learning will always win out over time. That's why poker is considered a sport, not a gambling game.

Skill wins.

So if you see yourself and your skill level at a certain point and it makes you angry, I am sorry. None of this is meant in any way to be personal.

This is meant to try to help the writers who want to move forward to understand what is ahead.

This is meant to pull back the mist a little and let writers peek into the minds of long-term professional writers.

And to help writers reach their dreams.

—Dean Wesley Smith
Lincoln City, Oregon
August 11, 2015

CHAPTER ONE

There are four basic stages of commercial fiction writing that are pretty clear. For this book, I just number them one through four.

I kind of think of them as places where writers live.

Basically, I'm an early-to-middle stage four writer. So is Kris. And we're working to get better all the time, as we always have.

Writers start in stage one and eventually work up into stage four if they keep learning and don't quit.

These stages will often have traits that carry over from one stage to another.

The lines between the stages are not dark and concrete, but are transitions that often take time to cross.

All of us, without exception, go through the early stages of fiction writing. No way around it.

And often writers can spend decades moving through a stage.

Or get stuck and have their career end in a stage.

So another way to think of this is like a journey.

A journey without an end point.

You never arrive, you never know it all as a fiction writer. Learning continues.

The key is never stop on the road. Keep moving and learning.

A Chess Example

To try to understand some of what I am talking about in coming chapters, keep in mind chess.

Those who have never played chess, or only played a few games, might know the moves of the pieces. But they can watch two chess masters and not have a clue what the masters are doing. The game is played on other levels than the prescribed moves of pieces.

When a beginning writer looks at a long-term bestseller, it is impossible to see what that writer did for book after book to get millions of readers every book. The books are just words, put into sentences. Right?

How hard can that be?

And chess pieces are just game pieces that move.

Just keep that in mind.

I Want to Jump Ahead Some Stages

Well, no. This question always comes up. No matter how much a beginning writer wants to get lucky and hit with some top selling books, which does happen, the skill level doesn't jump ahead.

We all go through the stages.

No matter how much of a hurry the writer might be in. And stage one writers are always in a hurry.

Now, that said, paying the price in the stages, the learning required to move through an early stage, can come from other places.

Often nonfiction professional writers can make a jump to professional fiction quicker. They might not be in the same stage with their fiction writing as they are with their nonfiction writing, but they can move quicker and start higher because they have "paid the price" in learning in nonfiction.

This also applies to those who started off writing plays, those writing for Hollywood, those coming out of advertising writing, and so on.

For those, the early stage or two were learned in other areas.

Stage One Fiction Writers

I went through this stage. We all start in stage one. I was no exception, never met an exception who didn't have a stage one period in one area of writing or another.

So what is a stage one commercial fiction writer? How can we spot stage one fiction writers?

Stage one writers believe fiction writing is sentences and grammar and punctuation.

That simple. The focus is sentence-by-sentence only.

Early on, all of us went through this. I was stuck in this period for seven years, from 1974 to January 1, 1982.

So what are some of the major traits that make you a stage one writer? Here are four major areas that might tell you if you have stage one issues or not.

1. Rewriting to Excess
The term many stage one writers use is "polish" when talking about this extreme rewriting.

Think rocks, folks, to understand this. You find a beautiful rock on the beach. It has color, it has sharp corners, it is unique. It drew your attention, after all, and made you pick it up.

So you are a stage one writer. You get home, toss that rock into a rock polisher, let it run with a bunch of other rocks, being polished down until finally, when it is finished, it is smooth and round and looks like all the poor other rocks you tossed in there with it.

With excess polishing of a story, you grind down any thought of originality, any possibility of author voice, and make the story same.

Sameness is dull.

A stage one writer's entire focus is on the words.

Stage one writers think that polishing the words makes for a better story. That is the belief.

It is wrong, but it is believed by millions.

Again, we all started there.

2. Extremely Slow

Even though stage one writers are in a hurry to be successful, by the very nature of stage one writing, of focusing only on the words and not story, stage one writers produce very little, if anything.

And that fits the myth that writing slowly means writing better stuff. (That shows no understanding of how the creative brain works. None.)

In the seven years I was stuck in this stage, I managed to produce two highly-polished short stories per year. And I was pretty focused at writing. Of course, all the stories were dull, no voice, no originality.

I had polished all that out in rewrites.

For seven years, I listened and tried to learn how to write from people who didn't know how to write creatively. I listened to every myth. There wasn't a myth I didn't buy into and try to do.

I was very, very slow. And I felt happy to get those two "perfect" stories out every year.

By all the myths, I was doing it right.

Sold nothing.

Had no career.

Of course, for stage one writers, it's always someone else's fault that they don't understand their perfectly polished story. Or it is some marketing thing now in indie that isn't working, and so on and so on.

Stage one writers always have an excuse for nothing selling.

Stage one writers believe they produce perfect stories and won't let anything but perfect out the door. So, of course it has to be someone or something else's fault their perfect story doesn't get the attention it deserves.

Of course.

And yup, I was no exception to that.

Seven long years.

3. Peer Writers' Workshops

Stage one writers tend to be in peer writers' workshops. And they often tend to write for the other members of the workshop.

They let someone who hates commas influence their work, or someone who hates too much setting up front change all their work.

This is like having ten different English teachers feed myths at you all at once.

Death of any good storytelling.

Total death.

And stage one writers tend to listen to suggestions from their workshops and then try to "fix" their story to make it better.

Yeah, writing by committee always produces great art.

Not.

There are "workshops" done by professionals, like the online workshops we do at WMG Publishing or Superstars done by Kevin J. Anderson or workshops done by Dave Farland, to name just three. If you find a workshop that is taught by someone who has been writing books for thirty years, those have value.

At our workshops, we don't let the other writers attending even speak about stories, even though most of them are selling professional writers. The only opinion that matters is the long-term professional instructors.

And we never let anyone teach who hasn't had a career in fiction writing in one area or another.

But peer workshops that are only full of stage one writers often will continue for a writer into early stage two before the writer finally goes, "that's silly."

I was attending workshops up into stage three, but only for quick audience reaction and learning business.

I never once tried to rewrite a story to the suggestion of a workshop. I at least managed to avoid that trap for myself. About the only one I missed along the way, I never found a peer workshop in my first seven years, thankfully.

And by the time I was into stage two and three, I mailed stories to editors before I ever took them to a workshop. That's why I learned that advice from workshops often kill stories. I sold a bunch of the stories that workshops told me sucked.

Luckily I mailed my story and didn't listen to people in workshops other than as a general audience reaction.

4. Concerned Only About Typing

Stage one writers have no idea at all about the look of a manuscript and how it relates to the story being told.

If they were taught in English class to put a paragraph every five lines, they do that. If they were taught that subject sentences are the key and can't do a paragraph until you get done with the subject sentence, they do that, having paragraphs that can often stretch for a page or more.

The idea of characters is not really formed for stage one writers, although stage one writers give voice to characters, but no learning about how to really do characters.

Stage one writers do character sketches ahead, thinking that's how it's done. And they mostly outline everything to death and follow their outlines because that's how it's done as well.

Pacing is an alien concept that might as well live on Mars.

Stage One Summary

Stage one writers have a focus only on the sentences, the grammar, the polish of a manuscript.

They give lip service to better characters, endings, and so on, but will spend ten drafts getting that "perfect" first line because they heard somewhere that was important.

All writers live for a time in stage one, or live in it while studying in other areas such as plays or nonfiction.

Some writers, with luck, go through it quickly.

Some of us, me included, take longer.

I really wanted to believe the myths that English teachers were teaching me. Desperately I wanted to believe them.

And I did, for seven long years.

But Dean, Didn't You Sell Two Short Stories in 1975?

Yes, I did. I was writing poetry at the time and selling it.

For my poems, I would struggle and rewrite a major "important" poem to death, work on a second one sort of, and then do a fun quick knock-off poem and then send all three poems out together.

I always sold the knock-off.

I never sold a poem I had worked on and rewritten. Thirty-some of the knock-off poems sold and I never caught a clue. My "good poems" didn't sell, and I stopped mailing poems in early 1976 to focus completely on fiction.

Well, somewhere in 1975 was when I first decided I wanted to try fiction.

So I wrote a quick story on my typewriter.

One draft.

Mailed it, no rewrite. (I had not yet bought into all the myths. I didn't know them, to be honest.)

Then I wrote a second story. Also fairly short.

One draft.

Mailed it.

Both of them sold right out. I had let the rough edges stay, my voice stay, my originality stay. Editors liked them and bought them.

Go figure.

Then, because they sold and I wanted to get better, I started learning the myths. And I started down into rewriting everything to death and writing slowly and focusing only on the words and sentences.

And seven years later I hadn't sold another thing.

For seven years I never put that together. Either with the poems I sold or with the two stories I sold. I was blinded by myths.

Completely.

And that's why I do the *Killing the Sacred Cows of Publishing* books. To help writers speed up through stage one.

CHAPTER TWO

Stage two of commercial fiction writers is again a stage we all go through. I was no exception, never met a writer who missed this one.

However, many writers can go through this stage quickly, often in a year or so. But at the same time, this is the place many, many millions of writers get stuck and eventually give up without ever reaching stage three and selling stories.

For lack of a better way of putting this, stage two is a transition stage.

The Major Traits of Stage Two Writers

—Focus is still solidly on the words.

—Writers are starting to see a change where the focus is shifting to understanding characters, plot, setting, and the other elements of a story. But again, the major focus is at the words and polishing to try to achieve characters, plot, setting and so on.

—Story is playing more of a part, but only slowly.

In other words, this is when writers start bringing their focus up and off the words and toward writing stories with real characters, emotional details, and so on. These are the early days of learning all this, but now the stage two writers are looking for answers, knowing that only focusing on the words no longer helps.

My Twilight Zone Magazine Stories

Now, as a stage three writer, later on, I ended up selling to the *TZ Magazine* and its sister magazine *Night Cry*. But something happened as a late stage one and early stage two writer to me with the magazine that bumped me solidly into stage two and then quickly beyond into stage three.

Back in 1981, the *Twilight Zone Magazine* started a new writer contest. At this point I had been a stage one writer for going on seven years, polishing and rewriting and thinking my work could easily win this new contest in this new magazine.

So I wrote them two stories for the contest. Almost an entire year's output in six months for me at that time and I was convinced both would win one award or another.

That fall I got the responses: Two form rejections.

(In hindsight, that's what the stories deserved because I had polished and polished anything original out of those two stories. They looked like everything else coming through the door to T.E.D. Klein.)

But wow was I angry.

I blamed everyone else and decided to quit writing. What was the point if my brilliance would never be found? I had given it seven years, after all.

Then one fine night at a science fiction fan meeting that was being held in my bookstore, someone said something about how Ray Bradbury wrote stories.

And then another conversation came up about how Harlan Ellison had just sat in a bookstore window and wrote a story that had won a major award without rewriting it.

So something finally clicked in my thick skull and I started finally researching how other professional writers actually did it.

Not how English teachers had taught me it was done, but how real professionals worked.

And then I found **Heinlein's Rules.**

Now I have a lecture through WMG Publishing about Heinlein's Business Rules, and at some point I might write a book about them. But at that point in the late fall of 1981, finding Heinlein's Business Rules sort of snapped my eyes open.

They were from a book in 1947 and they seemed so simple. But Heinlein in the article said the five simple rules were extremely difficult to follow, which is why there were so many aspirants who wanted to be writers and why there are so few professional writers.

I was, after seven years, damned tired of being an aspirant.

So as a New Year's resolution in 1982, I would follow Heinlein's Rules. I would write and mail a short story per week following the rules.

No exception.

One year later I was selling regularly and I have followed those simple rules ever since.

Five simple business rules.

And I agree with Heinlein. Almost no one can follow those rules. Everyone can make excuses that sound perfectly logical for them so they don't have to follow them.

But almost no one can follow those five simple rules.

Heinlein's Rules:

1. You must write.

2. You must finish what you write.

3. You must not rewrite unless to editorial request. (Editors are people who buy things, not someone you hire, folks.)

4. You must put your work on the market.

5. You must keep it on the market.

The moment I started following those rules, I moved quickly from stage one into stage two and then by 1983, about a year later, I had moved solidly into stage three and was selling.

Why? Because the rules forced me to stop focusing on the words and focus on writing stories.

If you are not focusing on words, what else can a writer focus on?

Answer: All the thousands of elements of storytelling, that's what.

The Monster Problem in Stage Two

Where millions and millions of writers get stuck and then quit in stage two is right at the focus point. They start to focus on the craft of storytelling, but they can't let go of the strong desire to only pay attention to the words.

After all, they ask, isn't writing typing words?

Stage two writers in this stage still write with grammar checker and spell-checker turned on.

Stage two writers are in a battle in their own minds. They are aware of the need for story and great characters and so on, and are learning them by taking workshops and buying how-to-write books.

But at the same time they cannot let loose of the intense myth that rewriting is critical, that every story must be polished.

So they learn character, then kill the story, learn great setting, then kill it by taking out character voice and so on, which is critical to setting.

To get out of stage two, you must slowly release the focus on words and realize they are just tools to use.

Carpenter Tools Analogy

Your desire is to be a fine cabinet craftsperson. So you focus on learning how to use hammers correctly. All the different types of hammers used to build finely crafted cabinets.

You become an expert with hammers.

But you think that learning hammers, learning how to pick the correct hammer for the job needed is all that is required to building a finely crafted cabinet.

You have been told over and over (by people who don't build cabinets) that to build a great cabinet, you must keep your hammers polished.

So you try to build a cabinet, but all you keep doing is, when something goes wrong in construction, you go back and focus on your hammers and polish them some more. Must be the hammer's fault, after all.

Sound silly?

Well, everyone in stage two knows how to write a sentence, has grammar and spelling under control enough to check spelling when a manuscript is finished. That was all learned in stage one.

So now put the words, the sentences, in your toolbox and move your focus completely to learning construction.

You must learn to trust your tools in stage two.

You must let go of the focus on the tool and just trust that in the process of writing, the tool will be there when you need it.

That's how you get out of stage two.

Ignore the typing, focus on the story, kill any idea of polishing.

And every time you have the need to go polish a story, just think of a cabinet-maker looking at his poorly constructed and designed cabinet and then polishing his hammers.

That won't fix the cabinet.

And polishing your words won't fix your story either.

Stage Two Summary

Stage two is a transition stage.

It is when a writer takes the focus only on the words and polishing the words and moves that focus slowly to learning story and characters and setting and the thousand other basic details that go into being a great storyteller.

The writer is moving from someone who only pays attention to typing to paying attention to story.

Many writers take about a year to move from full focus on typing to full focus on story.

But many writers never learn to trust their tools. Many writers never learn that the tools are there and just need to be used when the creative voice wants to use them. And not thought about other times.

Millions and millions of writers quit right here in this stage.

I was almost one of them.

CHAPTER THREE

As we move into stage three, it's time I bring in the poker analogy I promised earlier on in the book.

As I said, I have always had cards in my life. I paid most of my way through college with cards, and also played professional poker for a time.

The definition of a professional poker player is a person who makes most of his or her money playing poker. I am now a semi-professional since I make money at poker when I play, but I make most of my money these days from my writing.

In fact, here in 2015 I don't play much poker at all. Occasional trips to Las Vegas is all. I might go back more in the coming years. Time will tell.

But this poker analogy works very, very well. The stages of poker are almost exactly parallel to the stages of writing, and you don't need to know poker to understand the analogy. H

Honest.

For this analogy, I'm going to use the poker game called Texas Holdem. (Yes, spelling can be Hold 'em or Hold'em, but for this, I'll use the simple spelling.)

Texas Holdem is a seven-card game to make the best five-card poker hand.

At the start, each player around a table (usually 9 at a full table) is dealt two cards down, so only the player can see them.

There is a betting round.

The dealer places three cards face up in the middle of the table. (All players use those three cards.)

Another betting round.

The dealer places one more card face up on the table.

Another betting round.

The dealer places the last card face up on the table.

Last betting round.

All players are trying to make the best five-card poker hand from the five public cards and the two private cards in their hands.

Stage One Poker Players

Stage one or beginning poker players often don't even know a good poker hand or what beats what. They have no idea if the two cards that only they can see are good or not, and have no awareness of anyone else around them in any real fashion.

They might have seen a major player win with a certain hand on television and think that's a good hand without knowing why or how to even play it.

The focus of a stage one poker player is only on their two cards in their hand.

If they think those two cards are good, nothing else matters.

Nothing.

Just as stage one writers only have a focus on the words on the page with no real awareness beyond the words.

If a stage one writer thinks the words are perfect, the grammar correct, all commas are in the right place, then the story must be perfect.

Of course, just as stage one writers

find no readers, stage one poker players often have no idea why a pot with their money in it is awarded to another player. After all, they had an ace in their hand. Isn't an ace good?

Yup, about as good as having all the commas correct in a story.

Stage Two Poker Players

When a poker player moves into stage two, they are still, just as writers, focused far, far too much on the two cards in their hand that the other players can't see.

But awareness for the stage two player is starting to expand.

Stage two players can actually see the cards on the table and put them with their cards and maybe realize that their cards can't win in some situations.

Stage two poker players still lose far more than they win, but their awareness and knowledge is expanding. It is a transition stage, just as with writing.

Think of a bubble of awareness.

In stage one, the bubble was over the player only and his two cards. In stage two, the bubble of awareness has expanded out to include the cards face up on the table and knowing poker hands and so on.

In stage two writing, the focus is still solidly on the words. But the awareness has expanded out to include character and story to some degree. But when in doubt, the stage two writer always falls back on the words, trying to rewrite to fix a story.

You see this a lot in stage two poker players in things like the following example:

A player has two cards in his hand that combined with three other cards face up on the table make a straight. A straight is a decent hand, right?

Sure, but not when there are four cards on the board that are hearts. (A flush beats a straight.)

And even though the player has no hearts in his hand, he will call bets thinking he might win. That's like a stage two writer having a story fail and thinking if he just rewrites it, all will be fine.

The straight won't win against a flush and rewriting won't help a story.

The bubble of focus is still far too tight.

Stage Three Poker Players

I'm going to give the poker analogy before I start talking about stage three writers.

Think of the bubble of awareness I mentioned above. In stage three poker players, the awareness bubble has expanded to include everyone at the table.

Inside the awareness bubble, the player is watching what other people bet, how they play, what kind of hands they play regularly.

Often stage three poker players know or think they know what another player's two hidden cards are, and act on that knowledge.

The stage three poker player still has a focus on his own two cards, but has no problem in throwing away his two cards at the hint of a loss, and just not even playing for many hands in a row if good starting hands do not appear.

Stage three poker players understand the game, can glance at the five cards on the table and tell you what the best possible hand is for those five cards.

Stage three poker players can win, sometimes more than they lose overall depending on what level of stage three they are in, and who they are playing against.

Many, many professional poker players never leave stage three playing level. They don't need to. They are making a living.

So the awareness bubble has expanded out to everything on the table and the other people playing.

Still some focus on the cards, but the cards are more of a tool that a stage three player can take or leave, depending on the game, the stakes, and the others playing.

Cards in the hand are still important, but not critical anymore.

However, a stage three player would never think of playing a hand of cards without looking at the two cards they have. (Keep that in mind in a future chapter.)

Stage Three Writers

Think of the awareness bubble.

In stage three writers, the awareness has expanded out.

Now the awareness is on telling a good story, on having an interesting plot, on doing great openings, on writing great characters, on getting a reader into a story and holding them in the story.

Words now are still important, but only in the service of the story and nothing more.

Words can be tossed away at will, just as cards are tossed away in poker.

Traits of solid stage three writers:

—They have command of many, many different tools of writing that come out of the words and use those tools when needed. They no longer focus on the words. They only use the words.

—They have a solid grasp of story, of character, and of setting. And are constantly trying to get better at all three.

—They understand copyright and the business and sales. In other words, awareness is off the words and out into the world.

—They are writing at a decent pace.

—They seldom rewrite if at all (in the traditional sense of the term rewriting). Early stage three writers will still rewrite at times to fix story, but middle and late third stage writers seldom rewrite.

—Late third stage writers have often been around for some time.

Third stage writers often can make a living with their work. There are lots of ups and downs, but if the writer can weather those early ups and downs in this stage and learn the business and keep learning how to be a better storyteller, they tend to last for a while.

Third Stage is a Burial Ground for Writers

Sad to say that most writers who hit early third stage tend to stop learning. And that's where they stop and freeze down.

Eventually, sales dry up, their publisher drops them, they can't sell more books or their indie sales are not good, and they give up and go away.

Often stage three writers feel like they know it all, make a few sales, and just move on to other things because writing is too hard.

Or they accomplished their dream. No point in going on.

The history of publishing is littered with three-and-four-book authors who vanished. More thousands than I would ever want to try to count, sadly.

And indie publishing is not going to help this in any fashion. Early stage three indie writers are going to make a little money, have a market change kill their sales, and the writers will leave, not understanding that learning and sticking with it can get them up to a more sustained sales and craft level.

The awareness bubble keeps expanding all the way through the different levels of stage three.

For me, it took from 1984 when I crept into the lower levels of stage three and started selling until about 2005 to move through the levels of stage three writing and finally break through into the next level.

And during all those years I kept learning, experimenting, studying other writers.

Stage three writing is the place where writers sell. And if you keep learning storytelling, adding tools to your craft, and learn copyright and the business, you can have a nice, solid career for a few decades in stage three.

But to really stick around and become an old professional and a bestseller, stage four needs to be your goal.

CHAPTER FOUR

Almost all writers reading this will be in stage three.

If you see yourself in stage one, all focused on the writing and polishing of words, you can move quickly out of that once you understand the location you are stuck in. And then start making changes.

Change your focus to story. Stop polishing. Let your voice come through.

And stage two is the transition stage from the focus on polishing to the focus on story and characters and so on.

Stage three is huge.

It would be like crossing the United States and Australia combined. It's a ton of territory and a lot of things to learn. At one point someone suggested I try to break stage three down into levels and I just sort of laughed and shuddered at the same time.

Stage three is the learning and focus on story. On becoming a better storyteller.

I do entire workshops to try to help people move forward in just small areas of stage three such as character voice or depth or pacing or cliffhangers or ideas.

No way to break down stage three because one stage three writer will have a certain few skills mastered and be poor at others, while the writer sitting next to them will be poor at the skills the other writer has mastered.

Both writers are in stage three.

Expanded Awareness

As I detailed out in the poker analogy of stage three poker players being aware of everyone at the table and how they play, stage three writers are now gaining more and more awareness of story and business at the same time.

The bubble of awareness is just slowly expanding to include more and more skills that it takes to be a great storyteller and make money in this business of telling stories.

And the skills of sentence-by-sentence writing are more and more just taken for granted.

Sure, things like learning depth is a sentence-by-sentence skill in many ways, but it goes to the focus of story and character and reader reaction.

Understanding what a fake detail is might be down in the words, but it goes to story and character as well as reader reaction. What is learned in the basics of sentence writing in stage three all goes to service of story.

But the awareness bubble (for most writers) has limits.

And that is the problem.

The best way I like to describe this problem is that a writer walks into a huge lobby area of a building. As you first enter the building (or stage three) you have no idea at all that there are fifty or more stories of the building above that large lobby and the shops and stuff around the lobby.

The awareness bubble does not move past that one level. Writers just can't see the upper floors, and often don't even know they are there, let alone how to find a staircase or an elevator. They don't even realize they should look for one.

Writers at this level often stay in the lobby, happy with a few sales here and there.

Or they slowly become aware there is more above them, more things to learn. And these writers start looking for that staircase upward.

There are lots of floors of stage three above them. But sadly, most writers I have seen make the lobby and that's where they stay, eventually just drifting off into history.

My entire point of this book is in hopes that someone reading it is stuck in the lobby and realizes that they need to look for a staircase upward, that they need to get back to learning and studying other writers.

How do you find a staircase or elevator out of that lobby? By learning and studying and becoming aware that there are better writers out there than you.

And then studying them.

To find a way out of this huge lobby, you need to stop thinking that all long-term successful writers just got lucky and can't really write. Start asking yourself what is Cussler or Steele or Patterson or King or Oates doing right?

Get your taste out of the equation and study.

The staircase doors will start appearing.

And what is even more amazing, once you start climbing upward, you see things that you didn't even know existed. And the more that happens, the more you realize you really didn't know jack about telling stories.

How to Tell if You are in Stage Three?

Pretty simply, actually.

—Are you focused on learning story, learning character, learning depth, and on and on and on?

—Are you starting to have some success selling? Either indie or traditional.

—Do you have more than one or two books out?

—Have you cut down the number of rewrites, or found a better way, and want to get to the next story before you are almost done with the last one?

Death Spirals in the Lobby of Stage Three

There are three really, really common problems that early stage three writers have. In fact, I would say these two problems are the death of 95% of all stage three writers' careers.

It's like the writer gets into the lobby, looks around, and then turns and leaves.

Problem #1: Thinking that only original plots sell.

If you think this, wow do you need to really learn story and the history of story and so much more.

But the best way to do that is just stop thinking this and worrying about this. If you think all ideas are hard to come by and all need to be original, just take the Ideas online workshop that I do at WMG Publishing and I'll save you from this death in six short weeks. I promise.

I can hear the voices in your head saying, "But… but… but… I must have great ideas…"

That's your critical voice trying to slow you down, stop you, and if you let it, you are doomed from this one problem alone.

Problem #2: I don't need to learn that.

This is a thought pattern that gets nasty very quickly. It starts bringing in time and money and day jobs and so on and so on. This also is your critical voice trying to stop you or slow you down.

Critical voice only has one job and that's to stop you. Thinking you DO NOT need to learn something, anything, or practice something, is a golden road for your critical voice to stop you.

Learning never stops in this business. Ever.

My suggestion is this: If you hear yourself say, "I'm good enough in that area to not worry about it now." Then notice you said that, stop, and focus on that area. Learn it, make sure your critical voice knows that every time it attempts to pull that trick on you, you will go learn what it is trying to keep you from learning to improve your skills and selling.

"Good enough" is deadly in writing. Deadly.

Problem #3: Patience and lack of long-term perspective.

The thinking goes like this: *I've been at this long enough. It's not working. I've spent three years or five years or whatever at it. I need to walk away.*

Or even more stupid, sometimes I hear this expressed this way in the indie world: *My friends are all selling better than I am. I only made 300 sales last month, I'm failing, I'm going to quit.*

The door to the building is that big wide thing with people streaming in and out.

All long-term professional writers have learned to not be insulted by some two-or-three-year writer who proclaims they should be selling better than anyone. Or one of the one-or-two-year writers who got lucky with the right book at the right place and started selling quickly and think they are god's gift to writing.

I have worked since 1974 at this writing thing, learning and working and writing millions and millions and millions of words. When some three-year writer tells me I don't know how to write, or proclaims they are a better writer than Patterson, I just smile and turn away because I know they are already halfway out the door.

Harsh? Yes.

Not fair? Yes.

This is a business.

This is an art that takes decades to learn just the basics and you never learn it all. If you think you don't need those decades of learning because your English teachers told you that you had talent, then all I can say is "Goodbye."

I know that all beginning writers are in a hurry. I know that. I was as well.

So I suppose a true indication that you are well into stage three is that you understand the time needed to learn your art and business.

I hope you are not in any of those problems at the moment, or if you are, you can snap out of it, get back to learning, and expand your awareness to the fact that there are levels of writing you just can't see yet.

And then have the desire to see those new levels. After all, you made it through the first two stages. You can go higher and farther.

The Secret to Working Through Stage Three

Just tell the next story.

Do your best on every story you write, keep learning, keep practicing, and then just tell the next story.

Get that story you just finished out to sell to readers in one way or another.

And then just keep learning and tell the next story.

Make writing fun.

Make learning fun.

Make telling stories fun.

CHAPTER FIVE

Starting into stage four, the top stage.

I got a question after the last chapter when I put that chapter on my blog. "How many writers are in stage four?"

Think of stage four as a decent-sized town.

Selling stage three writers could fill a couple large cities. As I said earlier, most stage three writers never get past those first sales. To reach stage four, it takes an intense desire to keep learning and studying the art of storytelling.

And it flat takes years and years and millions and millions of words.

Sorry, just can't jump there. Not even slightly possible.

So What Is a Stage Four Writer?

—A writer in complete control of the art of storytelling.

—A writer who is still learning.

—A writer who is using techniques, often without knowing, that are advanced.

—A writer who is balanced in skills.

—A writer who has no giant weak areas in their storytelling.

—A writer who can handle any kind of storytelling technique a story demands.

—A writer who is a bestseller and has been for many, many years, if not decades.

—A writer who knows when a reader needs something before a reader knows they need it.

So what is the difference between stage three and stage four writers?

Often not much for advanced stage three writers. But still there are critical differences.

Stage three writers are often best-sellers, but fairly new at it. Stage three writers often have huge areas of their writing they are weak at and fear some types of storytelling.

Often a stage three writer will be very good at one area and will be using that all the time to keep selling without adding in the balancing skills.

And most importantly, a stage three writer is not always in control of a story.

Not from a critical place, but from a skill place.

More importantly, stage three writers have very, very little awareness of readers on the other side of the story. They may think of readers in marketing, but never in telling their own stories.

How to Explain This

To make this clear, I need to go back to the poker analogy. (And please, any professional poker player out there, give me some slack. I am being general here in a hope to help writers, not other poker players.)

As I said earlier, stage three poker players have expanded their awareness from the two cards in their hands out over the entire poker table to the other players and the five cards on the board.

Stage three poker players can often understand how other players are going to play, can often know what two cards another poker player has and so on.

Stage three poker players often make nice money.

Stage four poker players can do all that as well.

And so much more.

A stage four poker player is an expert at reading people in general. They know the types of players, they know the cards, and they will often know how a person will play before they sit down.

Not kidding.

There is a scene in the movie *Rounders* where Matt Damon (playing stage four poker player Mike McDermott) walks into a home poker game with some of his law professors. They ask him to join them and he declines (as he should and as I always do with friends). He stands there and watches them play a hand, then gives his professional advice.

They ask him how he knows to make that play and he explains clearly what every other player at the table is playing.

That scene was a brilliant and quick scene to understand the level of stage four poker players. It looked almost like a magic trick, but it was not, it was a great representation of some skills of stage four poker players. I will explain how Damon knowing all the cards relates to storytelling in a minute.

Stage four poker players play details, play motions, betting, and everything. And folks, there are only 52 cards in a deck, so simply seeing a reaction and a few cards can give a stage four poker player a clear read on another player.

But those players you watch in the top events on television play very strange cards in their hands that are not good "starting hands" by any book written for beginners.

Why?

Because the stage four players often don't care about the two cards in their own hand. (I have played more hands of poker blind than I ever want to think about, meaning I never looked at my two cards, even though I often pretended I did.)

Unless it comes to a showdown, meaning all betting is done and everyone turns over their cards, a stage four poker player won't much care about his own two cards.

A stage four poker player only cares what the other stage four poker player sitting across from him thinks he has.

Now understand, stage four and late stage three players often get into trouble with stage two players because those stage two players don't have the awareness to be convinced of something one way or another. Stage two and early stage three poker players just don't even understand the game they often watch on television.

A Real Life Example

I had bought into a $1,500 no-limit tournament at the World Series of Poker a bunch of years back. I found myself sitting across from Eric Seidel and on the left of David Pham, the *Card Player Magazine* player of the year the previous year.

Two top stage four players.

I did not know anyone else at the table and no one knew me.

There were over 80 tables. And as players got knocked out of the tournament, they had a list on a big board as to which tables would break to fill in the empty spots at other tables. Our table would not break until eight or nine hours into the tournament, if that.

So I was there on the same table with two of the top players in the world for at least eight hours if I could survive. They did not know me. I was like the other players to them, but they clearly knew each other.

So I just sat back, made a clear point of looking at my cards each time, and then tossed them away. I didn't even care what they were.

I had no intention of playing for at least the first hour of the tournament. Not because I was afraid, but because I wanted to set something up for the two top players and watch how they played as well.

Seidel basically only played a few hands in the first hour and everyone folded to him.

On my right, Pham was raising almost every hand and pulling most of the small pots, only getting into a few

fights at all with anyone at the table. And when Seidel was in a hand, Pham laid down his cards.

So finally, after one hour, Seidel and Pham clearly thought they had a clear read on me. They clearly thought EXACTLY what I wanted them to think.

I hadn't said a word, just folded every hand. They figured I was a tight player who was playing scared. I would have thought the same thing in their positions.

So after the first hour, on one hand, I glanced down and had a pair of kings. Pham raised, I re-raised him and everyone else on the table folded around to him. He nodded and without looking at his cards folded.

That one hand repaid all the blinds I had lost in the first hour.

What Pham was thinking was that I was a very tight player, an early stage player with a lot of patience, and would only play top hands, and Pham didn't want to fight with a top hand, especially so early in the tournament. (That was why I went with a pair of kings to start making my move, to make sure that if I did get called down to a showdown, I would have the powerful hand I wanted him to think I only played.)

I had made him believe he knew what cards I was going to play. And I noticed that when Pham folded, Seidel nodded. Seidel clearly had the same thought.

Two hands later, Pham raised again and I re-raised him again. This time I had two low garbage cards. But I knew he was a stage four player and all I cared about was what he thought I had, not what I actually had.

He folded again.

So for the next two hours, Pham took money from other players and I took money from him at times when he raised.

Not once did I get in a showdown with anyone in those first hours. Not one person ever saw my cards.

At that point in my life, I also had great peripheral vision and I raised Pham a couple of times when I noticed he hadn't even looked at his cards. I hadn't looked at mine, either, but that's beside the point. I was just playing with his mind.

In essence, we were playing cards without caring what our own cards were. Impossible to even imagine to a stage one or two poker player.

Players kept getting knocked out and leaving our table and leaving their chips behind with the three of us. At the lunch break, Seidel and Pham and I had the three large stacks.

After lunch, Pham changed his play from raising almost every hand and went to playing more like Seidel and I knew they had changed their read on me, so I changed to regular play, and the three of us took turns taking money from the others.

And never after lunch did I raise Pham or Seidel and they never raised me either. In other words, their read on me had gotten a little closer to my actual skill level and in the early hours of the tournament there was no reason to mix it up.

They knew exactly what I had done to them. I had led them to believe I was one type of player when I was actually another.

Mind control.

After nine hours, the tournament broke our table to send us to empty chairs at the twenty remaining tables. We walked together upstairs talking. (This was in Binion's and I went back to writing shortly after that tournament and have never had the pleasure to sit at a poker table with either of them again.)

So the key to stage four poker players, when playing other stage four players or good stage three players, is to make the other player think they understand and know what you have.

How Does This Apply to Stage Four Writers?

Simple and exactly the same.

Stage one writers only worry about the typing. The words.

Stage two writers are starting to worry about story, but still focus on typing and the words.

Stage three writers have expanded out to be aware of story and characters and they notice pacing and so much more. (Remember, stage three is a huge area that takes years to get through and most never do.)

Stage four writers could not much care about the words. Words are in the complete control of stage four writers and are only part of the tools the writer uses.

What is important to a stage four writer is what the reader is experiencing at any given moment in the story.

In other words, stage four writers' awareness has expanded outside the words, outside the story, outside of characterization, and to what the reader will be thinking and feeling at any moment in the story.

Stage four writers understand what will hold a reader in a story, understand when a question needs to be answered and answers it a fraction of a second before the reader thinks it.

Stage four writers will not allow the reader out of the story, and so much more.

Just as I controlled Pham's and Seidel's thoughts on that table for a few hours, stage four writers control readers' minds from word one of a story to the final word.

And often beyond.

CHAPTER SIX

Stage four in writing is hard, at best, to describe because for most writers, it is a level of craft that is impossible to see.

So how do you move through stage three and get to stage four writing?

Mostly, the answer boils down to one simple thing:

Read.

Read for pleasure.

Then when you find a book that you really, really enjoyed, go back and study it until you understand what the writer did to hold you in the book, what made you enjoy the book besides the subject.

Study at different times all aspects of the book.

For example:

—Understand the many, many, many different types of cliffhangers the author used.

—Understand the pacing of the scenes, the characters, the setting. (Yes, setting has pacing.)

—Understand the character voice, the cadence, the syntax, the pacing and choices of words and character tags.

—Understand the structure of the book, the movement through the book, the reason the author made the choices the author made.

You do all this after you read a book and really, really love it.

Read for pleasure, then study.

Who to Study?

This is where I am constantly shaking my head at newer writers. They are studying other newer writers.

Huh?

Newer writers are often stage three writers who had parts come together enough to make books work. If you are trying to stay in stage three, then study stage three writers.

If you are trying to move to stage four writing, study stage four writers.

Stage four writers are writers who have been producing for twenty or more years and who are bestsellers and write more than one book every few years.

Grisham is a great writer to study. You can see what he has done in his books and he is easy to study.

Koontz is a hard study because he's so subtle. But he, more than any other writer working today besides King, is a master of more techniques than you or I can ever imagine. So study him. His Odd Thomas books are great ones to study.

The list of stage four writers to study goes on and on.

Some bestsellers are not to your taste. Granted.

But if you think that a long-term bestseller such as Cussler can't write, and you are stage two or early stage three writer, you need to catch a very large clue.

And if you think Patterson can't write (when he writes alone), you need your writing mind examined.

Granted, long-term, major-selling stage four writers might not be to your taste. But they know what they are doing and you could learn from them if you open your mind.

There is a reason that hundreds of thousands of people buy every book a major bestseller puts out year after year for decade after decade. Figure out what that reason (actually it is a thousand writing skill reasons) is if you really want to get to stage four.

Study them.

And there are many stage four writers who fly under the radar for most people.

Many, many, many of us, actually.

A prime example is Joyce Carol Oates.

Another prime example is my wife, Kristine Kathryn Rusch.

Both would be worth your time to study. Those two write what they want and often the subject matter they tackle is not a subject that has a lot of readers. They don't care.

They write what they love and both have been major bestsellers for decades and both have won more awards than I can imagine. (And I see those awards stacked all over my wife's office and leaning against shelves and waiting to be framed and so on.)

In mystery, there are numbers and numbers of writers who are stage four and most students would not think to study them.

Lawrence Block, Edward Gorman, Barry Malzberg, to name just three of many.

Or study John D. McDonald's Travis McGee series. You'll have to reread those many times to start seeing the real genius of McDonald in those books.

Same guidelines on who to study applies to romance and westerns and so on.

So read for pleasure, study to advance your own art after enjoying a book.

Never study during a first read, unless a book is not to your taste subject-wise. For example, Danielle Steel is not to my taste, but I have purposely studied numbers of her books to really understand what she does and to learn.

Some Problem Areas Common in Stage Three Writers to Cure

Stage four writers are in control of their readers. Any reader in any walk of life or age or country.

Stage four writers control readers. Period.

Stage three writers are often writers who haven't learned even the basics of doing that.

A few examples:

—Fake Details.

Stage three writers often use fake details and thus lose control over their readers. Fake details come from stage one and stage two when writers think they need to add in setting, so they type it in instead of running the setting through the opinions and emotions of a character.

Example I use all the time in classes is the word "barn." A total fake detail because without emotions and descriptions through a character, every reader imagines a barn from his or her own past. And trust me, not all barns look the same.

The word "tree" is another commonly used fake detail. Example… *He walked among the trees.*

Check in with the image that appeared in your mind when I wrote that. It will be different for every reader.

But what I meant was… *He walked among the short Noble fir trees, brushing his hands over their tops gently, enjoying the silk feel of their needles and the thick smell of rich fir, knowing that in six months most of these tree would be gone, decorated with bulbs and lights in homes around the country and he would have enough money to barely live for yet another year.*

Yeah, trees is a fake detail unless you run it through the senses and emotions of a character.

Learning how to do that is just one step toward stage four.

One of many.

Another Major Area of Stage Four Writing

—Pacing.

Pacing is an area of writing that is impossible to see until you reach a level of skill that allows the mind to understand just the lower levels of the skill and art of pacing.

Lower levels of pacing are often used, without knowing, by stage three writers.

Hitting the return key, understanding that content drives the look of the manuscript, the length of the sentences, the size of the paragraphs. Many stage three writers work into this knowledge in the later areas of stage three.

But there is so much more to pacing than just knowing where to put a period and when to hit a return key. Those basics must be learned first, granted. But let me give you an example of a higher level, stage four level, of pacing.

This one area is easy to see, but impossible to implement at first.

How to see this one area of pacing: Go to an airport, park yourself off to one side in a chair looking at a busy hallway. The best place is just outside a security area as people are moving from the ticket counter to security.

Now with only pacing in mind, watch the people. And watch the pacing of the writing.

***

A woman chicken-steps past in high heels.
Click. Click. Click. Click.
Very fast.
Pulling a carryon.
Intent. Gaze forward.
Often phone or ticket in hand.
***

Next a man in jeans, a jacket, and tennis shoes strides past, seemingly without a care in the world.

His gait looks long, his shoes make no sounds, his eyes up and looking ahead.

He wears a backpack and seems to be in no hurry at all, a smile on his face as he enjoys the walk like a day in the park.
***

Behind the strider comes a man in a fairly cheap, off-the-rack business suit.

Too much cologne drifts behind him like a toxic cloud.

He walks with purpose, his stride medium. His cheap (but polished) shoes make a thumping sound in the hallway.

His tie pulled up tight against his neck. His coat buttoned to prescription.

His phone against the side of his head.
His dark eyes intense.

He acts like the phone call signals the end of the world.
***

Characters have pacing, just as scenes, chapters, setting, and dialog have pacing.

Yeah, I know, seems impossible to just do, and it is impossible to do from the critical voice. And rewriting always kills such things.

This must all be learned and then come out of the creative voice.

And I'm not even going to try to explain things like story voice, story tone, genre tone, and so on into meta-details.

You'll get there if you read for pleasure and then go study.

The Key and a Focus Point to Move Forward

Stage four is about control.

Just as I used the stage four poker players as an example of how they try to control what others think they have, stage four writers are complete mind-control artists.

Stage four writers make sure that no matter what question in a story a reader has, it is answered at the right moment.

So to start working through stage three and toward stage four, start focusing on control.

Learn the basics of pacing, learn depth and how to control readers with your openings, learn how to relay details through emotions and setting.

Control.

Do three things:

—One, read for pleasure, then study books you have read for the learning.

—Open your eyes when out in the real world and start seeing other people and paying attention to them. Pay attention to the patterns and the tags and everything.

—Learn business as you go because all stage four writers know the publishing business. You might get to stage four writing levels, but it will do you no good in this new world if you are also not a stage four business person.

And no, there is no business in this book. This is a craft book. I just wanted to make sure to mention that right here because it is that critical.

Stage four writers are balanced in all their writing skill sets and in their business.

And they are in control of all of it.

Takes time and a lot of practice, but you can get there.

SUMMARY

As I have said a number of times, no writer skips over any of these four stages of a fiction writer. We all go through them starting at the beginning if we ever get to stage four, the top level of fiction writers.

However, along the way, sadly, millions of writers get stopped in chasing their dream of writing sellable fiction at one stage or another.

So this book was my attempt to detail out the road that fiction writers walk.

And maybe for a few writers give some hints as to what is ahead.

And for another few writers, help the realization of what is happening with their writing is normal.

The Four Stages Once Again

Stage one writers only worry about the typing. The words.

Stage two writers are starting to worry about story and character, but still focus on typing and the words.

Stage two writers are still lost in thinking that polishing a story will help it. But they are in transition from the first stage to the third stage.

Stage three writers have expanded out to be aware of story and characters and they notice pacing and so much more. (Remember, stage three is a huge area that takes years to get through and most never do.)

Stage three writers early on start to understand words are tools and by the end of stage three the writers are so focused on story they often no longer see the words. And seldom rewrite.

Stage three writers can make a living for a short time, but this stage is where most writers leave for a thousand personal reasons.

Stage four writers could not much care about the words. Words are in the complete control of stage four writers and are only part of the tools the writer uses. What is important to a stage four writer is what the reader is experiencing at any given moment in the story.

So think of the journey in this fashion…

A writer starts by focusing only on the tools, then expands out to learn aspects of telling stories and finally moves to a position of controlling readers' minds.

Stage one and two writers are typists.
Stage three writers tell stories.
Stage four writers are entertainers.

It really is that simple.
And that hard.
I hope this book helps you with your journey. And can keep you moving forward and learning and having fun.

New to the Thunder Mountain Series?
The first novels are available in electronic format or print at your favorite booksellers.

Now Available
from all your favorite booksellers in trade paper and electronic editions.

Smith's
STORIES

DEAN WESLEY SMITH
USA *Today* Bestselling Writer

BLIND POET

The poet sits on the sidewalk, a fedora for tips in front of him.

He hands out poems to those who can see.

Some read his words one way, others another.

And some can't see his words.

At least not at first.

BLIND POET

ONE

HE LOOKED LIKE I USED TO LOOK: Shoes polished just right, blue three-piece suit with the correct button buttoned, hair stylishly short, combed up and off his forehead.

Empty.

He would never see my poem.

Even though he had sight, he was truly blind. His body was nothing more than the bare walls of a pure white room. He needed to fill that room with the battered furnishings of a real life, then live there.

He needed to push open that room by cooking his best meals, staining those white walls with layered smells. And with each meal he needed to invite someone hungry in to share the smells and the tastes and his company.

Then, and only then, could he fill that empty room.

But he hadn't.

He would never be able to see my poems. He was a selfish man. He had done nothing and given nothing.

I watched as he came down the sidewalk with his friends. I knew without handing him a poem he was just like I had been.

In fact, he would never think to ask for a poem. He would have no reason for doing so.

But one of his two friends would. A man I had given poems to quite often. That man had gray eyes and always wore a gray suit. He had a hurt so deep inside that no one around him could see it.

I knew it was there. I could smell the hurt like a piece of meat that had rotted and decayed and was poisoning everything about him.

I sat on the sidewalk with my back against the rough brick of the National Bank building and waited for them to reach me.

"Poet," the gray man said. "You got a poem for us today?"

"Of course," I said. "I always have a poem for those able to see."

"Great."

The gray man reached into his pocket, pulled out a roll of bills, and tossed a five into my battered fedora.

"Thank you for your kindness."

I looked up into his eyes as he took the flimsy white paper I offered. There was no telling what someone would read in my poems. It all depended on the reader.

The gray man stood on the sidewalk and I watched as he moved his gaze back and forth across the page like a pendulum of an old grandfather's clock. When he finished telling the time of my poem, he glanced down at me.

"Thank you," was all he said.

I understood, so I just nodded.

The man in gray then handed the poem to the third man while the empty man simply stood and watched, hands in his pockets.

The third man quickly scanned the page. "Strange. Really strange."

I wish I knew what he saw, but he gave me no hint.

Then the third man handed my poem to the empty man.

The empty man glanced at it, then flipped it quickly over and glanced at the back before turning it to the correct side again. Just as I had sensed, he could see nothing.

The empty man pretended to read. That's what I had done when I was first given a poem. I watched his light blue eyes and rugged features.

"Nice," he finally said to his friends without looking up.

Then he folded the poem and stuck it in his jacket pocket. "Now aren't we running late?"

The gray man nodded and the three of them moved off down the sidewalk talking of their business as if the stop with me had not occurred. That was the way of our society. No one paid attention to a beggar on a street corner who wrote poems that shouted at the deaf and splashed color at the blind.

TWO

I NEVER EXPECTED to see that empty man again. Those who are truly empty will laugh at the blank page and toss it carelessly into a wastebasket, not realizing the wealth obvious in the blankness of the sheet. I expected as much from this man.

I was wrong.

He was like I had been.

The empty man returned to my street corner at six that evening as I was getting ready to move toward the boarding house where I wrote my poems. It had been a good day giving my poems to the few who were interested in seeing something of themselves.

The empty man who now stood in front of me might have made a thousand dollars during that same period. I used to make that much empty money.

"Poet," the empty man said, reaching into his pocket, pulling out a five, and tossing it into my hat. "I'd like a poem."

I sighed. "Why?"

"Because the sheet you gave me this afternoon had nothing on it."

"So why would you like another?"

I could sense his anger. He wanted to prove to himself that I was just a fraud so he could go home to his white-walled world and laugh at the stupidity of his friends.

"You going to give me another poem or do I take my five back?"

"You may have another of my works," I said softly, "with or without your money. But you won't be able to read it."

"I knew it. Charlie was just pulling my leg. There really wasn't anything on that sheet."

"There was a poem there and your friend could read it. I'm not sure, but I think it was a good poem for him to see today."

The empty man nodded. "That's what Charlie said. I gave it back to him and he tried to read parts of it to me, but I couldn't hear him. I could see his lips move, but I couldn't hear a word he said. Strangest damn thing. Charlie was almost in tears as he read it, too."

I nodded. That was why the empty man had come back. I hadn't been totally wrong. He would have never done it on his own.

Not like I did.

"So why didn't I see the poem?" the empty man asked. "Special ink or something?"

"No," I said as I pulled out another poem for him. "Only those who have given can receive."

"Just what the hell is that supposed to mean?"

"It is your life," I said. "That is for you to decide."

I handed him another poem.

He glanced at it, then flipped the sheet over. He could not see the poem.

I could sense his anger like a fast river behind a very weak dam.

He crumpled up the poem and tossed it at my feet.

"You should be arrested for pulling a scam like this."

He reached into my hat and took back his five dollars, then stormed up the street, blowing other passersby out of his way with the force of his passage.

I picked up the wadded sheet and smoothed out the paper. I had done the same thing. But I had come back the next day and talked to the poet. I doubted if this empty man would return.

THREE

AGAIN I WAS WRONG.

He returned late the next afternoon. He nodded an uneasy hello and stood above me staring down at my folder of poems laying on the sidewalk.

Finally, he broke the silence that had formed as a shell around us holding out the noise of the city. "Explain how this works, would you?"

"What are you referring to?" I asked.

"The poems," he said, pointing at my folder. "Why can Charlie see your poems and I can't? I want to know how you do it?"

"I don't do anything," I said. "You can only receive if you have truly given. Very simple, really."

"No, you don't understand. I asked Jim, that's the third guy that was with me yesterday, what he saw on the page. You know what he said? He said he saw a bunch of scattered words that didn't mean anything."

I nodded to that.

"I want to know how you made Charlie see one thing, Jim another, while I couldn't see one damn word. What's the gimmick?"

I shook my head slowly. I could remember having the same feelings. I too had been unable to accept the fact that I was blind. Truly blind.

I too looked for any excuse or trick.

"There is no gimmick," I said. "You can only receive if you have given. You have given nothing. Therefore, you cannot see the poem and get what it has to give. I am truly sorry."

I could feel his anger. I expected him to suddenly kick out at me. That is the normal reaction for those who cannot understand something. They strike at it.

I expected as much from the empty man.

Once again he surprised me. With his face red, he reached into his pocket, pulled out a ten-dollar bill and tossed it in my hat. "Give me a poem."

I nodded and handed him the top one in my folder.

He glanced at first one side, then the other, then turned and walked up the street, the poem clutched tightly in his hand.

He returned at the same time the following evening with the gray man.

The empty man paid for the poem, looked at both sides of the sheet, then handed it to his friend.

The gray man took a long time to read the poem. I could sense it was speaking deeply to him. He finished, then reread the poem slowly. His face was the grayest I had ever seen it. The hurt that so damaged him was obviously moving closer and closer to the surface. One day it would explode into the light and he would be free from it. Scarred but free.

After he finished the second time, he handed the poem back to the empty man and started slowly up the street.

Again, the empty man looked at both sides of the page, then with only a quick questioning glance at me, moved quickly to follow his friend.

For the first time, I began to let myself hope. Not much, but just a drop like a thirsty man getting only a sip of cold water for his first drink.

Maybe this empty man would be the one.

Maybe he would learn how to give and by doing so, grant me the sight I so needed.

FOUR

EVERY EVENING the empty man came by for a poem. He always gave me five dollars and he could never see the poem. We very seldom spoke, yet inside him I could sense he was changing.

Slowly, fighting every step of the way, he was doing it.

The empty man had no idea how hard his battle was for me to watch. He had no idea how each day I dreaded him not returning. How relieved I was when he did.

I so wanted to tell him I had fought the same fight. But I was afraid I would influence the battle. He needed to go the path alone. The only thing I could do was remain the measuring stick he held up to see if he was winning or losing the fight from his emptiness.

Finally, one day, he sat down next to me with his back against the rough wall of the bank.

"Poet," he said, "you've repeated over and over that a person must give before he can receive. Right?"

I nodded.

"So not being able to see your poems has driven me batty. You know that, don't you?"

"I can see that you have become obsessed," I said.

"And I've bought a lot of your empty sheets, haven't I?"

"They were not empty."

He waved his hand. "Whatever. What I'm driving at is I think you owe me a few answers."

"If I can help, I will," I said. I just hoped he didn't ask me for answers I couldn't dare give him.

"Good." He turned to face me. "I've done a lot of thinking since I first got your sheets. You know, I had never given anything to a charity. Not once. But I've changed. Now I give. Every day it's more and more, not counting the money I toss in your hat. I'm giving now, so how come I still can't see your poems?"

"Maybe you're not giving enough," I said softly.

I could feel my stomach twist as my words passed across his face. I feared he would not have the strength and turn back into the white room inside himself. If he did so, we would both remain blind. Yet I had no choice. I had to tell him the truth.

"Not enough," he said, his voice again gaining anger. "You want more money from me, is that it? Now I'm starting to see the scam here. You—"

"No," I said.

I fought down my own panic and made my voice cold, made my words jab through him with the sharp points of icicles.

"From now on, you may have my poems for free. You could have always had them for the asking. I do not want your money. I have no need for money except to buy the paper for my poems and put food in my mouth. Any extra I give away."

"Then I don't understand," he said. "I've given hundreds and hundreds of dollars to charity. What more is there?"

"Only you can find the answer to that question," I said as softly as I could, as if the level of my voice might ease the cutting edge of the truth.

I watched the empty man's face and remembered how I felt when the poet had said that to me. I could remember how I had suddenly realized my fight had just begun. I hoped this empty man was as much like me as he appeared and would also understand.

"Damn," he said more to himself than me. He stood and reached out his hand. "May I have a poem?"

I nodded and gave him one. He glanced at both sides of it, then moved slowly up the street.

I could sense that he would have a rough night. Like a boat being tossed on a rough sea, he would battle to remain afloat. My only hope is that he would return for another poem tomorrow.

FIVE

HE DID.

And again the day after and the day after.

Every day he told me how much he had given away that day.

Every day it became a little more and a little more.

And the pages were always blank to his eyes.

He became my obsession just as I had become his. I talked with him, encouraged him, wrote poems for him that he could not see. The one minute we spent together became the opening and the closing of each of my days.

His success was my success. If he failed, I failed. His blindness was my blindness.

We became one.

Married.

A beggar and a businessman.

Finally, as I knew it must, and hoped it would, it ended.

He arrived two hours earlier than his normal time and sat down on the sidewalk beside me.

"You know, Poet," he said. "All this time and I don't even know your name."

"Does it really matter," I said. "I could be anyone."

"But you're not just anyone," he said. "You're the Poet."

We sat there in silence for a short time.

I watched the people pass and look down at the empty man with looks of contempt. I could understand what they were thinking. Why would a man in such an obviously expensive suit sit on the sidewalk next to a beggar. Of course, the passersby could only see the surface and not the true roles we played.

"I lost my job," the empty man said softly after a hundred people on the busy sidewalk had passed. "I have given away everything. Everything."

His last word sounded like the breath escaping from a corpse.

I nodded, but said nothing. I remembered how I felt at that moment. I too had given everything away. I too lost a job that I felt was the entire world. I did not like the next step. He would not like it either. But I felt confident he would take it.

ALMOST FIVE HUNDRED PEO-PLE passed us before he spoke again. "Will I be able to see the words now?"

"No."

"I was afraid of that," he said softly. "Even though I gave everything, I knew it would not be enough."

"It would have never been enough," I said, "because you were never really giving to give. You were giving only to receive."

He sat up and faced me. "What do you mean I never really gave. I gave everything. I just lost my job because I was so obsessed with this insanity. Do you know that everyone I gave one of your poems to could read it? You said I had to give before I could receive. So I gave. I gave money, time, my job, everything. So why can't I see one of the damn poems?"

"Because you never gave just to give. You were giving only so you could get. That was the difference."

The empty man looked hard at me.

I could see in his eyes that he was starting to understand. Truly understand. The knowledge washed over him like a summer shower on a dusty city street.

And with the knowledge, I watched him step from that simple white room inside himself and lock the door forever. He was still empty, but he was no longer trapped.

After a moment of staring at me, he slumped back against the rough wall of the bank and closed his eyes.

I went back to counting the passersby and handing out my poems to the few who wanted to see. It was everything I could do not to jump and shout at the empty man that he had made it. He had succeeded. He had pulled himself free. And if he would just take the next step, he would give us both true sight.

But I said nothing. I simply sat and counted people.

After almost seven hundred passed and I had given away three poems, he sighed and opened his eyes.

"What's next?" he asked softly.

I smiled at him. "The world," I said.

Then I took a clean piece of paper from the bottom of my folder, one that I had not written on, and handed it to him.

Puzzled, he looked at it and then at the pen I handed him next. "Write a poem," I said, tapping the paper.

"But I can't see the ink or the words," he said after a moment of frustrated scratching on the paper and banging of the pen.

"Neither can I when I write," I said. "But others will be able to see and understand what they need to understand from your words. That is giving."

I tapped his paper again. "Write."

I went back to handing out my poems to the few.

This time I did not count the passersby. It would be a long time until he would finish his first poem.

It is difficult to paint with colors you cannot see, use sounds you cannot hear, or touch emotions you cannot feel.

But I knew he would finish.

And when he did, I would finally have a poem to read.

More Cold Poker Gang Novels
available at your favorite booksellers.

Smith's
STORIES

DEAN WESLEY SMITH
USA Today Bestselling Writer

CAT IN WAITING
A Pakhet Jones Story

Pakhet Jones works as a superhero in the world of cats. She exists in the Poker Boy universe in Las Vegas and eventually works with Poker Boy.

Cats call the humans that take care of them companions. And do what they can to help them.

But sometimes it takes more to save a companion. Sometimes it takes Pakhet Jones.

CAT IN WAITING
A Pakhet Jones Story

ONE

THAT CREEPY LITTLE TINGLING FEELING made me want to scratch the back of my neck. Happened every damn time that someone was headed toward me, to disturb my perfectly wonderful afternoon in the sun.

How annoying.

I was in front of what I called my "office," Cabana #7 at the Beach at Mandalay Bay Casino and Resorts in Las Vegas. I lay on my stomach on a cloth lounge chair, my head, back, and legs soaking in the wonderful afternoon sun, making me almost purr in delight. Besides good sex, there just weren't that many things that made me purr, but an afternoon lying in the hot Vegas summer sun was one of them.

Around me, the sounds of the tourists and their kids playing was a comforting and familiar background noise, just like the waves in the huge wave pool rolling onto the sand beach that filled a large part of this vast casino pool area. I loved those sounds. They were like a lullaby easing me gently into my afternoon naps.

And getting to nap in my "office" was why I came here at least five afternoons a week.

I had reserved and paid for Cabana #7 three-hundred-and-sixty-five days a year, which cost me more than buying a house every six months. But they stocked the fridge with what I wanted, cleaned it like I wanted, and I knew it was always available no matter when I came by. Since I had more money than I knew what to do with, giving myself such a wonderful place to be in the sun seemed like as good a use as any. Living for over a hundred and fifty years could do that rich thing for a person if they were smart and crafty.

I was cat smart. I could save and hoard things with the best.

Problem was that some of my friends knew I could be found here. My real office was on the top corner of one of those plush, mid-rise buildings downtown near my condo in the Ogden. My secretary, Kit, who was a superhero in the secretarial world, ran things there like a clock. I actually owned the entire office building with one of my many companies, but almost no one but Kit knew that.

The tingling feeling on the back of my neck got worse. Damn, I hated leaving the sun. I really was a cat through and through.

So holding the thin top of my bikini in place, I sat up and tied it as Detective Hugh Halligan turned off the concrete path leading from the casino and waded through the sand toward my cabana. It was the seventh in the row, the farthest from the main entrance into the massive pool area and sandy beach. Kind of gave me an even greater sense of privacy.

Hugh was a stocky guy, clearly handsome in his time, but now somewhere in his fifties, he had squared up and was going bald. And the top of his head was always bright red most of the summer. I asked him once why he didn't wear a hat and he had just snorted.

He had on his standard black sports jacket that had to be damn hot in this intense sun and hundred-plus temperature. Hugh and I had worked many a case over the last few years together after he learned I had some ability with animals, especially cats. He had no idea I was a superhero in the world of cats. There just weren't many normal people on the planet that knew about superheroes or gods.

Hugh was not one of the few.

I actually worked for Becky, the god of cats. Over the centuries she had been known by a lot of names, but the most famous was Bastet, an historic Egyptian cat goddess. Now she just liked being called Becky. She seemed to have places all over the world, but still liked the hot sands of Egypt more than anywhere.

My skin was golden tan and I was completely bald, so my head was also tanned perfectly golden. At six-two, I towered over Hugh's 5-7 inch frame, and that was with his big old loafers on.

Some people say that I looked like a golden goddess, being so thin and tall and bald. And always being perfectly tanned didn't hurt that image. But I wasn't a goddess, just a superhero. And my looks had nothing to do with what I was good at, and that was cats.

Being a decent guy, Hugh did his best to keep his eyes on my face when I stood from my lounge and motioned for him to follow me back into the covered area of the cabana. It was about the size of a decent bedroom, wide open on one side, with a table and six chairs in the middle of the room and a counter to the right with a fridge.

A slight breeze of air-conditioning blew from the back of the room and outward, keeping the room considerably cooler than out in the sun.

I slipped a light, sheer white cover over my thin bikini that didn't hide much, but I knew for Hugh it helped.

"Sorry to bother you, Pak," Hugh said a moment after he sighed because of the blowing air conditioning in the cabana.

My full name was Pakhet Jones, but my friends called me Pak. In old Egyptian lore, Pakhet means "she who scratches." I fit that description just fine I am proud to say.

I handed him a bottle of cold water from the fridge and motioned that he sit down in the direct flow of the conditioner while I got a bottle for myself and sat to one side where the air didn't blow on me. I liked being warm. It had always been my nature.

"So for what do I have this pleasure, Detective?"

"I need some help with a cat," he said, looking a little more flushed than the moment before, if that was possible with his red scalp. He was clearly embarrassed he was here, which meant this was not his idea at all.

"Let me guess," I said after taking a sip of the cold water. "Commander Craig told you to get me."

Craig was a superhero in the world of detectives and at the moment was the chief of detectives in Las Vegas. I liked him a lot and if he would have liked women, I had a hunch he and I would have been an item along the way. But he was with Billy, his long-time partner and an even more wonderful person. Billy was a god in the world of advertising and the two of them had been together for decades now,

The Year of the Cat Collections
Don't Miss Any of the Twelve

even though both still looked under thirty as all gods did. We just stopped aging.

Hugh just shook his head. "I have no idea how you do what you do. But yes, he told me to contact you and you would help with this situation."

"So, what is this situation?" I asked, trying not to smile at my friend who was studiously studying his water bottle instead of staring at my mostly naked body across the table.

"Got a missing woman, lived alone in a big house up in Summerlin with a single white cat. We've been feeding the cat for the last few days while the search was going on, but now we need to catch the cat and close up the house."

"Can't catch him, huh?" I asked.

Hugh just shook his head. "And not a damn clue what happened to the woman either. Frustrating all the way around."

Something more was going on, of that I had no doubt. If the cat was being fed, it should have been easy to catch. But clearly this cat did not want to be caught for some reason. And cats always had a reason.

I took another drink of water and stood. "Text me the address and I'll meet you there in thirty minutes. Just got to change."

"Thanks," Hugh said, standing. "Really appreciate it."

With that he headed back into the sun and down the sand of the large beach toward the walkway.

I gathered up my beach bag and draped a towel over my shoulder and followed him. Just inside the casino entrance was a large women's room. I went into the women's room, then into a stall completely out of casino camera range, and jumped to my apartment in the Ogden in downtown Las Vegas.

I really loved being able to just teleport anywhere. I had learned that skill almost a hundred years ago and couldn't imagine now living without it. It was my favorite superhero power, right along with the ability to be invisible.

I could also turn into a cat, something I had learned about forty years ago working on a really rough case. A big female leopard. A not-happy female leopard. I do not use that power much at all, since there are few leopards near Las Vegas. And after the last time I used that power, I craved steak for breakfast for weeks.

I took out my cell phone, and while staring out of my front window over the Vegas Valley toward the Strip, I called Kit.

"Thought you were in your office," she said.

"Hugh found me. Craig's orders."

"You need Charles?" Kit asked.

"Fifteen in front of the building."

"Be careful," Kit said, and hung up.

Most of my conversations with Kit were like that. She was that good. And I had a hunch she was richer than I was. She just loved to work running offices and companies, just like I loved to be with cats and save cats and work with cats and own and fund shelters for cats.

It was what each of us did.

TWO

TEN MINUTES LATER I was changed into a business jacket and short blue skirt with matching heels and was in the limo. I looked like a businesswoman now.

I rode in the front seat of the long stretch limo with Charles as we headed out toward Summerlin on the freeway.

Charles, my limo driver, was also a superhero in the world of taxis and limos. He drove for both me and Kit and sometimes a few others. He had been a stage driver back in the old west and moved to limos in the 1920s.

He owned the largest fleet of limos in Las Vegas, which was going some, and I knew he had other businesses as well. But for me and Kit, he still drove us, because, as he said, that was what he did.

I really liked having a team of superheroes around me. We often worked to help each other solve problems in one of our areas and were all friends.

Charles was tall, my height at six-two, and I had never seen him out of his black suit and driver's black hat. His face was thin, but his smile real. He was looking at having to retire and put his companies behind shell companies because he had gotten a few questions about how young he still looked.

We had talked about it a few times and decided he would come back as his son, take over the company. Kit knew some people who could set up that kind of deep cover for him without a problem.

"So, a lost cat or something worse?" he asked as he got the limo into the restricted lanes of two passengers or more and leveled out at eighty.

"Got a hunch it's worse," I said. "Hugh came to get me under Craig's orders. Stick with me on this one. It feels odd and I might need your help."

"You got it," he said.

Ten minutes later and exactly thirty minutes from when Hugh had left the pool, we pulled up in front of a large, two-story desert-tan suburban home in a very exclusive section of Summerlin, which was already an exclusive suburb of Las Vegas.

"Lots are big here," Charles said as they both climbed out. "Homes aren't stacked on one another. All of them cost a million, easily."

To me, they all looked the same and I hated subdivisions with a passion. Originality didn't exist in these places.

Hugh pulled in right behind the limo. He was driving a newer-model Cadillac SUV. Clearly a detective's salary was doing fine for him, or he had family money. I had no idea. Had never gotten him to talk about himself or his family.

"Charlie," Hugh said, nodding to Charlie who was standing beside the car, ramrod straight. Then Hugh turned to me. "Appreciate you coming, Pak."

"Anything to help out when it comes to cats," I said.

He led the way up the hot sidewalk and unlocked the front door. We walked into a large entry way with high ceilings and a massive wooden staircase that swept up to the right like an old French design of a mansion.

Walls were off white, modern art of questionable taste filled a few walls, and a large table filled the center of the entryway, more than likely to just catch packages as someone came in.

I'm sure a lot of people found the home beautiful. I found it stupid and overdone.

"How long ago did the woman vanish?" I asked.

"Best we can figure about four days ago. Her daughter reported her missing."

At that moment a beautiful, long-haired white cat with wide blue eyes appeared at the top of the stairs.

"Aren't you a handsome Birman," I said to the cat.

You here to help? The cat asked.

Another of my superpowers was that I could communicate with cats with thoughts.

"I am here to help," I said aloud to the cat.

Good, the cat thought back at me and turned and vanished.

I shrugged at Hugh. "Guessing I am supposed to follow."

I headed up the stairs with Hugh following and Charles behind him.

Second room, the cat thought at me from somewhere I couldn't see him.

I pretended to glance into the first bedroom, then went into the second room. The cat was sitting on a wide windowsill near a massive large bed. Clearly this room was a master bedroom with large dressers and a walk-in closet to the right. But it also wasn't used. More than likely a house this size had two or three suite rooms like this one.

The room had a faint sick odor to it that I could smell, but I am betting Hugh and Charles could not.

She is about to pass, the cat said. *That will be sad.*

"Going to have to help me," I said to the cat.

The cat looked at the huge bed and I could feel the disdain at my stupidity for not being able to follow the smell.

I got on my hands and knees and pulled up the spread to look under.

At first I saw nothing, but the smell hit me like a fist in the face.

"Wow," I said, easing back from the bed.

"We've checked all the rooms two or three times," Huge said. "She's not in here."

I eased back into the smell like swimming upstream against a strong current.

Tucked way up under the headboard area was the shape of a figure. I could barely see her in the dark. From the smell, she had clearly soiled herself a number of times.

She wasn't moving at all.

I stood and turned to Hugh. "Call an ambulance. I think she might still be alive."

"She's under there?" Hugh asked, stunned, getting out his phone. "Crap, just crap!"

I then frantically started to pull off the bed covers and sheets to strip the bed down to the mattress.

Then Charles and I lifted the bed up and off the frame while Hugh made sure we were not hurting the older woman more.

We stood the mattress up against the wall, then went back for the box spring and quickly had that off the bed as well.

The woman, for some reason, had crawled under the top of the bed for something, gotten her sweater tangled up on the slats of the old-fashioned bed frame and got stuck.

All three of us quickly took the frame apart, gently untangling the sweater from it as we went until we had the woman on her back on the floor in the middle of the room.

Hugh quickly checked her. "Shallow breathing. Found her just in time."

At that the sound of an ambulance pulling up out front echoed through the big house and Hugh ran for the stairs to lead them here.

Charles and I just stood back, giving them room to get to her.

I turned to the handsome fluffy white cat still sitting on the windowsill, pretending to not care about all the activity.

I moved over to him and said, "May I?"

Yes.

I picked up the guy, surprised at how light and small he was under all that fur.

I held him, supporting his back feet as we watched the two ambulance crew come in and instantly start working on the woman. They got an oxygen mask on her and some IV going, then with Hugh and Charles helping, they lifted her over onto the gurney and wheeled her out of the door.

Hugh and Charles followed them out.

After a moment it was just me standing in the large bedroom with the big white cat in my arms.

I hope she will remain, the cat thought. *She is a good companion*.

"You most likely saved her life," I said.

I slept with her, would not leave her. It was all I could do.

I gave him a slight hug and I could feel him relax.

"It was more than enough," I said. "And more than anyone could ask for."

With that I felt him relax a little more.

I sat him back in the sun on the windowsill.

"I'll come back tonight with some food and some news as to how your companion is doing and when she will return."

He just lay down and curled up with a deep sigh in the sun.

I agreed completely. There was just nothing like a nap in the sun.

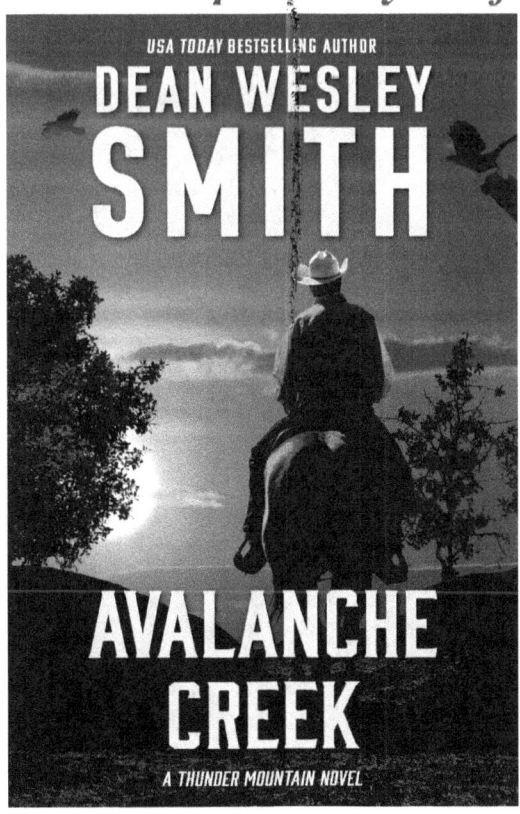
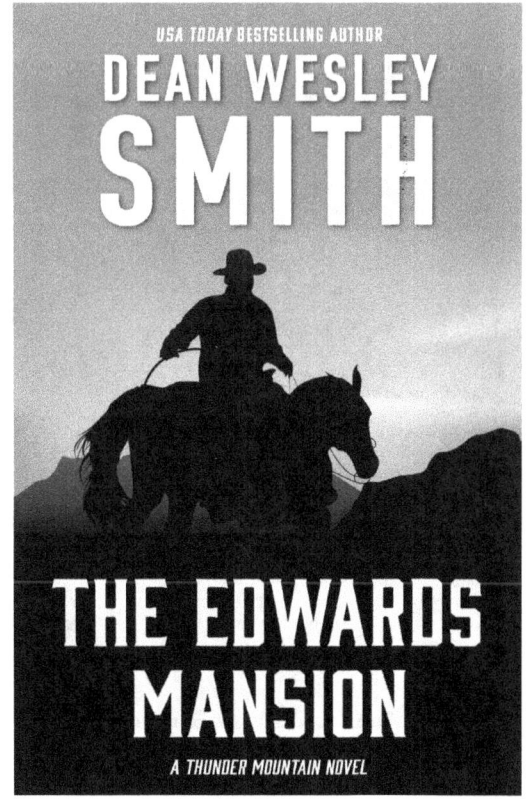

HEADS UP

A COLD POKER GANG MYSTERY

DEAN WESLEY SMITH

USA TODAY BESTSELLING AUTHOR

Retired Las Vegas Detectives Benson Cavanaugh and Bonnie State always worked alone before retiring. But joining the Cold Poker Gang task force push them to work together. Not something they easily want to do.

Searching for clues on a long cold missing person's case, they explore a shuttered old hotel and casino and find far more than anyone expected.

And that discovery takes them on a twisted journey through the past.

Another very, very twisted Cold Poker Gang mystery novel.

HEADS UP
A Cold Poker Gang Mystery

Heads up poker is a form of poker played between only two players.

Author's Note:
The characters in this book are fictional and any similarity to any person, alive or dead, is purely accidental. This is a work of fiction.

PART ONE
The Find

ONE

January 17th, 2019
Las Vegas, Nevada

THE OLD HOTEL NEVADA on Main Street in downtown Las Vegas seemed to be in hiding, almost ashamed to be seen. Only its seven-story oblong tower and a walled-off portion of the old casino was left standing. All the big Nevada-shaped signs with big "N" logos that used to cover the Main Street corner were gone, as well as the huge neon "Nevada" sign that had run across the top of the building proudly telling the world the Hotel Nevada existed.

Every entry on the ground floor had been walled in like a bad horror movie and painted a neutral light-gold color to match exactly the paint color of the entire building. Those old entrances looked as if they had always been walls.

Large, bright-colored billboards along street level now advertised restaurants, steaks, drinks, and gambling at the nearby Golden Nugget, the current owner of the old hotel. Those signs seemed to mock the remains of Hotel Nevada like memories of its past.

The ground floor casino area that used to front Main Street was now mostly a Golden Gate Casino parking lot, not even a bump in the pavement left of where millions were won and lost.

Driving past on Main Street, unless you knew the empty building used to be a major downtown Las Vegas casino, you would never notice it.

No one ever did.

It sat lost.

Hidden in plain sight.

All the room windows from the second floor up still had their drapes and looked like people might actually be in those rooms or sitting on the balconies of the seven-floor building.

No one ever was.

Some days a few of the windows were opened to air the floors out, causing the curtains to blow like ghosts. But there was no way at all into the building besides a heavy steel security door hidden in an alley near a large parking garage.

The Hotel Nevada sat empty.

Alone.

And completely ignored by everyone.

Recently retired Detective Benson Cavanaugh had gone past the old hotel a hundred times since it had been shuttered in 2012 and never gave the place a second thought.

At least not until tonight.

Now he held a red cold-case file with a picture of the old hotel before it was shuttered and what the hotel had looked like a few years ago, which is what it looked like still today. Why someone had thought to take a picture of the ghost hotel was beyond him.

Around Cavanaugh in the basement game room, fifteen or more retired detectives were talking, laughing, or staring at their cards. Two large poker tables filled the game room of retired Detectives Bayard Lott and Julia Rogers. A polished wooden bar from an old hotel filled one wall, and recessed lighting over the bar and the poker tables kept the room bright and yet homey-looking.

The room was climate controlled and even with that many old people in it, the air didn't feel stuffy or warm. And no one smoked, so the air was breathable.

Cavanaugh had fallen in love with the room the moment he had come down the stairs. One of those rooms you wish you had in your own home, but never could afford or find the time to put in.

Bowls of chips and M&Ms were scattered around the room and most everyone had a drink of some sort in front of them, a lot of it soda or water. These were all old detectives. Drinking alcohol, other than a beer or two, for most of them was a thing long in their past.

Cavanaugh felt the same way. He couldn't remember the last time he had had a drink past a small glass of wine at a good dinner.

Hell, he couldn't remember the last time he had gone out for a good dinner, actually.

The entire house had a faint smell of KFC. Cavanaugh had heard that Lott and Julia were KFC fans, but hadn't believed it until coming through the front door. That smell was easy to identify and damned hard to ignore.

Now he wished he would have eaten before coming. Chips just weren't going to hold him for long.

Cavanaugh could tell where there used to be a large-screen television on one wall, but Lott had told him it had been removed along with a couch and chair to make room for the second poker table as the Cold Poker Gang Task Force got bigger and more retired detectives wanted to actually play some poker each week.

Cavanaugh was the newest member of the task force. In fact, tonight was his first time at this regular Tuesday night meeting after just retiring from active duty and the tons of paperwork that went along with being a modern detective.

He had hated the paperwork. He knew of no detective who loved it, actually. But he flat loved the idea that on this special task force all they did was investigate and leave the paperwork to the active detectives when something was found.

Detective heaven as far as Cavanaugh was concerned.

Now, looking around at the room of retired detectives, he understood why they called this task force the Cold Poker Gang. Many of them actually played poker once a week and talked about the cold cases they were working on.

And Cavanaugh knew from his recent days as an active detective that this group closed a lot of cold cases and was respected throughout the city. And the Chief of Police backed the group completely while at the same time making sure it stayed out of the limelight.

Lott, the owner of this house, was sitting at one table, looking very serious at the play going on in front of him. Julia, his wife and partner, stood on the other side of the second table laughing with two other detectives. Lott and Julia had become a couple while starting this cold case task force. They and retired Detective Andor Williams now ran it.

Andor actually did all the work connecting the task force with the Chief of Police and getting the cold cases to hand out. If there was a problem or question, Cavanaugh was supposed to immediately contact Andor.

Cavanaugh had been standing at the bar for a good thirty minutes, just trying to soak in everything after the wonderful welcome he had gotten when he arrived. He felt like he belonged here.

Then, out of the blue, Andor, a short square man with wide shoulders and a bald head, had handed an official-looking red case file to Cavanaugh.

Cavanaugh would have sworn it was an original case file if not for the large red word "copy" stenciled on the cover.

"Glance at this file and I'll be right back," Andor had said, then turned away.

Andor was the oldest of the active Cold Poker Gang at seventy-three, but you could never tell he was that old. His energy was amazing and he walked anywhere like he would plow through a person in his way. Cavanaugh had heard of Andor and Lott solving some of the city's toughest cases back in the day when they were active partners.

Most of the detectives in the task force were in their late fifties and early sixties. Cavanaugh had retired at sixty-two with full benefits and health care, but he doubted he would have done that without knowing he could join this task force when he did.

Basically work was all he did in his life, all he had, and he loved it.

Cavanaugh knew most of the detectives in the room, if not personally, then by their fantastic reputations. Even though he felt welcome, he wasn't sure he belonged here with this caliber of detectives, but Lott and Julia and Andor had said he did, so Cavanaugh was going to give it a try.

Besides, he had nothing else to do. If he could solve cases working as a detective and not have to do the paperwork, he figured he didn't have much to lose.

But the case that Andor had handed him looked damn near impossible. A simple missing person's case of a Myra Stemple, age 23 when last seen coming out of a hotel on the Strip in 2009.

And even stranger was that her shoes, clothes, and purse, still holding over three hundred in cash, had been found three years later hidden in the back of a closet in the Hotel Nevada when it was being shuttered.

How the hell did that stuff get there? And how had it remained hidden for three years? Or had it just been put there a few days before? No way of knowing.

Or knowing what had happened to Myra.

That was clearly what Andor wanted Cavanaugh to find out.

Cavanaugh found it amazing those clothes and personal items had even been connected to a three-year-old missing person's case. Someone had been on the ball to manage that much.

Clearly the detectives on the case had done as much as they could, running into blank walls all the way along.

The case had been cold since 2012, but twice a year Myra Stemple's brother, a local attorney, went into the main station and talked to the detectives about the progress on his sister's case. More than likely his doing that got the case here to this task force.

At that moment Andor came back leading another detective who had been talking to Julia earlier. Cavanaugh recognized the new detective from seeing her regularly in the Main Street Station Casino buffet. He had had no idea until tonight she was a detective.

"Cavanaugh," Andor said, "meet retired Detective Bonnie State."

"Great meeting you," Bonnie said, smiling.

Cavanaugh somehow managed to say, "Nice meeting you."

Up close, Bonnie was one of the most attractive women he had seen in a long time. She had short brown hair, rich brown eyes, and a long face that looked like it smiled a lot. She was fairly tall, maybe only a few inches shorter than his six-two and she looked trim, like she worked out a lot, maybe even as a runner.

She had on jeans, tennis shoes, and a white blouse under a light tan blazer. He had no idea how old she was since her face showed very few wrinkles, but she was clearly old enough to be a retired detective.

And there seemed to be a force of energy around her. He liked that.

He reached out his hand and she shook it, her grip firm. She looked directly at him at that moment, then said, "Have we met?"

He laughed as he let go of her hand, even though a part of him didn't want to. "Trust me, I would have remembered, even at this advanced age."

He didn't say anything about seeing her a number of times in the buffet.

She laughed as well and blushed slightly.

Her laugh was wonderful, with a slight force to it that he had a hunch went with her energy and was part of her personality.

"Since you two are the new kids on the block," Andor said.

"I love it when someone calls me a new kid," Cavanaugh said, interrupting Andor.

Bonnie laughed and said, "Yeah, me too. Makes me feel all young and tingly again."

Cavanaugh just nodded. "Ah, to be young and tingly. Those were the good old days."

"Sure do miss the young part," Bonnie said.

"The tingly part wasn't bad either."

Andor just went on ignoring them both, "You two are now partners."

That statement took all the fun out of the air like a bad fart in a crowded elevator.

"I work alone," Cavanaugh said, suddenly feeling a little panicked.

No, scratch that. A lot panicked.

"So have I," Bonnie said. "Last ten years."

"Not on this task force," Andor said, smiling at both of them. "We work in teams of two or three, three being better since no telling when one of us is going to fall and break a hip. So get used to it."

Andor tapped the case file Cavanaugh had been looking at. "Sorry about that one right off. Someone had to take it. You two were just unlucky enough on the draw is all."

With that Andor turned and walked away, leaving the two of them standing there side-by-side, their mouths open.

Cavanaugh couldn't believe it. Twelve years as a detective working alone and now that he was retired, he ended up with a partner.

This did not bode well at all.

TWO

January 17th, 2019
Las Vegas, Nevada

RETIRED DETECTIVE Bonnie State loved the very idea of the Cold Poker Gang task force. And the moment she took early retirement, she got in touch with Andor about joining. He and Lott and Julia were all so welcoming, she couldn't believe it. They made her feel like she belonged as part of the group.

So she first had taken a trip to Hawaii for two weeks to celebrate retiring, and now was back with a slight suntan ready to go on this, her first night.

And she loved where the task force met, playing poker in what was basically a basement family game room, remodeled to hold a bar and two poker tables, but still just a family game room that she had to go through Lott and Julia's living room to get to. Doing that kept the feel of the task force really informal and clearly fun, even though over the last few years this task force had uncovered and solved some pretty major crimes and who knew how many small ones.

All she knew for a fact was that the Las Vegas Chief of Police was completely behind this task force and let them all wear their old badges and guns. And only active detectives had to do the paperwork on anything the task force found.

Over the last three years before she retired, she had gotten some credit for a cold poker gang solution or two, even though she had taken almost no part in the case as an active detective. The price she paid for the credit was that she got to do all the paperwork.

Seems the task force wanted to stay out of the spotlight as much as possible. Most of the population of Las Vegas didn't even know this existed. She really liked that attitude. Egos in here seemed to be at low ebb except when it came to hands of poker.

She looked around at the fifteen or so retired detectives laughing, talking, and playing cards. Everyone was enjoying themselves and that felt wonderful to her.

It felt like she had found a new home.

She was going to look forward to these Tuesday meetings even though she seldom played poker of any type. From what she had seen so far, the retired detectives at the table were very serious about their games. She wouldn't mind staying on the sidelines at all, at least until she got a little practice.

And maybe a few lessons.

Now Andor had asked her to come with him and they headed between the two tables to the bar where a tall, solid man stood staring at a file. He had a bald head and had on a seventies-style sports coat that looked slightly too large and had seen some wear. She had seen his type before. He liked to hide behind a costume and the wrinkled coat was his costume.

But his new and expensive running shoes told her a different story, as well as his new jeans.

When Andor introduced her to Cavanaugh, she had two emotions seemingly at the same time. First, his green eyes were wonderful, as was his face and smile. And second, she knew of him by reputation as one of the best detectives working in the valley and felt slightly overwhelmed finally getting to meet him.

Then Andor told them they were going to be partners and walked away, even though both of them complained.

She hadn't worked with a partner since her former partner got shot and had to leave the force on disability ten years before. She liked setting her own pace, using a small team she had set up around her to get things done. A partner, even someone as experienced as Cavanaugh, would just get in her way.

And clearly Cavanaugh felt the same way about her. Oh, this was going to be fun.

Finally he sighed and turned to her. "Detective State, I am really sorry about this."

"Call me Bonnie," she said. "I wonder if Andor knew we both worked alone?"

Cavanaugh sort of chuckled and shook his head. "Call me Cavanaugh. I try to hide my first name. And nothing escapes Andor and Lott and Julia. That's why when he told us, he ran and hid."

She glanced around. Cavanaugh was right, Andor had vanished in a basement room full of detectives.

"Neat trick," she said. "Think he's hiding under a table?"

"He didn't go behind the bar," Cavanaugh said, "so my guess is I think you might be right."

They both laughed, looking around the room and finding no sign of the stocky retired detective.

Bonnie realized she liked Cavanaugh's laugh. Not grating, just full of fun and clearly he laughed easily.

"So what case did he apologize for sticking us with our first time out?"

Cavanaugh handed her the file and she opened it while he sipped on a bottle of water.

Myra Stemple, single, missing since 2009, last seen walking out of a Strip hotel. Clothes found at the old Hotel Nevada years later. Case cold since 2012, totally forgotten except for the poor girl's brother who went to the original detectives twice a year.

Bonnie did what she called her first look at the case, just like she always did when handed a file. A combination of scan and quick read and a look at all the pictures. It took almost no time.

"Nothing much here at all," she said, closing the file.

"Yeah, thinking the same thing," Cavanaugh said. "Makes sense it went cold."

"So any ideas where we go from here?"

He shrugged and looked at her. "Got a hunch we better get to know each other a little better if we're going to be partners in this second life."

"Dinner?" she asked. "I'm just not having much luck with all the chips and M&Ms."

Cavanaugh laughed. "The KFC smell has been killing me. Got to learn to eat every week before coming here."

"Got that right," she said. "You got any favorite places in mind?"

He glanced at his watch, which she noted was expensive and fairly new. "How about the buffet at the Main Street Station Casino? Only about ten blocks from here and it's cheap and will be open for a few more hours at least."

"Wow, Detective, how did you know that was my favorite buffet?"

"A good detective never tells his secrets," he said, smiling.

"You saw me in there, didn't you?" she asked, laughing as they headed to say thank you to Julia before leaving.

"Damn," he said, "You're good."

"You don't know the half of it," she said, giving him a wink as she got to Julia.

Maybe, just maybe this having a partner might be fun after all.

THREE
January 17th, 2019
Station Casino Buffet,
Las Vegas, Nevada

THEY EACH DROVE and each paid for their own buffet before being shown to a table near a back wall. No one was around them.

The buffet was decorated in marble and tall polished wooden pillars to make it look like it was part of an old train station. There were lots of plants and massive chandeliers hanging from the high ceiling. The colors were browns and tans and everything felt welcoming. And the tables were spread out through two huge areas, one of the main reasons he liked it.

Plus there was a massive selection of food, mostly old-style Las Vegas buffet food, so any time of the day or night he could find something to eat.

The Main Street Station Casino itself actually had been pieced together with collectables from famous mansions, woodwork from Pullman cars, stained glass from museums, and even part of the Berlin Wall covered one wall in the men's bathroom. It was a very strange place even by Las Vegas standards and Cavanaugh loved it.

A second reason was the food was good and prices were old Las Vegas buffet prices. He could get breakfast for less than ten bucks and dinner under fifteen. Right now the Main Street Station Casino was a few blocks off of Fremont Street which accounted for the cheap prices, but in another year a new massive and modern casino would fill a couple of those blocks and Cavanaugh had no doubt the price would go up, as well as the crowds.

Cavanaugh loved sitting in the back of the large dining room so he could see the entire place and seldom did anyone sit around him. That was the case this evening. Neither one of them took off their light jackets, since both of them still had on their guns in under-arm carry and badges hidden under their jackets.

For some reason, now that he was retired, Cavanaugh felt even prouder to wear the badge and gun. When working, he just did it. Now he realized what a privilege it was to still be able to wear both.

Without a word other than both ordering iced teas from a waiter, they headed to the food lines. Cavanaugh filled his plate with some shrimp, a piece of prime rib, two chicken legs, and a few ribs. All protein. It was that kind of night. This place

lost money on him every time he ate like this, he was sure.

He made it back to the table before Bonnie and when she joined him she had a plate stacked high with a salad, a bunch of Asian dishes, and a slice of turkey. Numbers of times his plate looked exactly like the one she had just built, usually at lunch.

She pointed to his plate. "I do that as well, but tonight I seemed to crave a salad."

"How can anyone crave a salad?"

She shrugged. "Maybe the rabbit hasn't died."

Thank god he didn't have food in his mouth. He might have choked on it and then she would have had to save his life and that wouldn't be a great way to start a partnership.

She just sat there eating as if she hadn't said anything as he laughed.

After a moment, when he finally caught his breath, he said, "This partner thing might actually be fun after all."

"I was thinking the same thing," she said. "Something different after all the years of going it alone."

"Agreed."

For the next few minutes they just ate and Cavanaugh was stunned to notice the silence wasn't uncomfortable at all.

Finally Bonnie looked up and said, "Okay, should we talk about ourselves first or about the case?"

"How about a couple personal details first?"

She nodded and pointed to him. "Fire away."

He had no idea where to start, so he figured the basics would be as good as any, like a report of some sort.

"Sixty-two years old, I drive a three-year-old Cadillac, and I have a house I own free and clear just off Alta about a mile from here."

Bonnie nodded. "Nice neighborhood."

"Got it at a bad time, before the entire area started to rebuild."

He really liked his house, but at five bedrooms and three bathrooms, it was far, far too big for him alone these days. Actually had been for years. He just didn't know what to do, where to go, or even how, so momentum had kept him in the big place, living in just four rooms and closing off the rest.

"Married, kids, that sort of thing?" Bonnie asked when she saw he had drifted off slightly.

"Wife Karen died in a car wreck fourteen years ago," he said. "Drunk driver blew a stoplight. I have one daughter, Kathy, who is married and living in the Seattle area and works as an RN. No grandkids yet, might never be any. They don't seem interested."

"I know that feeling," Bonnie said. "Jacob, my only son, isn't married and has no interest in starting a family either. He lives and breathes for his computers."

"You married?" Cavanaugh asked.

"Divorced about eight years ago," Bonnie said. "Then just over a year ago he was killed in a boating accident, drunk with his current girlfriend, and he left all his millions plus some property to me and Jacob in his will. Guess he forgot to take

---

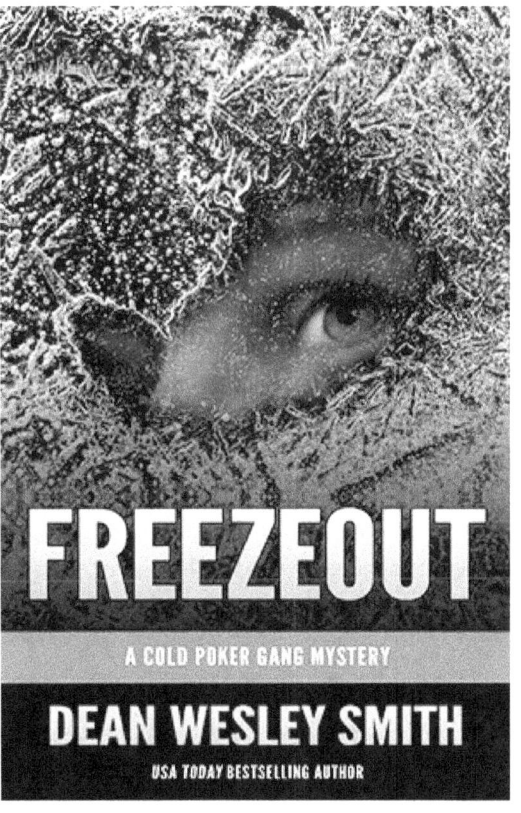

me off the will and the two million dollar life insurance policy as well."

"Wow," was all Cavanaugh could think to say.

"Why I could retire from being a regular detective after twenty years at the ripe old age of fifty-eight."

Bonnie went back to eating as if she hadn't said anything unusual at all.

"So clearly the two of us are like some of the other retired detectives in the Cold Poker Gang," Cavanaugh said. "We don't have money issues, which is nice, I must say, going into retirement."

"Can't agree more with that," Bonnie said. "Where did your money come from? And don't say twenty years of service."

He laughed. "I got my pension. It covers most things. But actually my wife got a lot of money when her parents died. She had been an only child. We both kept working and invested most of it. Bought a house, that sort of thing."

She nodded. "Smart, real smart."

"Where are you living?" Cavanaugh asked as he finished the prime rib and started in on the shrimp.

"Got a condo in the Newport Lofts not far from here, actually. But it's a small one-bedroom and I'm looking for something with a little more room."

"My place is five bedrooms and three bathrooms and a game room, formal living room, formal dining room, and family room."

"Just you there?" Julia asked, looking surprised.

"Yup. Too much space. And I have almost an acre of ground that costs me $300 a month to pay someone to keep up."

She nodded. "That is too much space."

With that they both went back to eating.

And Cavanaugh was feeling better and better by the moment about this new partnership.

FOUR

January 17th, 2019
Station Casino Buffet,
Las Vegas, Nevada

THEY BOTH WENT for desserts and when she got back, Bonnie noticed that Cavanaugh had pulled out the case file and had it on the table between them and was working on a piece of sugar-free key-lime pie. That was one of her normal favorites, but tonight she had gone for some apple pie with a little ice cream on top.

She might have more, she hadn't decided yet. She had had a good workout in the gym today and was craving more sweets.

She pulled the file over and opened it, focusing on the details this time instead of just a scan of the overall case. Cavanaugh gave her a few minutes until she slid the file back to him.

"Detectives originally did a good job with this one," she said. "Not sure what Andor thinks we can do."

"I'm not either," Cavanaugh said. "Maybe get lucky. You have any computer skills?"

"I can handle Facebook, sort of, and get my email and that's about it. But my son is a savant at computers and has offered many times to help me. And actually has at times over the last few years."

"Great," Cavanaugh said. "I talked with Lott and it seems the teams that have the most luck solving cold cases are the ones with great computer help. Pickett,

Sarge, and Robin have Robin and her husband's company. They are scary good with computers. Robin has offered to help us at times if we need her."

"Former Detective Robin Sprague and her husband?" Bonnie asked, actually surprised. "Don't they own that big security firm that guards all the bigwigs that come into town?"

"They do," Cavanaugh said, then finished off his pie.

"They weren't there tonight, were they?"

"Didn't see them," Cavanaugh said.

"Jacob freelances for the firm they own at times, when they need extra computer help. He helped with that ugly case in the tunnels they cracked last year."

"Jacob is that good?" Cavanaugh asked, looking surprised, which made Bonnie feel damned proud of her son.

"That's what he tells me."

"Think Andor might give him special clearance into police files to help us?"

"Can't imagine why not," Bonnie says. "He says he has extremely high security clearance in general and works for different parts of the government at times. Why?"

Cavanaugh pointed to the file. "Thinking we might be able to cross-reference some other similar missing persons cases from that time period and maybe even cross-reference some Jane Doe bodies around the year she vanished and also when they found her belongings."

"And maybe do a DNA match with the brother," Bonnie said, realizing that no DNA records were in the file at all because there was no body.

Cavanaugh nodded. "We need to interview him anyway and tell him what we are doing. Might as well get the brother to give us a sample. If we can get your son

into the system to do the cross-checking. If not, we'll call Robin."

"Damn," Bonnie said, "that's two more ideas than I had when I first read that file. You up for another dessert in celebration?"

He laughed. "Sounds perfect. And then we can swing back past the meeting on our way home and talk with Andor, get him going on the clearance for Jacob, if you are sure Jacob wants it."

"Far as I know, he might already have clearance," Bonnie said.

As she stood and headed for the desserts, she realized that for the first time in maybe years, she actually felt slightly excited about a case. An impossible-to-solve missing person's case. But something worth trying to solve no matter what.

And maybe, just maybe, that excitement was because she got to share the case with a partner. She liked that.

FIVE

January 17th, 2019
Las Vegas, Nevada

CAVANAUGH wasn't surprised that the two poker games were still going strong by the time they got back. The house had lost its smell of KFC and now had a faint odor of beer.

The meeting had started at seven and it was nine-thirty now. However, almost everyone who hadn't been seated in a game had left. Julia and Andor were the only two not playing left in the room and they were talking at the bar with a bowl of potato chips between them. Both of them looked up and smiled when Cavanaugh and Bonnie came down the stairs.

"How late does this normally go?" Bonnie asked, indicating the games.

"They are all old fuddies," Andor said. "It will all fade by eleven down to one game and be done completely by one. Everyone needs their beauty rest, you know."

Cavanaugh couldn't argue with that. He seldom was up past midnight these days himself.

"Got a question," Cavanaugh said. "How many members does this task force now have?"

"Twenty-four counting you two," Julia said. "About sixteen were here tonight, which is a little high."

"Wow, didn't know there were that many," Bonnie said.

"Still not enough to even begin to scratch some of these cold cases," Andor said. "And we lose a member every few months for one reason or another. So the group is constantly getting new blood, which helps us."

"Got a question of my own," Bonnie said. "My son Jacob is a computer expert who lives and works here in the city, mostly freelancing for either Robin Sprague's firm or for different government agencies. He tells me he has a very high security clearance. What would we have to do to get him access to department files so that he could help us?"

"Your son is Jacob State?" Andor asked, looking surprised.

Even Julia looked surprised.

Cavanaugh was pleased. Clearly they both knew Bonnie's son.

"That's his name, yes," Bonnie said, looking worried. "You know him?"

Andor laughed. "He already has complete access to all department and city files and has helped out a number of teams solve different cases."

Bonnie just shook her head and blushed a little, which Cavanaugh found to be nice.

"I just never thought to ask him if he knew about this task force," Bonnie said after a moment.

"Did you tell him you were joining?" Julia asked.

"No," Bonnie said, again looking embarrassed. "Guess me and the kid need to talk a little more, huh?"

All four of them laughed and Cavanaugh was very relieved. They now had the computer help and file access they were going to dearly need to solve cold cases in this modern world.

And that just made everything a ton easier.

Twenty minutes later Cavanaugh walked Bonnie out of the house and to her car. The night air had gotten colder and had a decent bite to it, and above them the stars were out clear and bright.

"Well, partner," Cavanaugh said, kind of stunned he had used that partner word, "got any suggestions for tomorrow?"

"Would you like to get together with Jacob?" she asked. "Tell him what we are doing and ask him for his help?"

"That sounds perfect," Cavanaugh said. "What's he going to think when his mom comes walking in with another man, let alone a new partner?"

"If he doesn't fall over in a dead faint," she said, smiling, "we'll be lucky."

Cavanaugh laughed. "As long as he doesn't ask me my intentions."

"Oh, he won't," Bonnie said, opening her door. "But he will ask me mine."

At that she grinned and said, "I'll call you in the morning, tell you where and when we are meeting after I talk to Jacob."

"Sounds perfect," Cavanaugh said.

By the time he was in his car, she was headed toward Alta and her condominium.

He followed her for a short distance and then turned the other way at Alta toward his house, which was only a quarter mile away.

For the first time in a long time, his big house didn't feel quite so empty as he unlocked the door.

And he didn't feel quite so alone.

SIX

January 18th, 2019
Mandalay Bay Shoppes
Las Vegas, Nevada

BONNIE had called Jacob and offered to buy him an early lunch at a wonderful Mexican restaurant in the Mandalay Bay Shoppes. It was fairly close to his place and easy for her to self-park. Plus the food was good and the portions large, and she usually took half of it home for another meal.

Cavanaugh knew exactly where the restaurant was, even though he said he had never tried it, and agreed to meet them at 11:30. She managed to get there at a quarter after eleven to get them a secluded table in the back where they could talk. She had ordered herself a glass of iced tea, and hot chips and salsa arrived less than thirty seconds after she sat down.

Cavanaugh found her five minutes later. She liked that he was the type to be early. They fit in that way.

He had on a slightly different seventies sports coat, just as wrinkled, just as out of style. Not a soul would give him a second look in that disguise, except that this morning, after the surprise of having a partner had worn off, she could really see him behind the disguise.

And actually, he was a very handsome man. Clearly in shape. He kept his head completely shaved, which gave him a distinguished look, and under the jacket he wore an expensive dress shirt, new jeans, and new and expensive tennis shoes.

If he took off the sports coat disguise, he would be a completely different person.

This morning she had put on a light green blazer over a white blouse and jeans and tennis shoes.

As Cavanaugh approached, he smiled, then looked around before taking off his jacket and hanging it on the back of the chair. She watched him move smoothly, like someone used to using his body. And with the wrinkled jacket off she could see his broad shoulders.

With those shoulders, the old-style sports coat made him look more square than in shape. But he clearly worked out. Maybe as much as she did.

She decided to take off her jacket as well. Both of them left on their underarm holsters and made sure their detective's badges were clear to be seen. Hopefully the waitress wouldn't be bothered by the guns.

"How are you doing this morning?" Cavanaugh asked as he sat down with his back against the wall looking outward.

"Actually a little excited about the case we're going to take a run at," she said.

"Yeah, me too," Cavanaugh said.

At that moment a waitress came by to ask for Cavanaugh's drink order and then as she turned away, Jacob showed up, so she got his iced tea order as well.

Jacob had a backpack over one shoulder and a Golden Knights sweatshirt on.

His jeans looked like he needed a new pair, but his shoes were expensive Nike, the latest running shoes.

He seemed to always wear basically the same thing and the backpack over his shoulder was like Cavanaugh's jacket, a form of disguise so that no one would pay him much attention.

She stood and hugged Jacob as they always did, then she turned and said, "Jacob, I would like you to meet my new partner, retired Detective Cavanaugh. Cavanaugh, this is my son, Jacob."

Cavanaugh stood, smiling, and shook Jacob's hand.

"Great meeting you," Cavanaugh said. "In the twelve hours I have known your mother, she has told me so much about you."

Jacob laughed and put his bag down and sat at the table. "No, she hasn't. She's not even sure what I do."

"But she's proud of whatever it is," Cavanaugh said. He smiled at Bonnie. "I'm sure."

"I am proud of him," Bonnie said.

Jacob turned to his mother and said, "I like this guy. Where did you find him?"

"At the Cold Poker Gang task force meeting last night," she said, smiling.

"Andor assigned you two to be partners, huh?"

Bonnie just sort of nodded, looking surprised, and Cavanaugh laughed softly.

Jacob looked at Cavanaugh. "You work alone, right, and Mom works alone. This could get real interesting real quick."

"So far no bloodshed," Cavanaugh said, laughing. "And how do you know so much about me?"

Jacob shrugged. "You were the active detective who worked with Robin and her partners on that crazy bomb and theft and

ancient storage unit with a sniper case, right? That was some fine work."

Bonnie noticed that Cavanaugh looked a little surprised and a little pleased at the same time as he nodded.

"Don't worry, Jacob does that to everyone," Bonnie said. "So Andor tells me you have full clearance to help us on cases?"

Jacob nodded and took a number of the chips. "I was hoping you would join the task force. Those old cases are fun to try to crack."

"Well, we have an almost impossible one, if you got the time?" Cavanaugh asked.

"I would love to help," Jacob said.

"Thank you," Bonnie said.

She had a hunch she was really going to like working with her brilliant son.

So now it seemed that suddenly she had two partners.

SEVEN

January 18th, 2019
Mandalay Bay Shoppes
Las Vegas, Nevada

CAVANAUGH really liked Bonnie's son, Jacob. Smart didn't begin to describe this kid. Scary smart would be a better way of describing it.

And hidden. The type of guy that unless you looked right at him, you would never see him.

Medium build, standard clothes for his age, standard student backpack, baseball cap, and a Golden Knights sweatshirt. He had a nondescript face, no beard or moustache, and his brown hair was just medium length and not styled in any fashion Cavanaugh could tell.

The backpack was the clue he was hiding. Jacob could walk past ten people and if those ten people were asked to describe him, they would just say, "A kid with a dark-colored backpack."

And nothing else.

Cavanaugh really liked that Jacob had worked with Robin already on a few Cold Poker Gang cases. Having Jacob and his computer skills as part of this team would give them a reasonable chance in this modern world.

Not that good old-fashioned detective work didn't usually do the trick. But with good computer access helping out, they could cut a lot of corners and find roads to investigate that they never would find otherwise.

Over the next thirty minutes they chatted and ate and Cavanaugh found out more about his new partner and how much she and Jacob really cared for each other. And respected each other. That was wonderful to see.

Cavanaugh wished his daughter Kathy was closer so they could spend more time together. But no way was Kathy leaving Seattle and no chance in hell was he moving into that sponge bath of a city. So they had to settle for infrequent visits.

He missed her and her mother sometimes more than he ever wanted to think about. So most of the time he just kept that stuff locked away so he didn't have to think about it.

"So what's this first case you two are working on?" Jacob asked as he finished his lunch and handed his plate to a passing waitress. Both Cavanaugh and Bonnie were only half done and Cavanaugh was full and planned on taking the other half home for dinner, while Jacob had eaten his entire huge helping.

Cavanaugh remembered when he could eat like that. Not anymore.

Bonnie handed Jacob the file and gave him a minute to look through it.

"Looks impossible," Jacob said when he finished.

"Thought the same thing at first," Cavanaugh said. "But we think we might be able to find a couple cracks with your help."

"DNA," Bonnie said. "We're going to go visit the brother and see if he'll give us a DNA sample."

Jacob nodded. "You want me to try to see if she's in the system somewhere with a familial match. I can do that."

"Exactly," Bonnie said.

"Also wondering if you could do a search of Jane Doe bodies turned up in the western states in the years from the time she went missing until her clothes were found," Cavanaugh said. "We're assuming the original detectives on this were watching for local matches, but there is no record they tried anything outside the area."

Jacob again nodded. "I'll get started on that, build a program to do the search for the western third of the country while you talk to the brother. I'll include the Vegas area as well just in case they missed something."

"You can do all that?" Bonnie asked.

"Easy," Jacob said. "Just will take me a little time to get into all the data bases I will need. And I've got a friend in a private lab in San Francisco who owes me a favor and could run the DNA of the brother quickly. Won't be in a chain of evidence, but figure if something gets going on this, we could always rerun the DNA through proper channels."

Both Cavanaugh and Bonnie just sat there staring at Jacob as he munched on a chip, clearly lost in thought.

All Cavanaugh could think was that this was going to be fantastic fun.

And no paperwork.

EIGHT

January 18th, 2019
Downtown Area
Las Vegas, Nevada

BONNIE HAD NO DOUBT at all that she was going to love working with Jacob and with Cavanaugh. After they left the Mexican restaurant, she had dropped her car off in her spot in the parking garage at the Newport Lofts condominiums and Cavanaugh had picked her up in front of the building. They had decided that there was no point in both of them driving everywhere and he liked to drive more than she did.

When they had been talking about it, Jacob had laughed and said, "If Mom never had to drive again, she would be happy."

He had been right, but she pretended to defend herself. The fact that Cavanaugh actually enjoyed driving was a relief. If she was going to have a partner, she might as well get some advantages out of it.

Besides the fact that she got to hang around with a handsome man who was funny and smart at the same time.

Cavanaugh told her that while he had been waiting for her to park, he had called Myra Stemple's brother Danny to tell him they were on the way.

Danny was a practicing attorney with an office in the downtown area near the Supreme Court building. She even knew the look of the office since she went past it many mornings on her run. The building was an old single-family home that had been remodeled into legal offices like every other home on the street. A sign in front announced the name of the law office.

As she climbed into the large black sedan and settled in, Cavanaugh said, "Brother's excited to see us. I told him we had no leads, but were starting a focused look at the case and he's willing to help in any way he can."

"Always nice to have family on board," she said.

She settled in as he got them through the city streets and headed toward the office. Cavanaugh drove with an assured manner, clearly relaxed, but very aware of traffic around him. She was comfortable instantly, which surprised her.

On a big screen on the dashboard were the directions to Stemple's office. But no voice said anything, just an arrow warned Cavanaugh when he needed to turn. He didn't seem to be paying it any attention.

"What kind of car is this?" she asked, glancing around at the comfortable dark-cloth interior and the massive array of electronics on the front dashboard.

"Cadillac CTS with all the markings taken off. Looks a little like an undercover cop car on the outside, especially with the dark color, doesn't it?"

"Why in the world would you want that?"

He laughed. "On one case a decade or so back I learned the hard way that if the person I was talking to saw a cop car pull up, I got more respect. Used to drive a big white SUV. Family looking thing. Caused all kinds of problems not counting the thing was a gas hog. Besides, I love Cadillacs, but didn't want to pull up in one of those either, so the guy at the Cadillac dealership customized this car for me a couple years back. I love it."

"I can see why," she said. "Comfortable."

"And it's got some special bells and whistles," he said, pointing to the electronic control panel. "Some of which I haven't even figured out how to use yet. Think Jacob could help me with that?"

She just laughed and shook her head as they pulled up and stopped in front of Danny Stemple's office. She had a hunch she was going to be finding out more and more interesting things about Cavanaugh with every day.

Stemple met them at the door, smiling, and welcomed them in. He was a short guy, not much more than five-two or so, with dark eyes and close-cut brown hair. Both she and Cavanaugh towered over him, but Stemple didn't seem to notice. He had taken off his suit jacket and wore a white shirt, expensive suit pants, and wide suspenders that looked slightly odd on such a short guy.

She and Cavanaugh made introductions and showed him their badges and he actually took a second to look at them.

His office was as she expected. What had been the living room of the older 50s home was now remodeled into a waiting room with expensive furniture and some lush plants in corners. A large desk filled one part of the room, more than likely for a receptionist or secretary, but no one was there now and it didn't look like anyone had used the desk in a very long time.

The room felt light and airy and welcoming. She would call it "lived-in."

Stemple led them into a side office that was clearly his and indicated they should take seats in front of his massive mahogany desk. On the walls he had numbers of degrees and citations from different organizations, but no family pictures at all, other than one near the window that

Bonnie recognized from the file as being of his sister. Not even pictures of parents.

Even though Cavanaugh and Bonnie were taller, when Stemple sat down behind his desk he was at their height. Most clients he would have sat above slightly. Very smart power move.

"Nice place," Cavanaugh said.

Stemple smiled and the smile actually hit his eyes. Bonnie could tell he was proud of his office. She wouldn't even be surprised if he lived in the back of the place. Clearly enough room.

"So you are looking into Myra's disappearance?" Stemple asked.

"We are members of a special task force," Bonnie said, "that looks into cases like your sisters. We now have a team on it, but we can make no promises."

Stemple nodded, but was still smiling. "Anything is better than doing nothing, so thank you. What can I do to help?"

"First off," Cavanaugh said, "we could use as much information about your sister as you have. What were her likes, dislikes, friends at the time she vanished, and so on."

"Got all that packed away in some boxes downstairs," he said. "As new information came to light, I added it in."

"You wouldn't mind if we copy all that?" Bonnie asked.

"Not in the slightest. I'll copy it for you, no problem. The original detectives on the case looked through it numbers of times, but didn't seem to find anything that seemed to help them."

"On our task force we're trained to look at things differently," Cavanaugh said.

Bonnie smiled. Cavanaugh knew exactly what to say to get the help they were needing.

"And one more thing after that," Cavanaugh said. "Could we take a swab of your DNA?"

"Familial match?" Stemple asked, nodding. "Glad to. And if you can get DNA to run on this old a case, you do have some clout."

With that Bonnie could only agree. The Cold Poker Gang did have some clout. But clearly her son had more.

NINE

January 18th, 2019
Downtown Area
Las Vegas, Nevada

CAVANAUGH was impressed with Danny Stemple and how he had offered to copy all the material he had in a few hours and get it all to them later in the day. And he gave them a DNA sample easily, excited that they were actually going to try that route.

But now, as Cavanaugh climbed into his Caddy and Bonnie climbed in beside him, he realized they were dead in the water. Talking with the brother had been the only thing that needed to be done that he could think of.

And they had just had lunch. It didn't happen often that he felt this sort of fish-out-of-water on a case. It happened, but he hated it every time.

"So any idea where to next?"

He started the car, but didn't bother pulling away from the curb.

Bonnie nodded. "After we mail off the DNA sample to where Jacob tells us, I was thinking the Golden Nugget?"

It took him a moment to realize why. "You think we need to get into the old Hotel Nevada to take a look at where her clothes were found?"

She nodded. "That's been bothering me since I read the file the first time."

Cavanaugh nodded. "I've been wondering why the detectives didn't track down who had checked into that room."

"Good question," Bonnie said. She glanced at the file, then said, "One of the lead detectives on this, Stan Carson, is a friend of mine. Let me ask him."

Cavanaugh watched as she pulled out her cell phone, checked something quickly, then put the phone on speaker so he could hear.

"Hey, Bonnie," Stan said when he answered. "How goes the life of leisure?"

"Actually back at work," she said. "I have you on speaker phone with retired Detective Cavanaugh."

"Don't tell me that Andor in the Cold Poker Gang put you two together as partners? Oh, Cavanaugh, I am so sorry."

"Thanks," Cavanaugh said, laughing. "But she hasn't hurt me this first day yet."

"Oh, give it time," Stan said. "So Detectives, what can I do for you?"

"We got handed the Myra Stemple case," Bonnie said.

"Andor really doesn't like you two, does he?"

Both Bonnie and Cavanaugh laughed, then Bonnie said, "We're trying to scratch at any breadcrumbs we can find. Wondering if there were records of who was checked into that room last where her clothes were found in the old Hotel Nevada?"

"Might be now," Stan said. "Never checked. When the clothes were found, all the records of the rooms were tied up in the massive bankruptcy of those five casino properties downtown. We couldn't access them without more court orders than we had the clout to get for a missing person's case."

Cavanaugh nodded. He remembered that bankruptcy and not being able to get records in the middle of it made sense.

"Took a couple years before all that got straightened out," Stan said, "and to be honest we just never kept track on that. Good idea if you can get them."

"We are also getting the brother to copy us all his records," Bonnie said. "And he gave us a DNA sample."

"Excellent," Stan said. "It would be a dream if you guys could give Danny some answers on his sister."

"We're going to try," Bonnie said. "I'll keep you up to date."

"Appreciate that," Stan said. "And Cavanaugh, watch yourself. Bonnie hates to take prisoners."

With that Stan hung up with both Cavanaugh and Bonnie laughing.

TEN

January 18th, 2019
Downtown Area
Las Vegas, Nevada

BONNIE SAT in Cavanaugh's Cadillac's passenger seat, running any kind of search she could figure out to run on her laptop to find any information about the Hotel Nevada. They were parked on the street on the Golden Nugget side of the old hotel and had decided that they needed more information about the place they wanted to look inside before actually going in.

Bonnie was feeling incredibly frustrated with each passing minute and nothing seemed to be coming up besides a few pictures of the outside, some mentions on a collectable casino chip site, and a brief mention on a dated website focused on old Las Vegas.

Beside her, Cavanaugh was running the same kinds of searches. And it didn't look like he was having any more luck than she was having.

The Hotel Nevada still looked like an active building if you didn't look too closely. It had been painted the same sort of light gold as the Golden Nugget and it still had curtains in all the windows of the seven-story building. But there was no entrance, no signs, nothing. On street level were big billboards advertising Golden Nugget restaurants and nothing more.

Where some of the old casino building had been was now a parking lot for the Golden Gate, which was next to the Golden Nugget. The Hotel Nevada had become a chameleon, blending in perfectly with the surroundings.

She knew she had driven by it hundreds of times and never once noticed it.

Finally Cavanaugh sighed and closed his laptop. "Got a hunch we're going to be saying this a lot."

"What's that?" Bonnie said, closing her laptop as well.

"This might be a job for Jacob."

She laughed and put her laptop away in its case and stored it at her feet with her purse as Cavanaugh put his laptop in a case and stored it on the backseat floor.

"So we're old," Bonnie said. "Old people aren't supposed to be good with computers."

Cavanaugh laughed. "I just hate being a cliché."

Bonnie pulled out the file of the case and opened it. "Her clothes were found on the third floor in room 317 in the back of the closet. What do you say we do what we are good at doing?"

"Talking to people," Cavanaugh said, smiling.

"Exactly," she said. "And looking at crime scenes."

"Not sure that is a crime scene," he said, shutting off the car.

"Pretty sure it's not," Bonnie said. "But can't hurt my ego pretending it is."

He laughed. "After that computer search, my ego needs all the help it can get."

She couldn't agree more about her own. That had been an amazingly frustrating hour.

And for the next hour the frustration continued.

They talked with a lot of different people at different levels of the Golden Nugget, but it seemed that no one on the property knew much about the old Hotel Nevada. Everyone knew it was owned by the Golden Nugget parent company. But no one seemed to know who to talk to or who might have keys or the ability to give them permission to go inside.

Bonnie felt almost as frustrated after an hour as she had felt with the computer search. Not that she could measure hours of frustration or that she even wanted to try.

Everyone at the Golden Nugget had been friendly and very willing to help. Just no one seemed to know how. It seemed that the Hotel Nevada was not only hiding from the city, but from the company that owned it as well.

No wonder no one had bothered to tear it down in over a decade.

Out of sheer luck, they did manage to talk to an employee pushing a cart up the alley next to the parking garage. He said nothing had been touched in the old hotel in the years he had worked there. And he had actually been inside it. Said the lower level was used for storage and the upper floors hadn't changed at all, with beds and dressers and curtains on the windows. He had called it "creepy."

He didn't know who could give them permission to go in though.

What they did learn was that at the time the Golden Nugget bought it in the bankruptcy sale, they did exactly what they planned to do with it. Immediately after taking control, they knocked down most of the old casino part, sold off that as a parking lot to the Golden Gate, made the building impossible for transients to break into, painted it, and then mostly just forgot it, leaving it as an area for future expansion.

A couple people did mention that someone must be going in and out of there, since at times windows were opened on the different floors and they had seen the drapes moving in the wind. But no one knew who that person was or what department to check with or who went in and no one even seemed to be able to find where the keys might be.

Only the guy in the alley gave them any clue to who it might be, but even he didn't know who to talk with and he no longer had keys.

If everyone at the Golden Nugget hadn't been so friendly and willing to help, the entire thing would have annoyed Bonnie beyond even the computer search. But at all levels the employees and managers wanted to help. But no one knew exactly how.

Cavanaugh and Bonnie did get some promises that the manager would find out and call them. Bonnie wasn't going to hold her breath on that. Finding out how to get into an old hotel for a cold case just wasn't on the top of busy hotel manager's job description. But knowing how friendly all the people they had met had been, it might actually happen.

As she and Cavanaugh headed out of the Golden Nugget Rush Tower and toward his car, he asked, "Some food?"

Now Available
from all your favorite booksellers in trade paper and electronic editions.

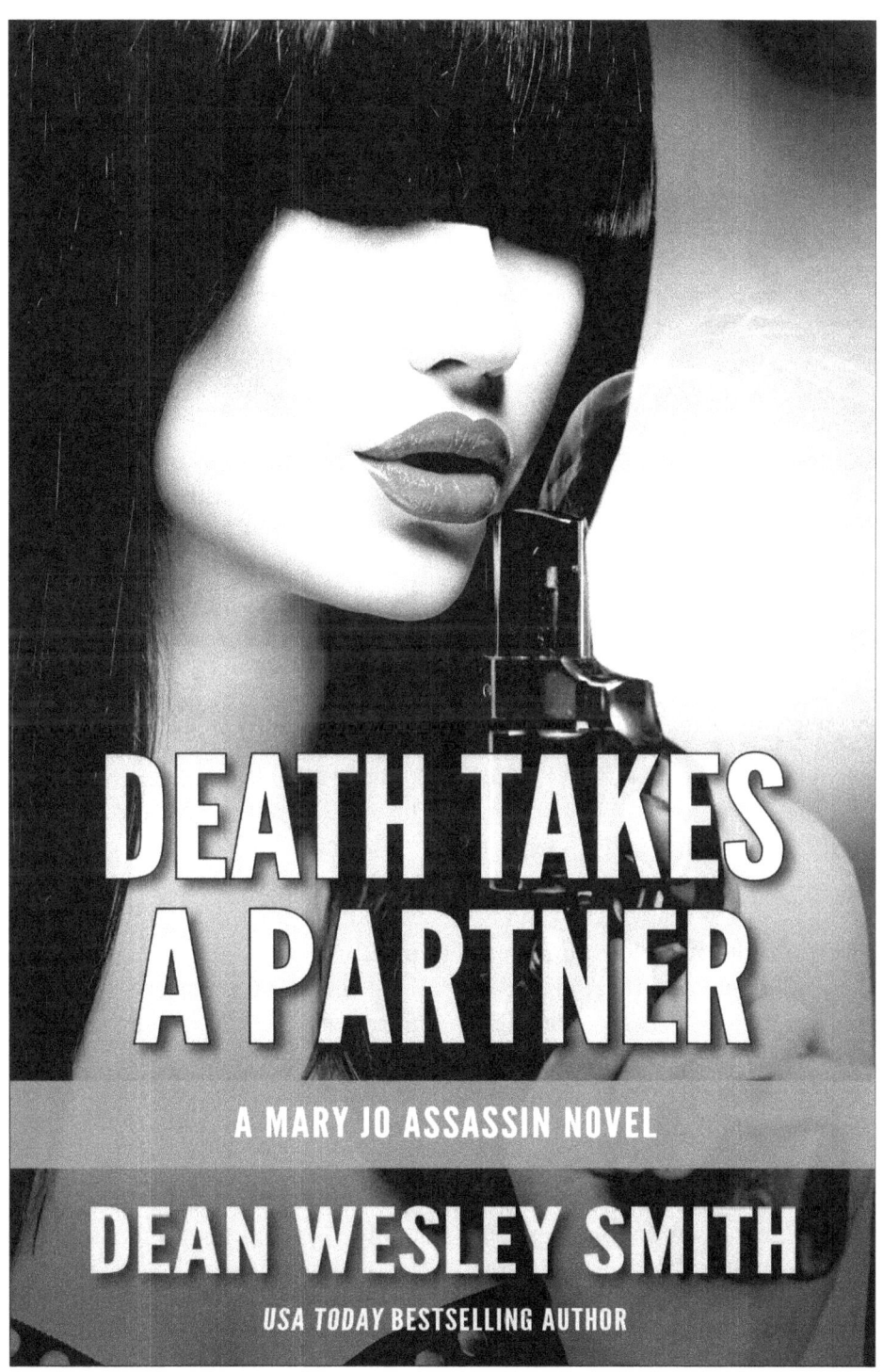

"Love to," Bonnie said. "But let's make it a distance away from that place."

She pointed at the Hotel Nevada across the parking lot from them.

"Agreed," he said. "I hate it when a building laughs at me."

She felt exactly the same way. Exactly.

ELEVEN

January 18th, 2019
Downtown Area
Las Vegas, Nevada

BONNIE didn't seem to care where they went for food, so he suggested the food court at the Meadows Mall on Valley View and she agreed, saying she had never eaten there.

"Just close for me," he said as he got them headed down Main Street toward Alta. "And a bunch of choices, all mediocre and cheap."

"Ahh, you know how to take a girl to the finest places."

He laughed. "I didn't suggest a food truck, did I?"

"Careful now," she said. "Don't be insulting some of my favorite places to eat."

They spent the next ten minutes of the drive to the mall and the walk inside debating which food truck at the First Friday Art Celebration was their favorite. It seemed they both had at least three. And they were all different.

After the conversation, the next First Friday he had a few new food trucks to try, of that there was no doubt.

The food court had ten different restaurants, including a McDonalds and what looked like a regular old burger diner. The food court smelled wonderful and the sound was only background, with faint mall music playing just under all the talking. About half the food court tables were full. He had seen it completely full at times.

They both went for the Asian and found a small table tucked off to one side of the food court where they could at least feel like they could talk in private.

He couldn't believe how comfortable he felt with Bonnie and how closely their likes and dislikes matched. The more time he spent with her, the more time he wanted to spend with her.

That was not like him at all.

And she even laughed at some of his jokes.

"There has got to be a way into that old hotel," Bonnie said after they got settled. "I'm finding it very weird that no one in the Golden Nugget seemed to know how, though, besides cutting the lock on that big steel door in the alley."

"It's someone's job to keep the place aired out, up to a certain level of fire code, more than likely use it for storage. Just got to connect with that person and then get his or her boss to give the permission."

Bonnie nodded.

"We might want to put in a request with their corporate offices," Cavanaugh said.

"And get their attorney and insurance agents involved?" Bonnie said.

"Ahh, real good point."

They ate in silence for a few minutes, the sounds of the mall swirling around them.

"Fire marshal," Bonnie said suddenly, looking up and smiling. "They would know how to get in there to do regular inspections. I saw fire stacks on the side of the building for water. They had inspection stamps on them."

Cavanaugh just laughed and nodded. "Dead right. And I got a good friend right at the top of the inspection side of the department."

He grabbed his phone and looked in his contacts for Sheck. He couldn't believe he hadn't thought of it earlier. He and Sheck went back a long ways, clear to the academy, such as it was in their day, and now Sheck was within a few years of retiring as well from the fire department.

Sheck seemed to know everything about every commercial building in this town and that was going some, considering how many casinos, hotels, offices, apartments, and condominiums there were in Las Vegas.

"Calling Chief Sheckley," Cavanaugh said to Bonnie, who looked surprised.

Cavanaugh put the phone on speaker between them.

"Cavanaugh," Sheck said, "I told you I'm too young to go fishing. I'm still chasing women."

"You're my age, you old fart," Cavanaugh said, laughing. "And I have you on speaker phone here with my new partner, retired Detective Bonnie State."

"Andor put you with a partner," Sheck said, laughing. "Oh, Bonnie, I am so, so, sorry. Is he being a gentleman? You tell me if he doesn't behave."

Bonnie laughed. "I think I can handle him, Sheck. And how is Katie doing? She get through that last hip surgery all right?"

Cavanaugh was sure his jaw hit the floor. Katie was Sheck's wife and clearly Bonnie and Sheck and Katie all knew each other.

Was there anyone in this town that Bonnie didn't know?

"She's doing great," Sheck said. "And mentioned last night that we hadn't seen you since you got back from Hawaii. Trip good?"

"Wonderful," Bonnie said. "I'll tell you both all about it soon."

"I'll make steaks if you promise that Katie and you will allow me to talk a little."

"A deal," Bonnie said, winking at Cavanaugh.

"What I really want to hear about," Sheck said, "is this thing you got going with Cavanaugh."

"First day and no bloodshed so far," Cavanaugh said.

"Check under your chair," Sheck said. "With Bonnie you might be bleeding and not even know it."

"Oh, Sheck," Bonnie said, smiling, "Am I really that bad?"

"Yes," Sheck said, laughing. "Now what can I do for the Cold Poker Gang's newest detectives today."

"Trying to get into the old Hotel Nevada," Cavanaugh said. "Folks at the Golden Nugget were great, but didn't seem to know anything about the old place."

"You working that case where the girl's clothes were found in that old place?"

"We are," Bonnie said, looking surprised. "How do you remember that?"

"It was one of my people who found them," Sheck said. "I happened to be there as well that day since I was making sure the place got shuttered correctly. Detectives on that case were impressive, being able to link them to that girl missing for three years."

"So anything to see in there?" Bonnie asked.

"Besides a warehouse full of stuff on the ground floor, old furniture and a ton of dust on the upper floors, not much,"

Sheck said. "But you two are the detectives and if you want to go in, I'll get one of my guys to take you in on an inspection."

"We would love that," Cavanaugh said.

"Be in the alley there tomorrow morning at eight," Sheck said.

"Thanks," both of them said at the same time.

"Oh, that's just frightening," Sheck said, and hung up.

"You think our friends are worried about us being partners?" Bonnie asked, laughing.

"Not worried so much," Cavanaugh said. "I think they are all terrified."

"Always good to keep them guessing," Bonnie said, laughing.

Cavanaugh flat agreed with that.

TWELVE

January 18th, 2019
Meadows Mall
Las Vegas, Nevada

BONNIE had really loved the look on Cavanaugh's face when he realized that Sheck was a good friend of hers. It seemed that the two of them knew a lot of people in common. She found it amazing they hadn't met before now.

But maybe, considering how solitary both of them had been over the last decade or more, maybe not that surprising. She just hadn't met many new people and she was finding being around Cavanaugh and being able to talk with someone far more enjoyable than she had imagined it might be.

Besides, Cavanaugh was smart, funny, and had the same focus and interests she did. What was there to not like?

Around them the sounds of the Meadows Mall food court were almost comforting. People talking and laughing, dishes and trays banging, unrecognizable music making sure that no space went without sound. She kind of liked it here. It wasn't that far from her place downtown and clearly no muss, no fuss eating.

And surprisingly, the food wasn't bad. A little too much sugar, as food court places tended to be, but not bad.

As they were both finishing, Cavanaugh got a call. He glanced at it and said to her, "Danny" before answering.

She liked how he was automatically including her as a partner.

"Oh, fantastic," Cavanaugh said to Danny after a moment of listening. "We'll be by in about thirty minutes to pick it all up."

He clicked his phone off and smiled. "All ready."

"Wow, that was fast."

Cavanaugh nodded. "Got a hunch he's been hoping for this day for a decade now.

Bonnie could understand that. She had a hard time imagining what it would be like to have a loved one just vanish without a trace. It had to be torture almost every day, like a wound that would never heal. She loved that this city had the Cold Poker Gang task force to help get closure to some families on these cold cases.

She just hoped that she and Cavanaugh could finally be the ones to find Myra, one way or another.

"So any idea what we might do with all the stuff Danny is giving us? He said it was four file boxes full. Going to take some sorting to make any sense of it."

She sat back. She hadn't given that any thought at all. She sure didn't have room for it in her small condo. Her kitchen table barely fit her and her morning coffee and an occasional case file she brought home. She really needed to find some place larger to live. But the thought of moving just sort of made her want to crawl back into bed and hide.

"How about," Cavanaugh said, "we work on it at my place. I got this large dining room with a massive table and a ton of light. We can spread everything out."

"It won't get in your way?"

He laughed. "That table hasn't been used since before Karen died. When Kathy and her family show up we either go out or camp around the kitchen table. In fact, I can't remember the last time I actually set foot in the dining room. Far as I know that table has been eaten by termites by now."

She laughed. "If it has, you have larger problems. But you sure having that stuff there won't be a pain? This case doesn't look like it's going to solve quickly."

"It would be fantastic to have that big old house used for something besides storing furniture I never use and me stopping by to sleep. But we're going to need to get some snacks and drinks of some sort to get us through working. I just never have much food in the place at all."

She laughed. "Neither do I in my condo. Jacob came by one day and asked if I was too broke to buy food. Coffee in the morning is all I need. And bottles of water."

"You think we might need to set up some new habits now that we are retired?"

She looked at him for a moment, surprised at the idea. Then she could see the little grin starting to form with a crinkle in the corner of his eyes and she laughed.

And he laughed with her.

And all the way to the car they talked about some of the habits they had as detectives that they were not going to change in retirement.

Or ever.

THIRTEEN

January 18th, 2019
Cavanaugh's Home
Las Vegas, Nevada

CAVANAUGH TOOK two boxes of the files they got from Danny and led the way into his sprawling ranch house through the front door with Bonnie carrying two more boxes behind him. He had parked in his driveway instead of pulling into his garage as he normally did. He figured it would be easier to get the boxes out and into the dining room through the front door.

Besides, the day had turned nice. Cool, not much wind, just nice.

He found himself surprisingly nervous to be showing Bonnie his home. Since Karen had died, very few people besides Kathy and her husband had been in the place. So he now found himself actually looking at everything. Almost like seeing it for the first time.

Amazing how a person could live in a place for years and never see it.

The heavy, wooden front door opened into a blue-tiled entry with a formal living room a step down on the left that only his housecleaning service people had gone into in the last decade. He never noticed that living room, or how the furniture looked dated and staged. At least it wasn't dust covered.

His television was in a family room on the other side of the kitchen. That was where he often watched a game or news while having dinner. He had a favorite recliner in there that he had to admit he had spent far too many nights in.

Just ahead from the front door was the kitchen with its large wooden kitchen table. His morning coffee cup still sat on the table beside the morning paper and a computer. He sat at that table every morning drinking coffee after showering and dressing, reading the paper and also following a few sites online. It was such an ingrained habit, he never gave it much thought.

"This way," he said, turning to the right from the entry and into a formal dining room. The massive dark mahogany table that filled the room could seat a dozen people easily and he remembered when he and Karen had bought it, having great plans to hold dinner parties, something they never once did.

At the moment the room was dark and felt completely unused.

He dropped the two boxes on one end of the table and moved two of the heavy chairs back against the wall to give Bonnie room to put down her boxes.

He then clicked on the massive chandelier and was glad to see the housecleaning service had the table polished and dust free.

He moved to the drapes on one wall and opened them, adding even more light to the area.

Now it seemed almost welcoming instead of a dark-feeling tomb that he walked by every day and never noticed.

"This will work great," Bonnie said. "And wow, big place."

"A museum for turn-of-the-century furniture," he said. "I should charge for tours, make a fortune in my retirement."

She laughed. "You going to charge me for a tour?"

"First one's always free," he said, smiling.

And with that he could feel his tension easing. He showed her the kitchen, the closest bathroom, the bedrooms down the hall, and then out onto the back patio through a large sliding door from the kitchen.

"Wow," she said, looking out at the acres of trees and landscaping. "I didn't know this much land was still open in this area."

"All the houses along here have this size acreage. Land was fairly cheap back in the late 1950s when this place was built. And they tucked all the houses up close to the street so that made these back areas seem even larger. You ought to see some of the estates over closer to Alta. Tennis courts, pools, you name it."

"You got room for all that back here," Bonnie said.

"No idea what I would even do with a pool." He indicated the rocks and cactus areas with a gravel path running through it toward the back of the lot. "That used to be all regular lawn and flowers and such and I had it all removed and changed to low-water landscaping about a decade ago. Left this one small lawn area here near the back patio, but I think I'll have it changed out when I get around to it."

"I think it's all fantastic," she said. "Were you and Karen happy here?"

"Never got the chance," he said. "We bought it, got a great deal, actually, and had just started to work on it and make it our own when she was killed. So I have no real memories or anything of her here, other than some of the furniture that we bought together."

"That's kind of sad," Bonnie said.

Cavanaugh just shrugged. "I suppose that's one reason I didn't move. It quickly became just my place and it didn't constantly remind me of Karen. And Kathy never really lived here either. We bought it when Kathy went for her first year in college."

"Kind of a large bachelor pad, don't you think?"

"Never one to shy away from excess," he said, waving his arm around at the large space.

"Well, I think it's beautiful," she said.

"Thank you," he said. "Appreciate that."

And he did, very much, actually. He couldn't remember the last time he had shown this place to someone. So her liking it felt great.

"So should we dig into that paperwork?" she asked, turning to go back inside.

"Unless you have any other ideas," he said, following her and locking the back sliding door.

She shook her head. "Just got to tell Jacob we have Danny's DNA swab and ask him what to do with that?"

"And we do need snacks and something to drink," Cavanaugh said, moving to the almost empty fridge.

"So let me call Jacob, ask where he wants us to send the sample, grab some snacks and come back and dig in."

"Sounds perfect," he said as she took out her phone.

And it did.

FOURTEEN

January 18th, 2019
Cavanaugh's House
Las Vegas, Nevada

BONNIE WAS AMAZED at Cavanaugh's place. She doubted he had any idea how much it was worth, or that he even cared. But the place was huge and in that style they called "Mid-century Modern." And its location was in one of the old, historic neighborhoods.

And even though the furniture was all twenty years old and mostly brand new, the place still had a comfortable feel to it and that surprised her even more than the size. She could understand why Cavanaugh had kept it, even though it was far, far too large for his needs.

For any one person's needs, actually.

Jacob had given her the address on where to ship the DNA sample and who to ship it to. So they had packed it up, addressed it and dropped it at the main post office downtown, then stopped at the grocery store for snacks and some Diet Coke for her and combination iced tea and lemonade for him. To her that had sounded disgusting, but when he gave her a sip it actually was pretty good if you liked sweet lemon in your tea.

Jacob called just as they got back to Cavanaugh's place and unpacked the drinks and snacks and were getting ready to get to work on the files. She glanced at her watch. It was just after five in the afternoon and they had already done a lot of things in their first day.

"Found a few things you need to know on my searches," Jacob said after she put her phone on speaker so Cavanaugh could hear.

"There are twelve Jane Doe bodies in the western states. All are possible matches from the time period. DNA will help with that."

"Shipped it an hour ago," Bonnie said.

"Good," Jacob said. "But you guys may have another issue on your hands."

Bonnie glanced up at the stern look on Cavanaugh's face. She didn't like the sound of that at all.

"Issue like where to have dinner," Cavanaugh said, "or with the case?"

Jacob laughed. "Mom, I think you have met your match with snark."

Bonnie just laughed and shook her head at Cavanaugh, who shrugged.

"When I cross-referenced," Jacob said, "what Myra looked like in size, hair color, age, and so on, I found another eight missing persons cases that matched hers almost exactly in a five-year period. All in Las Vegas, all unsolved. Hers was the last I found so far, but haven't gone past 2012 in time."

"Oh, shit," Bonnie said.

"My feeling exactly," Jacob said. "Want me to check with Andor and get you all the files on those?"

"Yes, please," Cavanaugh said.

"Yes," Bonnie said.

"And your old hotel connection might just be real," Jacob said. "Three of those women's clothes were found in the old hotel before it shut down. In the same room. It was a dump those last years before it went into bankruptcy, from what I can tell. So no telling what information can be trusted or not."

Bonnie flat didn't know what to say. Nine different women, nine families without answers all these years. It just twisted her heart.

"Fantastic work, Jacob," Cavanaugh said into the silence.

"Thanks," Jacob said. "But got a hunch we're just getting started on this one. I'll get in touch with Andor and get those files to you. Where are you at?"

"My place, sorting the stuff from Myra's brother," Cavanaugh said.

"Copy that," Jacob said. "And sorry, Mom."

"Don't be sorry," she said. "Fantastic work."

"Thanks," he said and hung up.

Bonnie just shook her head, staring at the four boxes of information on Myra.

Eight more?

"I think we just kicked over a beehive," Cavanaugh said. "No wonder people were worried about us being together."

That broke her thoughts of the eight women and she laughed and smiled at her new partner. "And we're not even done with the first day yet."

"Now I'm starting to get worried," he said, laughing.

Then he went to the first box, took off the lid and started sorting.

And she joined him. Nothing to do but get back to work and follow the leads.

PART TWO
The Hotel Nevada

FIFTEEN

January 19th, 2019
Shuttered Hotel Nevada
Las Vegas, Nevada

CAVANAUGH now wished he had brought a heavy coat. He stood out of the wind, tucked against the cinder block alley wall of the old Hotel Nevada, trying to stay warm in the high-forties morning air. The clouds looked like they threatened rain and there was no sign at all that the Vegas sun would appear anytime soon.

He had gotten here early, at 7:30. Maybe a little too early. If he got much colder, he was going to have to go back to his car to warm up.

Standing here now, by himself like he had been for the last ten-plus years, he still wasn't sure that yesterday hadn't been some sort of strange dream. Working and spending the day with Bonnie had been easy.

And actually fun.

He couldn't remember the last time he had spent an entire day with the same person, let alone enjoyed it.

And she had seemed to enjoy being with him as well, which was even stranger. None of his stupid comments had bothered her at all.

After Jacob's bombshell of a call yesterday afternoon, they had spent the next few hours getting a start on sorting all the information about Myra that her brother had given them. Neither one of them really knew what might be important and what wasn't, so they just read and sorted.

And having Bonnie working in his house felt odd for a few minutes and after that it felt perfectly natural. And when he realized that, it surprised him. But he decided to just not question it and focus on the case.

It seemed that Myra Stemple had led a pretty normal life up to the day she had disappeared. She had decent grades in high school, graduated from UNLV with a degree in accounting and immediately went to work for one of the large tax agencies in town.

She had stayed single, although she was dating at the time of her disappearance. But the detectives on the case had cleared her boyfriend of any suspicion without a problem, since not only were they seemingly in love, but he had been on the East Coast when she vanished.

There were lots of pictures in the boxes, as well as letters and such. It seemed that when their parents had died while Myra was in college, she and her brother had gotten even closer. No wonder Danny spent so much time focusing on finding his sister. She was the only close relative he had.

But there hadn't been one thing in the boxes that might show that Myra was in any kind of trouble that would cause her disappearance.

At just after six, Jacob had arrived with copies of files of six of the eight other missing person's cases.

What had jumped out at Cavanaugh on first glance at those new files was that the clothes of three of them had been found in the exact same room as Myra's clothes.

And years separated the finds.

What was it about that room?

He had no hope that they would discover it today, but he did want to get in there and get some pictures of that room anyway. Clearly the cases were connected.

"Morning," Bonnie said from just to his right as she came into the alley and tucked against the building like he was doing. "Damn cold out here."

Bonnie had on a blue, heavy ski-parka jacket, ski gloves, and a matching stocking cap. Her cheeks were slightly red from the cold already. And he was surprised at how happy he was to see her.

"At least you were smart enough to wear a jacket," Cavanaugh said. "And gloves and a hat."

"Watched the weather this morning with my coffee," she said. "Maybe some snow up in Summerlin."

"Lucky for me I don't have to stand out here much longer," he said, pointing to a guy coming down the alley toward them.

The approaching guy was short, walked with a quick stride, and also had on a heavy coat with a fire-marshal insignia on the front, and gloves and a hat. Cavanaugh felt downright underdressed for this meeting.

"Morning, Detectives," the guy said as he got closer. "My name is Alistair. Sheck told me to give you an inspection tour of this place. But still need to see some badges for insurance purposes."

"Nice meeting you. I'm retired Detective Bonnie State working with the Cold Poker Gang task force."

Alistair took off his glove and shook her hand and glanced at her badge with a nod.

"Retired Detective Cavanaugh. Same task force."

He showed Alistair his badge hooked on his belt under his jacket, then shook the guy's hand as well.

"Thanks for helping us this morning," Bonnie said.

"Place was due for its monthly inspection anyway," Alistair said, shrugging. "You two can just go explore while I do that."

"Do we have to tell anyone in the Golden Nugget we are in here?" Cavanaugh asked.

"They know we're going in this morning. They might send someone over, but often they don't."

With that he turned and walked down the alley between the old hotel and the Golden Nugget parking garage to a massive metal door. He took out a key and unlocked the door and pushed it open with a loud scraping sound that echoed between the old hotel and the parking garage,

making a note on a clipboard as to the time and the condition of the door and lock.

"Hope you got flashlights," he said, pulling one out and clicking it on. "This place can get as dark as an Egyptian tomb on the lower levels, not that I have ever been in one of those tombs."

"You clearly haven't lived then," Bonnie said.

Alistair glanced at her. "You been in one?"

"Oh, heaven's no," she said, smiling at him.

Alistair laughed and shook his head. "Detectives."

"Retired detectives," Cavanaugh said. "We've had a lot of years to practice being smartasses."

Alistair laughed. "I'll remember that. Now how about flashlights?"

"Got a light and a spare," Cavanaugh said, pulling both out of his pocket. He wasn't sure if Bonnie would think to bring one or not.

"Same here," she said, smiling at Cavanaugh as she pulled two out of her pocket as well.

So they were starting off on their second day thinking alike. Too strange.

"Then all set," Alistair said. "I'll get you to the center staircase area and after that you are on your own. Once you get up a floor it will be light because there is a center light well that runs the length of the interior of the building."

"Thanks," Cavanaugh said.

And with that they stepped inside the old Hotel Nevada, flashlights illuminating the shapes of furniture and tables stacked in the large room and covered in tarps.

"Those things look like covered animals," Bonnie said, almost in a whisper. "This is going to be weird."

Now Available
from all your favorite booksellers
in trade paper and electronic editions.

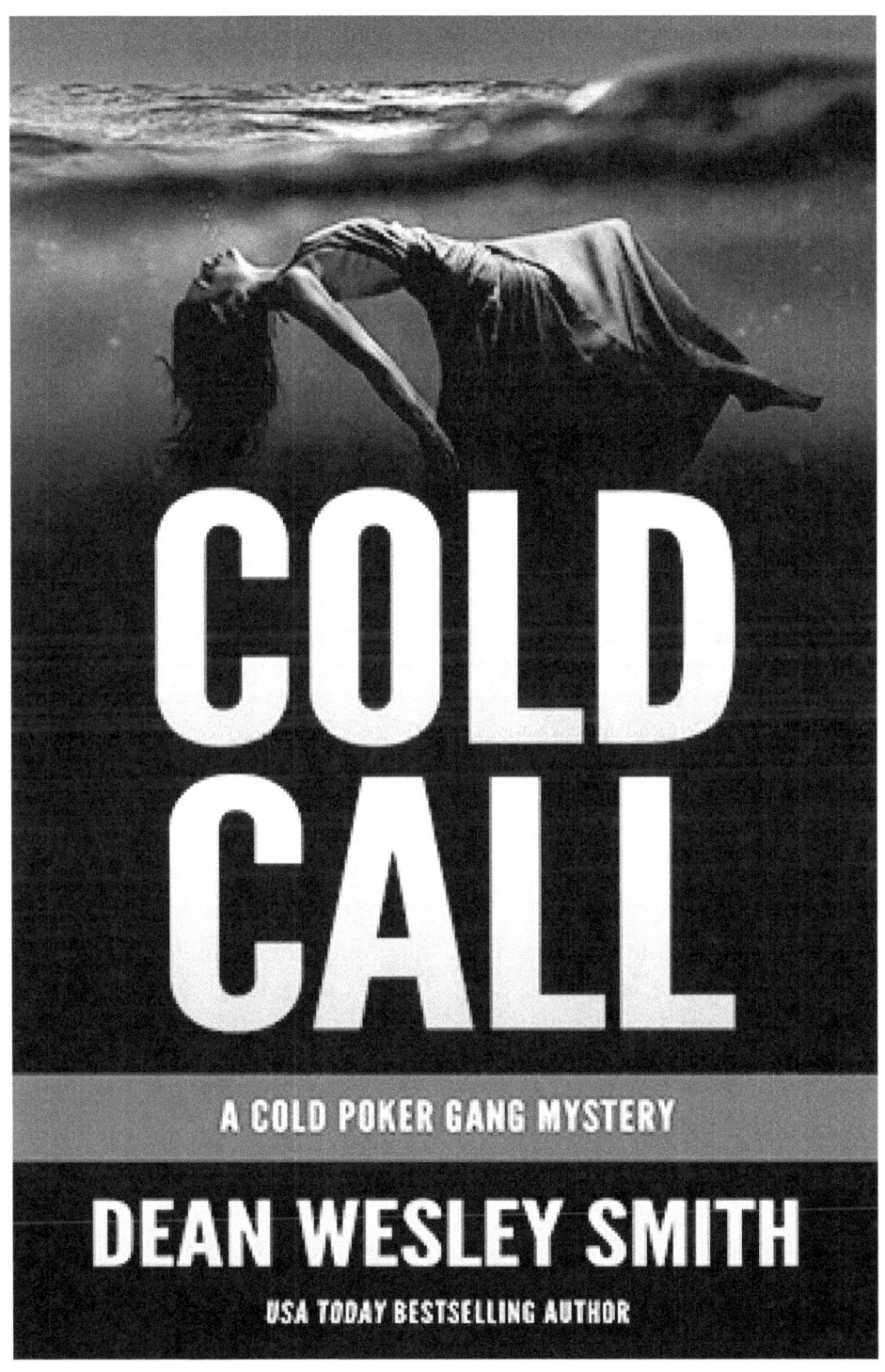

Cavanaugh couldn't disagree. Right off, this place felt like one of the strangest and creepiest buildings Cavanaugh had seen.

And considering this was in Las Vegas, that was going some.

SIXTEEN

January 19th, 2019
Shuttered Hotel Nevada
Las Vegas, Nevada

BONNIE HATED the feeling of the old Hotel Nevada almost from the first step from the back alley and into the storage area. Alistair had closed the alley door behind them and locked it. All three of them had flashlights on and the beams didn't seem to push back the gloom much at all.

"This way," Alistair said, moving down a wide aisle between stacked furniture and through a couple double doors until finally they emerged into a large lobby area. The ceiling was low as had been the case back in these old hotels and casinos, and she was sure she could still smell the odor of a million cigarettes. The place looked dingy and worn out, like all the cigarettes had just dulled everything.

Or that might be just layers of years of dust. With a flashlight, she couldn't tell. She was betting it was a little of both.

Where large doors had been on one side was now nothing but a wall of plywood, clearly built to block the entrance from Main Street. Only faint light reached the large room from down a wide staircase on the right.

On the left was another wide archway that led into what had been part of the casino. Nothing remained in there except for more stored furniture under tarps. The tile of the lobby under their feet, once polished, now showed dirt and scuff marks and just looked as dull as the walls and ceiling.

The old mahogany front desk filled part of one wall with a wall of keys to the rooms behind it. The keys still hung on the pegs as if waiting for some ghost to take one and stay in a room.

She had no doubt that the front desk and the wall of keys would end up at some point in someone's home as a decoration piece. But past the desk and back key wall, she couldn't see much else in here worth saving.

The entire place had a smell of extremely dry dust and a little smell of something sour, which wasn't something normally smelled in Las Vegas. And just their movement had dust swirling in the beams of their lights. She was going to need another shower by the time they got out of here.

"Enjoy yourselves," Alistair said, shaking his head. "I honestly hate this place and wish they would just tear it down."

"Can't say that I disagree," Cavanaugh said.

Bonnie just nodded. There just wasn't anything about this old hotel to like. It wasn't old enough to be a real historical attraction. It just sort of reminded her of a period of downtown Las Vegas that was going to be better forgotten and as quickly as possible.

"Thanks," Bonnie said as Alistair turned to go into the old casino area. She and Cavanaugh headed for the staircase. She was really, really glad right at this moment that she had a partner on this case. Doing this alone would have almost been too much. She could have done it, but having Cavanaugh beside her at this point felt much better.

And clearly he was thinking the exact same thing.

"Having a partner is coming in real handy right now," he said as they started up the stairs, moving slowly to not stir up too much dust.

"How's that?"

"I fall through the rotted floor, I got someone to pull me out."

"I'm leaving you," Bonnie said. "I haven't known you long enough to stay in this place for that."

"Now I see why you haven't had a partner for a long time," Cavanaugh said.

"They are scattered in old buildings all over town," Bonnie said.

Cavanaugh laughed and they kept climbing slowly.

"Wow, this is even creepier," Cavanaugh said as they reached the second floor landing.

They didn't need their flashlights anymore since light streamed into the hallway from every door. Both of them clicked off their lights and tucked them in a pocket.

The hallway went off in two directions, covered with what looked like a 1960s patterned carpet, now faded and dirty. Light sconces on the walls were spaced between every door and the hallway seemed very narrow compared to modern hotel hallways.

She moved over and looked into one room without going inside.

The door had been blocked open with a chair and the drapes were open on the window, making the room light, even though outside the day was dark and cloudy.

One bed tucked against the left wall, two old and worn end tables were on either side of the bed. A small round table sat in front of the window with one chair.

Everything had a gray tint of dust.

"This might have been an expensive room in the day," Cavanaugh said.

"Yeah, afraid I stayed in far too many just like it," Bonnie said.

"We really are that old, aren't we?"

"Not a nice thing to say to a woman," Bonnie said, laughing. "But yes, we are. Annoyingly so."

"No argument from me there."

They both turned and, in silence, went up toward the next floor, the only sound the wind hitting the windows and the creaking of the stairs as they headed up.

"Same layout as the floor below," Cavanaugh said.

Bonnie pointed to the sign on the wall. "317 is in this direction."

Bonnie led the way in the narrow hallway until she found the room where Myra's clothes, and three other missing women's clothes had been found over the years.

It looked just like any other room, only it was a corner room tucked in over the alley and had a window facing Bridger Street where they had both parked.

The bed was on the hall wall, the table was under the window, and the bathroom door was open showing an old claw-foot tub and rusted toilet and sink.

The closet door was closed, so Bonnie moved over and opened it.

It was narrow and deep.

Bonnie took out her flashlight to see the back of the closet and when she clicked it on she staggered backward.

"What?" Cavanaugh asked.

"Clothes," she said, keeping her light on the pile of women's clothes tucked in the back of the closet.

"Shit," Cavanaugh said, softly.

She knew instantly what those clothes meant.

There was another missing girl somewhere.

SEVENTEEN

January 19th, 2019
Shuttered Hotel Nevada
Las Vegas, Nevada

CAVANAUGH FELT stunned to his core at the sight of those clothes stuffed in the back of the closet on the dark wood floor. It had been one thing to read about finding Myra's clothes and the clothes from three other missing women, but seeing a pile of clothes there now, in this hotel that had been shuttered since 2012, felt like he had been slapped.

"Now what in the hell do we do?" Bonnie asked softly, more to herself than him.

"I'm calling Andor first off," Cavanaugh said, pulling out his phone. "We need to know what the procedure for the task force is for something like this."

She nodded and a moment later he had Andor on speaker so Bonnie could hear. Cavanaugh quickly explained where they were and what they had found and the circumstances of finding clothing in this same closet with other missing women.

"We might have a serial killer or worse here," Cavanaugh said. "God only knows what is going on."

Bonnie nodded.

"Two days together and you two are already causing a shitstorm," Andor said. "I'll get an active detective headed your way and I will give him your phone number."

"Going to need a forensics team on this as well," Bonnie said.

"That's the active's call. Meet the active in the alley in ten."

Andor hung up.

"Feeling really naked right now without gloves," Cavanaugh said. "Got some in my car."

"And we need to tell Alistair what is happening and what we have found," Bonnie said, staring at the pile of clothes in the closet. "Get him out of here as well."

There was something off about the clothes and the closet, but Cavanaugh knew he didn't dare touch any of it.

"Does that look like more than one woman's clothes?" Cavanaugh asked, kneeling down and shining his flashlight on the pile from a lower angle.

"I was thinking the same thing," Bonnie said from behind him, shining her light on the clothing as well. "At least two, maybe three or four."

"Damn it all to hell," Cavanaugh said.

Cavanaugh used his phone to get a bunch of pictures of the room, the clothes, the hallway, the room number, everything.

Bonnie did the same.

Cavanaugh figured it would never hurt to have duel sets of images on this mess.

Then they headed back down to the darkness of the main floor.

"Alistair!" Cavanaugh shouted when they reached the bottom of the stairs. Dust was still swirling lightly in the air in the flashlight beams from when they had been down here before.

"Back here," came the answer from behind the main desk.

Feeling like he was in a cave, Cavanaugh followed the sound until they found Alistair inspecting some pipes that ran through the ceiling in an office area behind the old front desk.

"Seen any signs of break-ins?" Bonnie asked him. "Now or over the last few years?"

"Nothing at all," he said. "This place is sealed up as tight as it comes and the Golden Nugget security patrol the outside so no one would have time to break in even if they tried. Why?"

"We found some women's clothes in the back of that same closet on the third floor where other women's clothes had been found," Cavanaugh said.

"Shit," Alistair said. "Just shit. I was with Sheck when we found the ones as the place was being shuttered. How the hell did someone get in here?"

"We were hoping you had an idea on that," Bonnie said.

Alistair just shook his head.

Around them the dust from the three of them moving around was swirling and Cavanaugh felt like he was starting to breath more dirt than air.

"Active detective on the way," Cavanaugh said. "He might order in a forensics unit as well. Better tell the Golden Nugget security what is happening."

"I'll do it," Alistair said. "Done here anyway."

The three of them headed back through the lobby and then out through the storage area to the door on the alley. Outside the wind and the biting cold air hit them as Alistair turned toward the Golden Nugget.

"I'll stay here by the door," Bonnie said. "You get us some gloves. You have evidence bags as well?"

Cavanaugh nodded and headed for his car. He wasn't sure if he was feeling numb from the cold or from what they had found. He couldn't wrap his mind around what it meant just yet.

Or more likely he didn't want to think about what it might mean, that a lot of women were missing and likely dead.

And besides those clothes in that empty room upstairs, he and Bonnie didn't have one idea where to even start looking.

EIGHTEEN

January 19th, 2019
Shuttered Hotel Nevada
Las Vegas, Nevada

BONNIE STOOD against the block wall near the back door to the old Hotel Nevada, facing the Golden Nugget parking garage, waiting and trying to think through what they had just found.

More than one woman's clothes, stashed in the back of a shuttered hotel room's closet. A hotel that very, very few people had access to.

And more than likely there wasn't a thing she or Cavanaugh could do about it since they were retired and an active detective had been called in, as should have happened.

Even if they were allowed to continue, she had no idea how, besides finding out who had keys to the old hotel. That would be step one, but with nothing else, that would end up a dead end very, very quickly.

And for some reason she didn't think anyone with official access would be the person leaving those clothes.

And what had happened to the women?

Why that room?

Cavanaugh came back down the alley from his car and handed her three pair of evidence gloves that she stuffed in her pocket.

"Got some evidence bags in my pocket," he said.

She nodded.

At that moment a blue Jeep SUV pulled up near the mouth of the alley without blocking it with a dash flasher on.

Bonnie breathed a sigh of relief. She knew that SUV. It belonged to Detective Isadora Fawn. Like Cavanaugh, she only went by her last name with friends.

She was a five-two red-haired powerhouse who tended to talk fast and laugh a lot. She had worked alone since her last partner retired four years ago. Bonnie and Fawn had talked a few times about teaming up, but never got around to it before Bonnie retired.

Fawn climbed out of her SUV and started toward them with a smile on her face. She had on jeans, tennis shoes, and a ski parka and looked closer to a college student going skiing than a fifty-year-old detective.

"So Andor stuck you with this lug," Fawn said, coming up and giving Bonnie a hug.

Fawn then hugged Cavanaugh, who was laughing.

"I see she hasn't done obvious damage yet."

"Why is everyone so worried about my health around Bonnie?" Cavanaugh asked.

"They know me," Bonnie said.

"Got that in one," Fawn said. "So Andor told me it is both of your second days on the task force and you are already causing troubles."

"Andor's fault," Bonnie said. "He gave us the Myra Stemple missing person's case."

"The one with the brother checking in regularly?" Fawn asked.

"That's the one," Bonnie said. "When they were shuttering this place back in 2012, they found her clothes in the back of a closet on the third floor three years after she vanished."

"Well that's flat creepy," Fawn said.

"It gets worse," Cavanaugh said. "We had Bonnie's son Jacob pulling missing person's files and three other women's clothes were found in the same closet over a five-year period before this place got shut down. The cases never got connected until Jacob did it."

"All from missing women?"

Bonnie nodded. "And all in the same closet in room 317. She pointed up. "That room right there on the Bridger Street side."

"Well shit," Fawn said.

"So we wanted to take a look at the room," Bonnie said. "So we got Sheck to send Alistair to do a fire inspection and let us look around while he was at it."

"And…" Fawn said. "Oh, shit, don't tell me."

Fawn's face went pure white, which made her red hair stand out even more.

Bonnie and Cavanaugh both nodded. "More clothes tossed in the same closet. Looks like there might be enough there for three women, maybe more."

"Andor never should have let you two near each other," Fawn said.

She reached inside her coat and pulled out her radio. "Dispatch, I need a forensic team to the old Hotel Nevada, on the alley side. Stat. And five or six uniforms to help with a search."

She nodded, clearly listening on the earpiece in her right ear, then said, "Copy that."

She put the radio back inside her jacket.

At that point Alistair and two Golden Nugget security officers were headed up the alley toward them. One was tall, in a suit, and clearly in charge.

Fawn waited for them and flashed her badge. "Make sure no one goes in or out of this place without my permission, or the permission of one of these detectives. Understood? And Alistair and both of you, if you were ever in this building, I'm going to need your prints to clear you."

"What happened?" the tall guy in a suit asked.

"We'll brief you when we figure that out," Fawn said. "I have uniformed officers on the way. Have them wait here for our return. But while that is happening, one of you can get me a list of every employee with a key and access to this old place."

Then she turned to Bonnie and Cavanaugh. "Want to show me what you found.

Bonnie nodded and handed Fawn an extra flashlight.

"Oh, this will be fun from the looks of the dust already covering you two," Fawn said, shaking her head as she clicked on the flashlight.

"Fun if you like horror mansions at a carnival," Cavanaugh said.

"Amazing Bonnie hasn't killed you yet," Fawn said as Bonnie held open the door for Fawn, smiling at Cavanaugh.

"The day is young," Cavanaugh said, winking at Bonnie and following Fawn inside.

"Got that right, Detective," Bonnie said.

From just inside the old hotel, Fawn snorted and then laughed.

NINETEEN

January 19th, 2019
Shuttered Hotel Nevada
Las Vegas, Nevada

CAVANAUGH was impressed at how Detective Fawn just took control of the situation. She should have, but with two other long-term detectives already on the scene, she might not have. But she understood at a deep level the place of the Cold Poker Gang task force and realized almost instantly that she might be dealing with an active crime scene that he and Bonnie could do nothing with.

Not sure what crime yet, but better to treat the scene correctly right from the start and Fawn had realized that instantly.

It took them a long minute in the dark to reach the staircase and a short time to climb to the third floor and make it down the hall to room 317. Dust still swirled in the air and Cavanaugh had no doubt that once a forensics team and a bunch of uniforms got in here to work and search, the air would be more dirt than breathable.

"We better have everyone searching put on masks," Cavanaugh said.

Fawn nodded. "Going to need a shower after this one."

She quickly inspected the hallway, then went into the room. Bonnie and Cavanaugh followed.

"You touch anything in here?" Fawn asked.

"I opened the closet door with bare hands," Bonnie said.

Fawn nodded.

Cavanaugh had zero hope that any kind of fingerprints would be found that would help them in here. But better to take them all and eliminate the prints like Bonnie's just to be sure.

Now all three of them had on gloves.

Cavanaugh and Bonnie had just not thought that this room would be any more than a place clothes were found years ago when they first came in. How wrong was that assumption? Wow.

Fawn went to the closet and shined her light into the back of the closet at the pile of clothes.

Cavanaugh stood back by the bed, just trying to take in the entire thing.

Bonnie stood near Fawn, watching and ready to help with anything Fawn might need.

From where Cavanaugh was standing, he could see that the closet was deep. A long-gone hanger bar had clearly been across the front. There was a light fixture on the ceiling of the closet, but the bulb was missing.

On the right, beside the closet, was a bathroom with a tub/shower, an old porcelain sink, and a stained toilet. No shower curtain remained and from the looks of some of the old linoleum on the floor, there was rot under the sink and near the tub.

Then Cavanaugh noticed something. Both the bathroom and closet back walls were on the alley side of the building. Both should have been even with the other. But the bathroom was deeper.

Significantly deeper.

He went into the bathroom and tapped on the wall between the bathroom and the closet. It was covered with faded old flower-print wallpaper that had peeled in a couple of places showing the boards under it. In the back corner, beyond the back of the closet, it sounded as hollow as it did when he knocked on the closet wall area.

"What are you doing?" Bonnie asked, looking in at Cavanaugh. "We thought we had a woodpecker in here."

"Bathroom's deeper than the closet, yet both back walls are on the alley wall."

"Plumbing stack maybe?" Fawn said from the closet side, her voice an echo.

"Too much extra for that alone," Cavanaugh said.

Bonnie stood back into the middle of the room and Fawn joined her, both studying the depth of the closet, then the bathroom. Cavanaugh stepped back out of their line of sight to give them a clear look, making sure as he did that he didn't step on any area of the bathroom where the floor might be rotted through.

"Go to hell," Fawn said. "He's right. Shine some lights in here," Fawn said.

Cavanaugh came out of the bathroom and both he and Bonnie shined their flashlights on the back wall of the closet.

Fawn took a number of quick pictures with her phone of the clothes and the back wall of the closet. Then being very careful to not touch any of the clothes in the pile, she reached over and tapped on the back wall of the closet.

It clearly sounded hollow.

She shined her own light along the edges, then with a slight push on the right side of the wall, there was a click and the back wall of the closet opened slightly.

She stepped back, shaking her head.

"This just gets creepier by the moment," she said.

Cavanaugh could only agree with that.

"That's what we need in this place," Bonnie said. "Hidden passageways."

"What we really need is to get forensics in here first while we search the hotel," Fawn said. "Then we can see what is behind that wall."

"All right if we help?" Bonnie asked a half moment before Cavanaugh could.

"Oh, trust me," Fawn said as she turned and headed for the door. "You two aren't getting out of this damn dusty horror show anytime soon."

"Something about our mess, we get to help clean it up?" Cavanaugh said, laughing.

"Got it in one," Fawn said as she turned and at a fast walk headed down the hall through the swirling dust in the air.

Cavanaugh really, really liked Detective Fawn. She pulled no punches, all business, and yet was willing to bend rules a little.

Cavanaugh glanced at Bonnie as they followed Fawn down the hallway in the swirling dust Fawn was kicking up. Bonnie was looking intent and worried.

He felt exactly the same way.

TWENTY

January 19th, 2019
Shuttered Hotel Nevada
Las Vegas, Nevada

BONNIE and Cavanaugh stood off to one side in the alley with Alistair as Fawn gathered the uniformed officers that had arrived. Bonnie could see that Cavanaugh already had dirt covering his bald head and the shoulders of his suit jacket and she could see the dirt on her coat as well. They were going to be a mess by the time this was over.

All they would need next would be for it to start sprinkling and they would turn into large walking mud balls. Oh, fun.

The alley was crowded now with the uniformed officers and three security

personnel from the Golden Nugget, plus one of their hotel managers.

Bonnie had been impressed at Detective Fawn's ability to see a strange situation and take charge instantly. Bonnie hoped that in the same circumstances she would have been able to do the same.

At that moment, the forensics van pulled up into the alley.

"All right, everyone listen up," Fawn said, her voice loud and carrying. "No one goes into this building without a mask and gloves. This entire building needs to be considered an active crime scene until further notice."

Nods all around and a stern look from the manager of the casino. Bonnie couldn't blame him. She was sure this wasn't the way he wanted his morning to go.

"I need the uniformed officers to start on the top floor, search every room, work together, make sure you don't miss anything as you work your way down to the main floor. Take notes as you go that you will turn into me. We are looking for anything that seems out of place from an old shuttered hotel like this, including clothing. No detail is too small to report to me. Understood? I will be in and out of room 317."

The uniforms nodded.

"Move slow to stir up less dust," Fawn said. "And thank you all for the help."

She nodded and the uniformed officers dawned mask and gloves as they went in, each clicking on a flashlight as they entered.

At that point the two women wearing protective white gear from the forensics team approached Fawn. Bonnie recognized both of them from different crime scenes over the last few years, but didn't know them by name. She did know that they were both good at what they did and very efficient.

"For the moment we got clothes that might be from crime victims in the back of a closet in room 317," Fawn said to the two forensic team members. "More than likely more than one victim. Retired Detective State touched the door handle to open the closet."

They both nodded. Bonnie knew her fingerprints were on file and they would be easily eliminated.

"The back wall of the closet opens. Just process the clothes and the closet and room itself for now. I'll deal with wherever that closet opening goes to. Once we figure that out, you can process it."

Again they both nodded and put on masks and headed inside without saying a word. That was exactly the way Bonnie remembered them. They never seemed to talk much.

Detective Fawn then turned to the hotel manager and his security team. "I'll brief you on all this as soon as I know more. But if I could ask a favor, would you have your people set up barricades at both ends of this alley and post someone in the parking area of the Golden Gate near the corner of the building there?"

"Glad to, Detective," the manager said and turned to his people.

Detective Fawn then turned to Bonnie and Cavanaugh and Alistair.

"You three get the fun job," she said, smiling. "You get to search the basement or basement levels."

"You thinking that space behind the closet leads down there?" Bonnie asked.

Fawn nodded. "As likely as anything. "But before you hit the basement, see if the closet on 217 opens like that as well. And check the one on the floor above. You know where I'll be."

They all nodded.

Fawn handed each of them masks and gloves and headed into the swirling dust as they put them on.

Bonnie was so not looking forward to going into the basement of this place. But she knew she had been in worse and thankfully she was not claustrophobic.

Plus she wasn't going in alone.

And besides, someone had to do it.

She was just thankful Fawn hadn't sent them home for the day. She had had the right to, and very well could have. But having two experienced detectives and an experienced fire marshal on a search couldn't hurt.

At least Bonnie hoped it couldn't.

TWENTY-ONE

January 19th, 2019
Shuttered Hotel Nevada
Las Vegas, Nevada

CAVANAUGH hated closed-in places, so the idea of going down into an old building's basement did not excite him in the slightest. But at this point, since this had become an official active crime scene, he felt lucky to still be here and helping. He knew there was a pretty strict line between what the retired detectives could do and the active cases. Andor had made it clear that they weren't supposed to cross that line.

Cavanaugh wasn't sure what Andor was going to think of them still helping, but they would find that out later. It had been Fawn's call, after all. And in her spot, he would have made the same call. In fact, he had on one of his last active cases working with Cold Poker Gang detectives.

The exact same call and it had almost gotten one of the retired detectives killed. But at the moment he wasn't going to think about that.

The closet in 417 was the same depth as the bathroom.

The closet in the back of the room under 317, number 217 had the extra space, but no back wall that seemed to want to open. He and Alistair both tried different methods, including how Cavanaugh saw Fawn open the wall above.

"So looks like there is a chute of some sort back there," Bonnie said as the three of them stood looking into the closet. "Going from room 317 down."

"But there is no place for it to come out in the basement," Alistair said. "Just nothing below this end of the building."

"Half basement?" Cavanaugh asked.

"Built for the utilities and such," Alistair said. "Come on, I'll show you."

They followed Alistair down the stairs and into the dark main floor, then behind the old front desk and to a corridor. Their flashlights were now barely cutting through the swirling dust.

A closed door led to the left off the corridor and Alistair opened it and started down a fairly narrow staircase.

Alistair led the way checking his footing as he went down each step. The staircase turned about halfway down toward the alley side of the building and at the bottom they ended up near a wall on the alley side.

"There's got to be another way into this basement," Cavanaugh said after a moment. "You couldn't get equipment up and down this staircase."

"Sidewalk lift opening," Alistair said. "It was walled off when they shuttered the building and the opening in the sidewalk paved over."

The basement actually didn't have the low ceilings that Cavanaugh was expecting. And since the three of them were moving slowly, they hadn't stirred up much dust yet. But it did smell of mold and rot and he was very glad he at least had the dust mask on.

They all stopped at the bottom of the stairs. Alistair shone his light to the left. "That way is Main Street and that is where the lift entrance was walled over."

Cavanaugh could see it clearly and at a glance he could tell it was solid.

"Paved over on the sidewalk as well?" Bonnie asked, studying the wall.

"Can't even tell it was ever there now," Alistair said. "That's not how anyone got in here."

"And see the footprints in the dust?" Alistair said, moving his light down in front of them and then farther into the room. "Those prints are mine from six months ago when I inspected the pipes down here."

He traced his steps in the dust with his flashlight from the staircase over to an old pump system, then back.

"No one else has been down here," he said, taking his light and moving it slowly along the floor.

Cavanaugh could see clearly that he was right. The only footprints besides Alistair's were at the bottom of the stairs where they had all stopped.

"And that's the alley wall side," Alistair said, shining his light on an unbroken concrete foundation wall fairly close to them.

"But that's a good twenty or more steps closer to the center of the building than that alley wall," Bonnie said.

"Half basement," Alistair said.

Something wasn't feeling right to Cavanaugh.

A seven-story building sat above them. That foundation wall they were looking at was in the middle of the building.

"There's another room on the other side of that wall," Cavanaugh said. "We just need to find the entrance to it."

"It isn't down here," Alistair said. "That wall is as solid as it comes."

"Let's walk the perimeter to make sure, then head upstairs to see if we can find another staircase down," Bonnie said.

All three of them, moving slowly to not kick up much dust, walked all the way around the outside of the room, looking for anything that seemed out of place.

Nothing.

Alistair was right. Everything was as solid as it looked.

But it was when Cavanaugh got back to the staircase and noticed a full-sized storage door under the staircase that things got stranger if that was possible.

He tried to open the door without luck.

It wouldn't open.

Locked.

"Stuck," Bonnie said.

"Or locked from the other side," Cavanaugh said.

He glanced at Bonnie, then at Alistair. "We need to go tell Detective Fawn what we have found and ask her what she would like to do with that door."

Bonnie and Alistair nodded and with that they waded their way back up through the thickening dust in the air and then once again back up the staircase to the third floor.

TWENTY-TWO

January 19th, 2019
Shuttered Hotel Nevada
Las Vegas, Nevada

AS BONNIE climbed the staircase slowly behind Cavanaugh and Alistair, trying to ignore the dust building up in her eyes, it dawned on her that maybe Jacob could help.

She got to the landing and standing beside Cavanaugh in the narrow hallway against a faded wallpapered wall, she quickly called Jacob.

"Hi, Mom," he said.

"Need a quick favor if you can manage it," she said.

"Fire," he said.

"We are in the old Hotel Nevada and we found more clothes and a hidden passageway."

"Oh, this is really twisted," he said, laughing.

His laugh sounded strained and she could tell that her words had bothered him.

"Any way you might find and send me quickly the original floor plans for this hotel."

"Great thinking," he said. "I'm on it."

And he hung up.

"Really good thought," Cavanaugh said as she tucked her phone back in her pocket. "Think he can find them?"

"If anyone can," Bonnie said, "I'm starting to think Jacob can."

"I'm starting to agree with you on that," Cavanaugh said.

"Okay, standby," Detective Fawn said and a moment later the two forensic team women came out into the hallway.

"Bonnie, Cavanaugh, need your lights in here," Fawn said. "Bonnie, take a movie of me opening this thing, would you?"

"Glad to," Bonnie said as she moved into position standing on the right side of the closet door. Cavanaugh stood on the left, shining both his flashlights at the back wall.

Fawn was kneeling in the closet. Clearly it had been completely dusted for prints and all the clothes were bagged and out of the way.

Bonnie made sure her phone camera was recording, then said, "Ready."

Fawn eased forward and pushed open the back wall of the closet.

The opening was about four feet tall. And beyond it Cavanaugh's lights showed a metal ladder going down.

Fawn eased forward and shined her light down into the shaft. "Looks like it goes all the way to the basement," she said. "Film that."

She backed out and let Bonnie move into the closet and aim her camera downward. Then she also backed out carefully.

"Let's let the forensics team in here to dust that area," Fawn said.

"We might know how to find the bottom of that," Cavanaugh said. "But we have a locked door."

Fawn nodded. "You two go back down into the basement. Alistair, could you come with me to talk with the manager."

"Will do," Alistair said. "That is an area the fire department should have been inspecting, by the way."

Fawn laughed. "Damn, I love devious thinking."

Fawn told the forensics team to only work on the area they could reach without going downward at all, then to standby outside. Then Fawn and Alistair headed down the hall.

Bonnie and Cavanaugh followed.

The dust in the hallway was getting thicker by the moment and she could hear the uniformed officers moving around a floor above them as they worked their way downward in their search.

Thank God the day wasn't hot. This kind of dust would have formed mud on them if mixed with sweat. Now all it was going to do was clog drains as they all showered it off.

She and Cavanaugh were just about to head down the basement stairs when Bonnie's phone rang. It was Jacob.

"Found the original plans," he said. "Sending them to you now. I made them large enough so you could see details, so on your phones you're going to have to scroll around a lot."

"Thank you," Bonnie said. "We'll call you and fill you in as soon as we get out of this horror show."

"Got you," Jacob said. "I'll keep digging."

Cavanaugh and Bonnie went on down into the basement, then Bonnie brought up the plans Jacob had sent.

It took both of them a good minute before they could figure out what-was-what. When they finally did, Bonnie pulled up the basement plan.

"No wall there," Cavanaugh said. "That had originally been concrete support posts."

Bonnie nodded. He was right.

"And the closet in 317 shows no back access area."

"So this wall and that back access was put in after this place was built for some reason," Cavanaugh said.

"I really don't think I want to know the reason," Bonnie said.

In fact, she was sure of it.

TWENTY-THREE

January 19th, 2019
Shuttered Hotel Nevada
Las Vegas, Nevada

USING BONNIE'S phone, Cavanaugh and Bonnie studied the original floor plans of the Hotel Nevada as best they could over the next ten minutes. The phone clearly wasn't the best way to try to study floor plans, but at least they had them and as far as they could see nothing looked out of place.

Except for the secret passage to the back of the 317 closet and also whatever was behind that block wall that didn't exist on the original plans. Who built them and why was a major question.

The major question that just might lead them to what happened to all the women whose clothes ended up in that closet.

Cavanaugh was really beginning to worry about what exactly they might find on the other side. He kept trying to push the worst thoughts out of his mind, but with the women's clothes upstairs and that many women missing, the fear of what they would find just sort of kept eating at him with each passing minute.

Both he and Bonnie had called this old hotel a horror show. It might just live up to that name shortly.

The light grew brighter as Alistair came down the steps carrying a crowbar and hammer followed by Detective Fawn and the two forensic women. The two techs had helmet lights and Adrian and Fawn had flashlights.

Those lights added to Bonnie and Cavanaugh's, and the basement room seemed almost light in all the swirling dust.

Bonnie showed Fawn the floor plans they had gotten from Jacob while the two techs worked over the door area, making sure all prints were taken and cataloged.

Finally they stepped back and Fawn held up a key.

"Golden Nugget manager claims this is a master key to every door in the place," she said. "But if it doesn't work, we have his permission to break down any door in here we need to."

With that she went over and inserted the key into the lock on the door under the stairs. It turned with a loud click that echoed in the basement.

"Go to hell," Fawn said as she turned the handle and opened the door.

She stepped back so that they all could see that beyond the door was nothing more than a storage area, empty.

The techs stepped inside and did a quick dusting for prints and anything else, then came back out.

Cavanaugh had a hunch that if this was an entrance into that other room, it also was hidden. Clearly Detective Fawn had the same idea.

She went into the closet and to the back wall, shining her light along all corners.

"Cavanaugh, State, some more light in here, please?"

Cavanaugh let Bonnie step all the way inside the small storage area, then he stayed in the door, shining his light on the back wall where Fawn was working.

After a moment she said, "Here it is."

She pushed and with a click the back wall swung away silently.

There was a faint light on the other side.

Fawn looked back at both of them, a frown on her face. She indicated they should be silent and then drew her gun.

Now Available

from all your favorite booksellers
in trade paper and electronic editions.
The book that started the Cold Poker Gang.

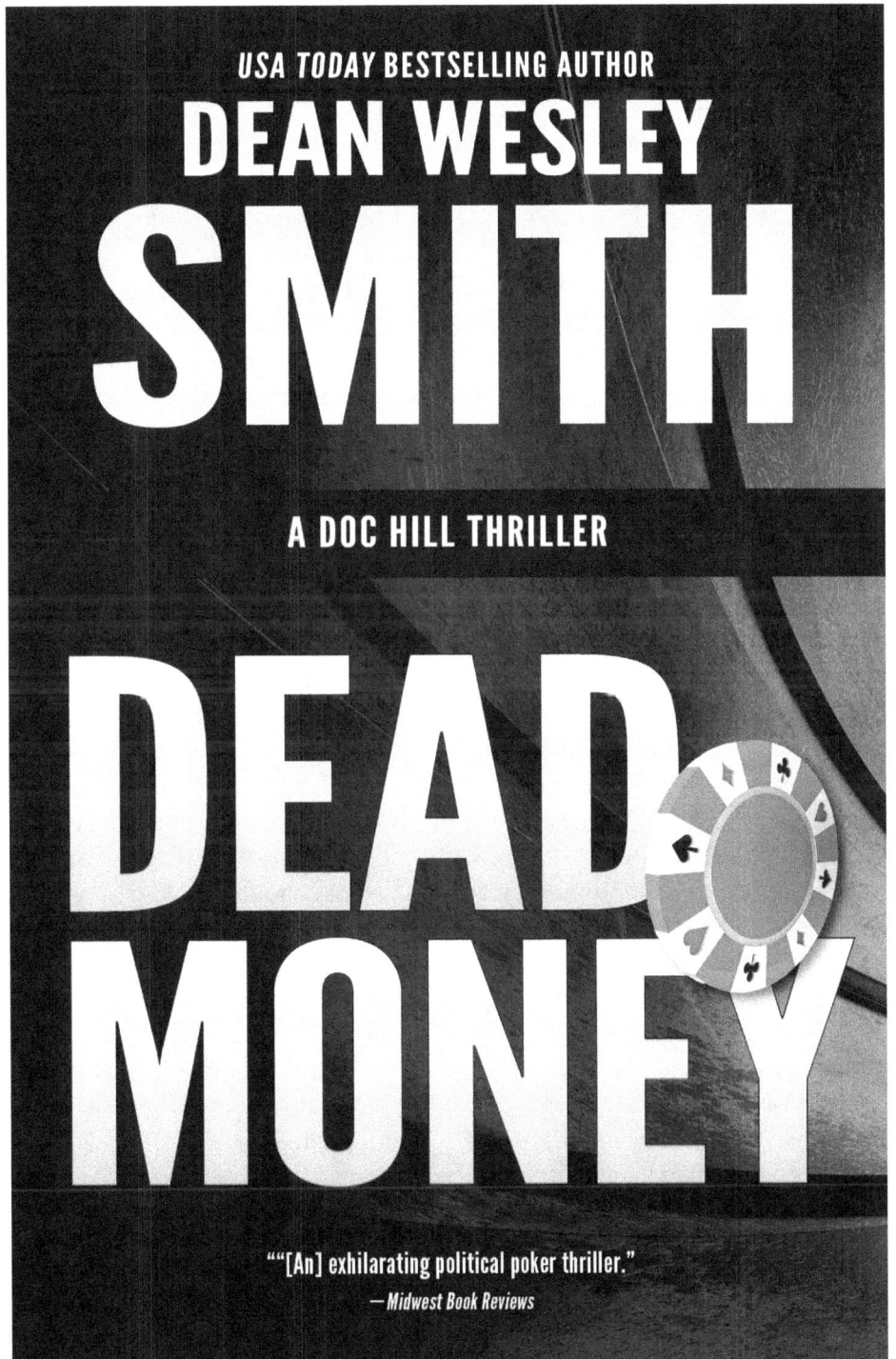

She pointed to Bonnie to follow her and go left. She pointed to Cavanaugh to follow and go right.

He nodded and drew his gun. Second day on the task force and he already had his gun out. This was not something he had ever expected to do.

Fawn counted down with her fingers.

Three, two, one.

Then she went in with a shout, "Police!

Bonnie followed and ducked left, Cavanaugh went right.

What greeted them on the other side was just about as far from any horror show Cavanaugh might have imagined.

An apartment.

A fairly nicely furnished one at that with one light shining over the kitchen counter like a nightlight.

No one home.

Fawn made sure by checking the bathroom, then put her gun away and clicked on a switch by the bathroom door.

Lights came up, fairly bright and warm.

And no dust besides the little bit that they had brought in.

Cavanaugh just shook his head. This old building wasn't supposed to have power running to it. Clearly that was wrong.

There were two beds, neatly made against one wall. Beside each bed was an open closet with nothing but empty hangers. A washer/dryer stacked combo sat beside one closet.

The kitchen looked fairly modern and had a nice granite island with a couple bar stools tucked up to it. A large wooden kitchen table filled one corner with eight chairs around it. A number of couches formed a living room area with a large-screen television hung on one wall.

The place looked more out of a modern house beautiful than a hidden room in the basement of a shuttered hotel.

Cavanaugh walked over to one side where a metal ladder went up the wall and into the ceiling and shined his light up into the hole. Looked like it went up to the third floor, from best he could tell.

Detective Fawn moved over to the kitchen counter and pointed to some bleach and Lysol cleaning solution and a neatly washed stack of rags. "Looks like this place has been scrubbed down of any trace of anything."

Cavanaugh nodded. "I was expecting us to find a horror show in here."

"Not sure if we didn't," Bonnie said.

Detective Fawn only nodded at that.

TWENTY-FOUR

January 19th, 2019
Shuttered Hotel Nevada
Las Vegas, Nevada

BONNIE didn't know what to think about the modern apartment they found under the old hotel. Clearly the apartment was linked to the missing women in some way or another. And finding an apartment was a thousand times better than finding bodies, which was what she had expected to find.

But this was far, far stranger.

Detective Fawn now had the techs working the room, but it was clear that the room had been sanitized completely. Why? Again Bonnie had no idea at all.

Fawn and Cavanaugh and Bonnie were standing in the middle of the room and Alistair had gone back out to the alley.

"How was anyone getting in here?" Cavanaugh asked, looking around slowly. "The hotel above is locked up as tight as I have ever seen a shuttered building in this city and the Golden Nugget security patrol it."

"So there is another way in," Fawn said. "That way is toward the Golden Nugget."

She pointed over the kitchen.

"Nothing coming in from that direction," Bonnie said. "And that way is the parking garage of the Golden Nugget. But maybe something out to the alley?"

"That way is Main Street and that other basement room," Cavanaugh said, pointing at the wall with the dining room table. "So nothing in that direction."

"So what is left is that way, toward the Bridger Hotel or along the alley in that direction."

"You two search the wall along the alley," Fawn said. "I'll take this television wall."

The techs had already finished with the wall above the beds and the closets, leaving a fine white dust where they had been. Bonnie took out her flashlight and studied the cracks along the closets near one bed, then how the bed itself was situated, looking for anything.

Then she saw it, but wasn't sure at first if she wanted to. Under the bed, on the concrete floor, was a throw rug. Similar rugs were scattered in different places around the room to make the room feel warmer, instead of just bare concrete.

Using two gloved fingers, Bonnie carefully lifted the corner of the rug. Under it was a wooden floor.

"Damn it all to hell," Bonnie said. "You two need to take a look at this."

She held the rug up until both Cavanaugh and Fawn could see, then dropped it.

Fawn turned to the techs. "This bed been checked completely?"

One of the techs nodded.

Bonnie stood and she and Cavanaugh quickly picked up the bed and moved it to one side.

"Going to need you to check this carpet and what is under it," Fawn said to the techs.

Bonnie watched as the two forensics techs went over the rug and area under the bed quickly, clearly finding nothing.

Under the rug was a wooden trap door that looked heavy and solid and Bonnie was worried that they were going to have to get in some help to open it. But it turned out they didn't because as Detective Fawn moved the latch, the entire heavy wooden floor swung sideways and into a recessed opening without her even touching it.

"Shit," Fawn said, jumping back as the door moved into place.

Clearly the door was on some sort of electric motor that ran silently and allowed the door to open with the bed still sitting over it.

The smell of dampness and cold came up out of the now open dark hole.

Fawn and Cavanaugh both clicked on their lights at the same time and aimed them downward.

Bonnie had no real desire to see what they would find down in that hole. Again her worst nightmares of far too many women's bodies came right to the front.

In the hole a fairly steep and narrow staircase went down and toward the alley. It looked long, longer than a normal staircase.

"Ever get the feeling we've found the staircase to hell?" Cavanaugh whispered.

"Or worse," Bonnie said, almost too silently for anyone to hear.

Fawn glanced at Bonnie, then at Cavanaugh. "I go first," Fawn whispered as she drew her gun. "Bonnie stay behind me and to my right, Cavanaugh behind Bonnie and to the left."

Bonnie nodded and for the second time she had her gun in her hand.

All three of them still had on gloves and Fawn put her mask back over her mouth as she started down.

Bonnie and Cavanaugh did the same.

As Detective Fawn neared the bottom of the stairs, a light clicked on, showing a narrow, but lit tunnel that headed off toward Bridger Street and beyond.

Bonnie had no doubt that they had found the entrance to the secret room. It was a tunnel under the right side of the alley.

The tunnel was lined on all four sides with blocks and smelled like damp mold. It was only as wide as one person, but tall enough that they didn't have to duck for anything.

It looked like it also had been kept clean. Not even cobwebs gathered in the upper corners.

"We have to be thirty feet or more underground," Cavanaugh whispered. "Under the old utilities and everything."

Fawn nodded, putting away her weapon as Bonnie and Cavanaugh did the same. "Stay here."

Fawn quickly went back up the staircase and told the two forensic technicians where they planned on going. "Go back to the alley and wait for us. Tell the uniformed officers there that I want them posted every fifty steps along the alley for a block on the other side of Bridger."

Then Fawn came back down the stairs.

Bonnie was impressed at how Detective Fawn was handling this entire situation. They didn't have one ounce of evidence of any crime, yet she was handling this as a dangerous situation, which it clearly might be.

A hidden room and tunnel under an old hotel clearly was suspicious, not counting the women's clothing they had found.

The tunnel did not go any farther toward the Golden Nugget than the staircase, so with Detective Fawn leading, they turned toward Bridger Street.

Every thirty steps a light hung from the ceiling, giving them enough light that they didn't need their flashlights, something Bonnie was very grateful for. She couldn't remember being this tense in a long time and she couldn't imagine going along this tunnel with flashlights.

After about forty steps, Cavanaugh said, "We're under the street now."

"You two are going to owe me for this," Fawn said, shaking her head. "I hate tunnels and caves."

"That makes two of us," Bonnie said.

"Make that a solid three," Cavanaugh said.

They kept moving, Fawn and Bonnie watching ahead down the tunnel while Cavanaugh continued checking behind them.

All Bonnie kept thinking was that she hoped this nightmare would end soon.

This was not at all what she had expected to be doing when she joined the Cold Poker Gang. Not even close.

TWENTY-FIVE

January 19th, 2019
Under Downtown Las Vegas
Las Vegas, Nevada

CAVANAUGH FLAT hated contained and closed-in spaces like the cement-block-lined tunnel they were moving through. And he hated even more knowing he was at least thirty feet underground.

The tunnel had clearly been built a long time ago, which didn't give him a lot of confidence about how safe it was, even though it looked solid and clearly had been cleaned regularly.

And it really didn't help that Bonnie and Detective Fawn hated this place as well. The tension among them was so thick, it might flood the tunnel all by itself.

He just wanted this done and over with, but at the same time he was impressed at how methodical and careful Fawn was being.

"My guess is that we've just passed the alley side of the Bridger Hotel," Cavanaugh said.

"Tunnel seems to be going directly down the alley," Bonnie said.

"I think you're both right," Fawn said.

He had been keeping track of how far they were going and he had a good sense of the distance above ground between things. He just never expected to be using it underground in a secret tunnel.

"Almost to the end," Fawn said, again drawing her gun.

Cavanaugh could see what she was talking about. Ahead of them the tunnel ended in another staircase that went to the right and up steeply.

"This is going to end up in the Little Hotel Boarding House," Cavanaugh whispered.

For the longest time the Little Hotel had been a problem because of squatters and the homeless, but it was on a registry of historic places, since it was one of the oldest hotels in town, so no one seemed to know what to do with it.

"That place has been shuttered almost as long as the Hotel Nevada," Bonnie whispered.

Detective Fawn got to the bottom of the stairs and looked up, seeming to hesitate.

Cavanaugh knew why she was hesitating. They had permission to be in the Hotel Nevada. They had no permission to go into the Little Hotel.

"I may be wrong about this going into the Little Hotel," Cavanaugh whispered to Fawn. "I was just estimating how far we had come and guessing how far the Little Hotel was down the alley."

Fawn nodded and smiled at Cavanaugh. "We have a need to see where this ends, right?"

"Those women's clothes," Bonnie said. "No telling what we might find."

Fawn nodded and started up the staircase. She clearly felt she had enough to make entering the Little Hotel viable in a court case, if this ever came to that. So far they had no crimes at all.

This staircase was a lot longer and clearly went all the way up instead of coming out as the other end did in a basement.

Cavanaugh stayed at the bottom, gun drawn, watching back down the tunnel.

This was their basic training and right now he wished he was in Fawn's position, but she was the active on this case and she needed to go first.

Bonnie followed Fawn, giving her room, yet backing her as she went up in the narrow staircase.

At the top, a light was on, putting Bonnie and Fawn in shadows.

Cavanaugh watched as Fawn felt around the edges of the door at the top, then glanced back at Bonnie and nodded.

She pushed a button and a sliding door opened with a scraping sound.

With one last look down the tunnel, Cavanaugh headed up the stairs two-at-a-time, getting to the top as Bonnie went through the open door behind Fawn and went left.

Cavanaugh went right.

They were in one of the worst-smelling rooms Cavanaugh could ever remember.

Rot and pee and decay. All combined.

And the room was empty, except for the pee stains and the signs of an old homeless camp against one wall.

It was pitch dark and Bonnie and Fawn had their flashlights on.

Fawn went over and tugged on the door that led into the hotel.

"Locked and bolted from the other side," she said.

"So there has to be another way in and out of here," Cavanaugh said.

They had come up in a corner of the room that looked like nothing was there until the wall had slid back showing the staircase and the light beyond.

"This wall is the alley side," Cavanaugh said, indicating a wall beside where they had come up.

All three of them shone their lights along the wall until finally it was Bonnie who found it.

The door out was tucked right against the square that covered the staircase. She clicked a lock and pushed and a narrow section of the wall just opened outward.

Bonnie stepped through and into the paved alley, followed by Fawn.

Cavanaugh wasn't far behind feeling completely relieved to be back out in the overcast light of the cold Vegas day.

Near them a surprised uniformed officer stood, hand on his gun.

"Don't let anyone get near or go in that door besides the forensic techs until I tell you otherwise," she said to the officer.

Then she turned back toward the crowd on the other side of Bridger Street.

Cavanaugh fell in beside her on the right, Bonnie on the left.

"I got no crime and three days of paperwork," Fawn said.

Cavanaugh understood that completely.

Bonnie nodded as well.

"And I expect that before I get done with that paperwork, you two will tell me just why the hell that room and tunnel exist."

Cavanaugh was glad that Fawn wasn't making it all an active case and thus getting them out of the way.

"Maybe we can also figure out what the hell happened to all those women," Bonnie said.

"Yeah," Fawn said. "That would be damned nice. You owe me at least that much for all this crap."

Ghost of a Chance Series Available...
These novels are available in electronic format or print at your favorite booksellers.

PART THREE
The Boyfriend

TWENTY-SIX

January 19th, 2019
Dinner at the Wynn
Las Vegas, Nevada

BONNIE HAD NEVER enjoyed a shower more than the one she had taken after getting back from the Hotel Nevada. It was three in the afternoon and she was hungry, tired, and so dirty, she couldn't even believe it.

Waves of dirt just washed off her and she had ended up washing her hair twice just to feel clean. She had a hunch it might take a few days before the feeling of being covered in dust would pass, no matter how many showers she took.

Plus she couldn't quite process what they had found. First the clothes, then the secret tunnels and apartment. And yet with all of that, not one ounce of evidence of a crime.

Nothing.

It was going to be a headache for the Golden Nugget to close off that tunnel, and for the owners of the Little Hotel to deal with it on their end. And no telling what the city would do with the part that ran under the alley and street.

What annoyed her most was that she didn't even have any idea what it all had been used for. Her mind went to the worst case, especially with the connection of missing women and the clothes. But if someone was killing women, why leave their clothes?

And no sign of any kind of foul play anywhere.

No sign of anything, actually.

None of it made any sense at all.

She and Cavanaugh had decided that they would go out for an early dinner to talk and have Jacob join them. Cavanaugh had said he would buy, since he wanted to go to someplace upscale and away from that old hotel.

Far, far away.

And she had completely agreed.

So he suggested the Wynn Buffet and they had decided that she would pick up Jacob and meet him there.

And as she and Jacob walked from the parking garage into the wide, tall hallways of the Wynn, with the sounds of the crowds and everything clean and immaculate and very bright, she realized Cavanaugh had been right. This was exactly what she had needed after spending the day in the underside of Las Vegas.

The hallways had huge tan chandeliers, bright purple and orange and brown colored carpets, the combination of colors that would look stupid anywhere but an upscale Las Vegas hotel. Here the colors gave the place a sense of lightness and fun.

The buffet was down a side hall and decorated in bright, almost carnival colors. Even the chairs were multi-colored and the lighting was bright and felt almost cartoonish. Even the massive real plants seemed fake in the strange colors.

Yet it all worked. She wasn't sure how, but it did, and it lightened her mood with every step.

She had never eaten here, but she sure liked the feel of it.

"Do I want to ask what this place costs?" Jacob said, looking around as they were led inside.

"No," Bonnie said. "Just enjoy the food."

Cavanaugh was already seated and he waved to them with a smile as they approached and then stood. Seemed deep down he was a real gentleman and he had cleaned up well and even had a newer-looking sports coat on that seemed to fit him better than his older regular ones. He really was a very handsome man.

Especially in the bright light like this.

Bonnie dropped her coat and Jacob his pack on chairs.

"Food?" Cavanaugh asked, laughing.

As one they headed for the massive buffet lines.

Bonnie decided to start with a small Caesar salad and some corn soup. She planned on going back two or three times in this place, so no point in pushing it. She was so hungry, she might overeat if she didn't pace herself.

And just the routine of getting some food and the quality of everything around her calmed her. Plus everything smelled wonderful and looked even better.

That old hotel covered in gray dust, the hidden room, and the tunnel had really gotten her wound up; more than she had realized, since she had this ability to just block those kinds of things to do the job.

Once they all got seated, Jacob said, "So, Mom wouldn't tell me about what happened. So spill it you two."

For the next ten minutes, as they ate, she and Cavanaugh told Jacob about the entire morning, from finding the new clothes, which he already knew, to finding the secret room.

"So that's why you wanted the floor plans?" Jacob said, nodding.

When they got to the tunnel, Jacob's eyes got larger and he just shook his head.

"No bodies, no blood, nothing?" he asked.

"Nothing," Cavanaugh said, finishing off a piece of beef and pushing his empty plate to the side where it was picked up almost instantly by their waiter.

"Thankfully no bodies," Bonnie said.

They all agreed with that.

Telling the story again, sitting here in the Wynn, actually helped Bonnie clear out some of the tension and she could tell that Cavanaugh was relaxing as well.

"Still processing that there was no sign of any crime at all," Jacob said.

"Yeah, me too," Cavanaugh said.

"Absolutely nothing," Bonnie said. "Poor Detective Fawn has a ton of paperwork to do and not a thing, not even a case name, to go with it."

Cavanaugh laughed. "Yeah, would not want to do all that paperwork from this morning. But no crime is why we can still work the case. We solved nothing. Our missing person case is still just as cold as a polar winter night."

Bonnie nodded. "If we had found any sign of a real crime, at that moment we would have been headed home and moving to a new case."

"So you have any luck with anything?" Cavanaugh asked Jacob as he finished off the last of the ribs he had on his plate.

Jacob shook his head. "No luck unless you consider eliminating possible victims as luck. The Jane Does I found do not match any of the missing women from the clothing found in the hotel."

"And any luck finding a connection with that room?"

"Nothing," Jacob said. "In fact, almost nothing was ever recorded about that hotel. The place was like a ghost hotel."

"That's what I was calling the place," Cavanaugh said, nodding.

"You got some history?" Bonnie asked, surprised.

"What little I could find," Jacob said. "It was built in the 1960s using the name of the first Hotel Nevada that had originally been on Fremont Street. That first historic hotel with the same name gets all the attention."

Bonnie nodded to that, as did Cavanaugh. She actually knew a lot about that old hotel. One of the famous ones.

"This new incarnation had troubles right from the start," Jacob said, "mostly because of the location across from the bus station and off Fremont Street. It changed hands a few times, open and closed a few times, before ending up in that massive bankruptcy and shuttered. Not even the gambling license was saved for more than one year. Golden Nugget, after they bought it, just let the gambling license go back to the state. Not worth maintaining was their stated reason."

"So a perfect place to hide, almost in plain sight," Cavanaugh said, nodding.

Bonnie agreed. "And I have a hunch that the 317 room was the regular entrance to that apartment until the place got shuttered."

"Tunnel was there ahead of that," Cavanaugh said. "I'm guessing that room and the tunnel was built as the hotel was being built."

"I agree," Bonnie said. "Kept off the plans, something I am sure in that period of time was easy to do with a little well-placed envelopes of cash."

"But why?" Cavanaugh asked.

"Got a hunch the answer lies with the women who are missing," Bonnie said. "What makes them similar?"

"And are they even alive?" Jacob said. "That apartment sounds more like a way station to me, a place to vanish and then move on into a new life for one reason or another."

Bonnie looked at Cavanaugh who was deep in thought.

"There were no restraints anywhere in that apartment," Bonnie said.

"And two beds," Cavanaugh said.

"And closets for clothes," Bonnie said.

"And three ways in and out," Jacob said. "That doesn't sound to me like a place you hold someone prisoner."

All Bonnie could do was nod. Damned if Jacob wasn't right.

She had been so expecting them to find bodies in that tomb of a hotel, another alternative had never occurred to her.

What happened if Myra wasn't dead? Then where was she?

And even more important, why would she decide to vanish?

TWENTY-SEVEN

January 19th, 2019
Dinner at the Wynn
Las Vegas, Nevada

CAVANAUGH FELT much, much better after the first thirty minutes in the Wynn Buffet. After leaving the old Hotel Nevada, he had gone home and taken a very long shower, just trying to get the feeling of that old place off of him. The dust, the smell of mold and rotting wood, and then the strangeness of that apartment and tunnel felt like he was carrying an oppressive weight on his shoulders.

The shower helped.

Clean clothes helped, and now sitting, waiting for Bonnie and Jacob in the Wynn Buffet, with all its bright lights, even brighter colors, and its energy and having so many people enjoying life around him made him feel better by the moment.

The buffet was nothing if not colorful, almost carnival bright colors, purples, reds, bright oranges, which contrasted perfectly with all the gray and dust and darkness he had been in all morning. Plus the entire seating area he was in was surrounded by growing flowers and live ferns and other decorative plants. So with each passing moment he felt like the weight of that old downtown hotel was lifting from him.

Bonnie and Jacob came to the front and worked their way toward him through the tables. He waved and smiled and stood as they got closer.

Wow, she was even more beautiful than he had realized when they first met. Her short hair, clearly freshly washed, fit her face perfectly and she had on tan slacks that matched her tan blazer. She walked like a person completely in charge of her surroundings, and completely confident with every movement.

What had surprised him was that even in all the stuff this morning, they had continued to get along, and after just two short days he liked being with her more than away from her. Not exactly sure what that meant, but it was certainly something brand new for him. He hadn't felt that way about another person since Karen was killed. More than likely, if Karen was somewhere watching right now, she would laugh and say, "About damned time."

And all Bonnie's friends thought of her as a force of nature and he liked that even more. If nothing else, working together was going to be wonderful fun. Challenging, but fun.

They got food and then over that first course told Jacob everything that had happened during the day.

It was Jacob that finally hit on what had been bothering Cavanaugh. That room hadn't been part of kidnapping women. It hadn't been a prison. It had been a way station to help women disappear.

That was the only thing that really fit.

And if that was the case, who and why and for how long? Cavanaugh's guess was the room and tunnel and secret passage to room 317 had been built at the same time as the hotel. So whatever this was all about had been going on since the sixties.

And had clearly been going on after the hotel was shuttered.

The three of them talked about that until Bonnie decided to go back for another round of the fantastic food. Cavanaugh and Jacob decided to do the same and this time Cavanaugh went for a second helping of the barbecue ribs and some shrimp. Bonnie made herself a shrimp cocktail and got some fresh halibut and Jacob came back with a plate so mounded, it was hard to tell what any of it was.

Oh, to be young and able to eat like that again.

"So," Cavanaugh said as they all started to eat, "if what we are thinking is correct, Myra Stemple so feared something, she went underground and started a new life."

Bonnie and Jacob both nodded.

Then Bonnie turned to Jacob. "Could you do a search of all unsolved missing women cases since the mid 1960s."

"Cutting out all the ones that were found, or likely murdered?" Jacob said.

"Sure. Any other parameters because that is going to end up with a massive list."

Cavanaugh agreed with that.

"How about," Bonnie said, "make a main list of missing women who had some sort of effects found, like the clothes in the closet."

Jacob nodded without missing a bite, then said, "I'll do the big list and the smaller list."

Something bothered Cavanaugh about the Myra case and he couldn't put his finger on it.

"Any chance it would be possible to cross-check the missing women with prior complaints of abuse on them?"

"Sure," Jacob said. "Another list and I'll get you a master list of the women with something found after they vanished who also had filed some sort of abuse claim. That should be a small enough number to work with."

"Thank you," Bonnie said, smiling at her son, who seemed to just ignore the thanks and kept eating.

Bonnie looked at Cavanaugh and smiled and rolled her eyes.

"I saw that," Jacob said.

And with that, the last of the horrid day in the old hotel vanished from Cavanaugh's mind and he relaxed completely into the good food and great company.

TWENTY-EIGHT

January 19th, 2019
Dinner at the Wynn
Las Vegas, Nevada

BONNIE KNEW that Cavanaugh had been so right when he suggested dinner at the Wynn Buffet. The bright lights, the wild colors, the feeling of all the people around them living normal lives was the perfect antidote to the dust and darkness and craziness of that old shuttered hotel. Bonnie was feeling better by the minute, and a second helping of food certainly hadn't hurt.

And Cavanaugh's company was perfect as well. In only two days, she had come to think of him as her partner. And she liked it when he was around, liked his sense of humor, his serious intensity, and how his mind worked through one detail to the next like a great detective.

The fact that she found him attractive didn't hurt either.

At one point, she and Jacob talked about their old cat Thomas and how they both missed him and Cavanaugh had asked her why she didn't have a cat now.

"Never felt it would be fair to the cat," she said. "You know how it is, gone every day all day."

Cavanaugh nodded to that and said, "Same reason I never got cats either. Was thinking I might at some point now that in theory my schedule will slow down some."

"Yeah," Jacob said, "how's that working out for you so far?"

Cavanaugh laughed and so did Bonnie.

So they talked about cats for a time, then finally Jacob brought the conversation back to their case. "I doubt that Myra will end up on the list with abusive complaints in her past."

"I figured as much," Bonnie said. "The original detectives would have found something and put it in the file."

"But if we are right about that room," Cavanaugh said, "she was running from something and I'm betting, if I had to bet, that it is her brother."

"If we are right about the room," Bonnie said. "And it feels like we are. But if we get a DNA match back of a Jane Doe to Myra's brother, that will change everything."

Cavanaugh nodded. "So for the moment we go forward with two theories. Theory one, that room was a staging area to help women disappear purposefully. Or second, that room was a form of prison."

"Or showroom," Jacob said, casually between bites. "If this is all about a sex trafficking ring, that room could have been used to display the women or girls that were for sale."

Bonnie just stared at her son.

He shrugged. "Sorry, it is a possibility, especially here in Las Vegas."

"He's right," Cavanaugh said. "Three major theories."

Bonnie sat back and sighed. "And until we find Myra Stemple, one way or another, we will never really know which theory is correct."

"Yeah," Cavanaugh said softly. Then he said, "And on that happy note, I need some dessert."

Bonnie laughed and stood with him. "Wait for me."

"Oh, great," Jacob said, shaking his head. "Now they have to help each other pick out desserts."

"And what's wrong with that?" Bonnie asked, laughing.

"Just too damn cute," Jacob said.

Bonnie smiled at Cavanaugh as they headed toward the desserts. "Who knew we were cute."

"I don't think anyone has called me cute since I was eight years old," Cavanaugh said.

"Don't let it go to your head," Bonnie said, laughing.

"Too late," Cavanaugh said, laughing with her. "Way, way too late."

TWENTY-NINE

January 19th, 2019
Cavanaugh's Home
Las Vegas, Nevada

CAVANAUGH HAD just gotten home after the wonderful dinner with Bonnie and Jacob when his phone rang. His place seemed empty, more so than normal and he had resisted turning on the light in the dining room where all the files were for the case.

He wanted to work, but without Bonnie that didn't feel right for some reason. He was amazed at how in such a short time he had grown to really like having her around and working with her.

He glanced at his watch. It was just after six in the evening. Still very early.

"Hey, partner," Bonnie said. "You up for spending a few hours on those files from Myra's brother? I'm so full I don't think I dare do anything but work."

"I would love the company," Cavanaugh said. "I was wondering what I was going to do the next few hours as well. You already dropped Jacob off?"

"Just did," she said.

"Front door will be unlocked. I'll get some coffee going."

"Perfect," she said. "See you soon."

He hung up and suddenly the big house didn't seem so empty.

"Wow, you are sort of really sad," Cavanaugh said to himself.

He whistled the entire time he got a pot of coffee brewing and just about the time it was done, Bonnie knocked and pushed open the door.

"Kitchen," Cavanaugh shouted and a moment later she appeared.

"Damn that coffee smells good," she said as she came in.

"After that meal," Cavanaugh said, "it just sounded good to me as well."

"Have I told you how much I like this place," she said as she took the mug of coffee he handed her, looking around at the large kitchen and the door out to the back.

"Thanks," he said, letting the compliment sink in a little. "You are one of the very few who have seen it, so that means a lot to me."

"Means a lot that you would let me see it," she said, smiling at him, then sipping on the coffee.

He took a sip from his mug as well and it tasted heavenly. Sometimes, like in the morning, coffee was just coffee. But other times, like after a fantastic meal with good company, it took on a different, better taste that he appreciated, and this was one of those times.

"So you think we actually might find something in all that stuff Danny gave us," Cavanaugh asked as he led the way to the dining room and turned on the overhead lights. The four boxes were right where they had left them on the massive dark mahogany dining room table.

"If she was taken by a sex-trafficking ring," Bonnie said, "nothing here is going to help us."

Cavanaugh agreed with that.

"And if she was abducted and killed?" Bonnie asked.

"We might find a hint as to why or some connection in here."

"Exactly," Bonnie said. "But if she wanted to disappear on purpose, I'm thinking it's what we don't see that will be important."

"You thinking the brother was an abuser of some sort?"

"Just one of many possible theories," Bonnie said. "But that lack of family pictures on the wall and that lack of receptionist kind of got me wondering."

Cavanaugh nodded. "And the mention that the place had a basement was strange as well. Not many houses in this area have basements."

"And all three of those things are perfectly innocent on the surface," Bonnie said.

"What does your super-detective sense tell you?" Cavanaugh asked her, smiling.

"That I need to take off my cape, turn on my super-detail vision, and look through all this stuff," Bonnie said.

"Super speed, too?" Cavanaugh asked.

"Nah, detail vision can slow a woman right down."

Cavanaugh just laughed, shook his head, and turned to the boxes. Bonnie just smiled at him, a light in her eye as she sipped her coffee.

He knew when to stop and he had a hunch that stopping right there was the perfect place on that conversation.

THIRTY

January 19th, 2019
Cavanaugh's Home
Las Vegas, Nevada

BONNIE COULDN'T really believe how comfortable she felt in Cavanaugh's home. She had just relaxed when she had gone through the front door and smelled the brewing coffee. And his shout that he had been in the kitchen just felt right, like they had been doing the same thing for a long time.

Comfortable, just everything about Cavanaugh and his home made her feel. Comfortable and respected.

She had no idea what was happening with her being around Cavanaugh, but at the moment she decided she wasn't going to question it, just enjoy it.

They spent until after eight in the evening and two cups of coffee each, going through the papers Danny had given them. From everything Bonnie could tell, Myra had been a good student in school and liked her job. But by the time they finished, Bonnie could see a couple of pretty glaring holes in all the information.

She and Cavanaugh went back into the kitchen and sat at the kitchen table, Bonnie nursing the last of her second cup of coffee and Cavanaugh sipping on a bottle of water.

"What did you think?" he asked.

"Where was she living when she vanished?"

Cavanaugh nodded. "I wondered that as well, and it wasn't in the case file either, so my gut sense is that she was living with the brother. And I noticed there was not one mention of the boyfriend in her brother's stuff."

Bonnie nodded. "That was the second thing that jumped out at me. I don't think the brother knew about the boyfriend."

"The file cleared the boyfriend of any possible wrongdoing because he was back east when she vanished," Cavanaugh said. "But that doesn't mean he wasn't involved."

"Think Jacob could find the boyfriend?" Bonnie asked, smiling.

"I think he could find a dime under a couch in New York if it was referenced on the internet. I was shocked that he found those floor plans of the hotel so quickly earlier."

Bonnie glanced at her watch. It was just a little after eight. So she took out her phone and called Jacob.

"Yup, we're working," she said in response to what Jacob said when he answered. She clicked on speaker. "On speaker with Cavanaugh. We're wondering if there is any chance you could track down the boyfriend."

"Hang on," he said. "Might take me a minute."

With that they could hear computer keys clicking, but Jacob said nothing more.

Cavanaugh just smiled at her and mouthed "Amazing."

She agreed with that completely. She had always been proud of Jacob and liked him as a person. But now, after only a day of working with him, her respect for her own son was growing by the minute.

"Name is Devon Daniels," Jacob said. "He now lives outside of Seattle. Married to a Missy Craig, one kid. Sending you a picture of the family and their address. Seems he does something for Boeing."

"Thanks," Bonnie said.

"And should have the lists for you tomorrow," Jacob said. "And my friend in San Francisco got the DNA sample, will have a preliminary result back to me tomorrow as well so that I can run for familial matches."

"Thanks," Cavanaugh said. "Really appreciate it."

"And thanks for the dinner," Jacob said.

With that he hung up.

Bonnie clicked off her phone, smiling.

"I really like your son," Cavanaugh said. "Efficient, blunt, and wastes no time on anything."

"Yeah, I kind of like him as well."

At that moment Bonnie's phone dinged. It was the picture and address of the boyfriend.

She opened the picture and just sat there, staring, not really believing what she was seeing.

"Want to grab that file picture of Myra?" she said to Cavanaugh.

He nodded, looking puzzled, and went and got it, sliding it across the kitchen table at her and then moving to stand behind her.

She looked at it, then at the picture Jacob had sent her.

"Son of a bitch," Cavanaugh said softly.

"I think we just solved our missing person case," Bonnie said, looking at Missy Craig, aka Myra Stemple.

"I think you may be right," Cavanaugh said, softly.

THIRTY-ONE

January 19th, 2019
Cavanaugh's Home
Las Vegas, Nevada

"SO WE SOLVED the missing person case," Cavanaugh said, moving around and sitting back down at the kitchen table across from Bonnie. "But I'm not sure we should tell anyone yet."

Bonnie nodded. She had been getting to that same conclusion almost instantly.

The silence in his kitchen was thick, but not uncomfortable as they both sat and tried to work out their next move on this case. He had spent many an evening and sometimes mornings sitting here at this table doing the same exact thing, working

over a case, sometimes taking notes, but mostly just thinking.

Clearly Myra had wanted to leave, and had gone to extreme measures, with a long-standing group of some sort or another, to do so. That means she considered herself in mortal danger, and others who knew about her situation did as well.

But there was nothing in the files or in Myra's history that showed any type of abuse or danger.

"This isn't witness protection," Bonnie said, after a moment, pointing at the photo on her phone.

"That secret room and tunnel certainly had nothing to do with witness protection either," Cavanaugh said. "And her clothes and purse and things were found in that closet years later, more than likely dumped when someone was cleaning that room. She was running."

"And running scared," Bonnie said. "And if I had to guess, I think she was more than likely running from the brother."

"Agreed," Cavanaugh said. "If they were as close as the brother led us to believe, she would have told him."

"And on one level his desire to find her seemed just normal family-like stuff, keeping in touch with the detectives and all. But when looked at through the lens of her running, it seems damned creepy. Especially if he suspected she had run to escape him."

Cavanaugh nodded.

At that moment Bonnie's phone rang. She glanced at it and put it on speaker. "Got both of us."

"You notice that picture I sent looks exactly like the missing woman?"

"Yeah, we were just talking about that and what to do," Bonnie said.

Now Available
from all your favorite booksellers
in trade paper and electronic editions.
The first Cold Poker Gang novel.

KILL GAME

A COLD POKER GANG MYSTERY

DEAN WESLEY SMITH

USA TODAY BESTSELLING AUTHOR

"So my guess was right and that secret room is part of an Underground Railroad to help women escape."

"Looking more and more like that," Bonnie said.

"So any ideas?" Jacob asked.

"The brother," Cavanaugh said. "Any chance you can do a deep dive on him without letting him know. He's an attorney, so be careful."

"And that office of his," Bonnie said. "We noticed that when Myra vanished, she had no official address. Does the brother live in his office and when was that basement under it built?"

"Got it," Jacob said. "Back with you in the morning."

Bonnie clicked off her phone and looked up into the wonderful and intelligent green eyes of Cavanaugh. "So got any ideas of what we do next?"

He nodded. "We call Andor and tell him why we need to keep it quiet. Then we make a trip to Seattle."

"To talk with Myra?"

"Only Myra is going to know why she had to vanish. And if we promise to keep her secret, she might just tell us."

Bonnie nodded. "My stomach is twisting on this one. I'm thinking that brother was doing something awful to his sister."

"And maybe others since," Cavanaugh said.

"Damn, you had to say that, didn't you?"

"You were thinking it," Cavanaugh said, smiling.

With that she could only nod, because she had been thinking it. She hated that she had, but she had been. Just where all the years of being a detective took her.

THIRTY-TWO

January 20th, 2019
Main Street Station Buffet
Las Vegas, Nevada

CAVANAUGH and Bonnie had talked for another hour before she had headed home. After she left he had watched a little television and fallen asleep in front of the nightly news before dragging himself to bed.

Now, this morning, he felt almost rested and was waiting for her and Andor in the buffet at the Main Street Station. The crowd around him felt like he actually had some privacy in the table they had given him in the back. The massive high ceilings and antique decorations gave the place a comfortable feel very different from the Wynn's over-the-top colors and massive plants.

He liked this place better.

He had gotten here thirty minutes early and was just sipping on an iced tea when he saw Bonnie come in. He waved her over since he had already paid for her and Andor's breakfast.

She looked great this morning, even more than normal it seemed. She had on a blue jacket that somehow matched her jeans and when she saw him, her smile had lit up her face. He was betting his smile did the same for his face.

Only a few days and he just couldn't believe how much he was enjoying being with her, both working on a case and just being together. And how attracted he was to her.

"Thanks for breakfast," she said as she joined him.

"I'm celebrating not having to go into a dirty, dark, shuttered hotel looking for secret rooms this morning."

She laughed. "I got happy this morning as well when I realized the same thing. So a pleasure to join you in that celebration."

At that moment Andor came in the front and Cavanaugh waved him in, indicating he was already paid.

"You buying?" Andor said as he got to the table, moving through the other tables like he might knock them over. "This can't be good."

With that he turned and headed for the food lines. Bonnie and Cavanaugh both laughed and followed him.

After they all had gotten a distance into their breakfasts, Andor said, "Okay, besides smoothing over finding the hidden rooms with the Golden Nugget and the mess for poor Detective Fawn and days of paperwork she has to fight through, what can I do for you two?"

Cavanaugh slid him the folder with the image of Myra Stemple, then the image of her with her husband and kids.

"That was her boyfriend before she vanished," Bonnie said.

"Son-of-a-bitch," Andor said. "She ran."

"The secret room and tunnel we figure was part of an Underground Railroad of some sort," Cavanaugh said, "to help women escape from abuse."

"So who was abusing her?" Andor asked. "And that means some of those other missing person's cases are runners as well."

"The ones with the clothes found in that closet," Bonnie said. "More than likely."

"Better than the alternative," Andor said.

Cavanaugh could only agree to that.

"Our best guess is that Myra was running from her brother," Bonnie said. "We have Jacob doing a careful dig into him, but we haven't heard back on that yet."

"So let me guess," Andor said, "you are thinking of going to Seattle to talk with her."

Bonnie nodded. "And we need to keep what we have found secret until we figure out who she was running from and why."

At that moment Bonnie's phone cheeped and she glanced at it. "Jacob."

She put the phone on speaker and said, "You got me and Cavanaugh and Andor on speaker."

"Let me guess," Jacob said. "Main Street Station Buffet."

Cavanaugh just shook his head and laughed.

"So we're predictable," Bonnie said, laughing as well. "What did you find on the brother?"

"No records at all of a basement in that office building," Jacob said. "If there is one, it was built under the public reporting."

Cavanaugh glanced at Bonnie who nodded.

Andor said nothing.

"He owns the building outright," Jacob said. "He has very few clients that I can figure, and makes very little money. He basically does nothing much as an attorney at least in the public records."

"How is he surviving?" Bonnie asked.

"No idea," Jacob said, "He had no obvious gambling issues, no sports issues, and without the right kind of warrants, I couldn't check his banking accounts."

"Thanks, Jacob," Bonnie said. "We really appreciate it."

"One more thing," Jacob said. "None of the women whose clothes were found in the old hotel have any matches to Jane Doe bodies. It's looking more and more like every woman who went through that secret room was a runner."

With that Jacob hung up.

The sounds of the buffet came crashing back in on the table as Cavanaugh sat there silently, thinking.

"Looks like you two need to head to Seattle," Andor said. "And sooner rather than later."

He took out his cell phone and hit a number in his contacts. "Hi," he said after a moment to whoever answered. "Got a pretty critical case that Cavanaugh and State have uncovered. They need a ride to Seattle."

He nodded. "Perfect. Thanks!"

With that he hung up and looked at Cavanaugh, then at Bonnie. "Be at the private terminal at the airport in one hour. I got you a ride to Seattle and back today. Now it is time for dessert."

With that he stood and headed for the food lines before Bonnie or Cavanaugh could say a word.

"He does that on purpose, you know," Bonnie said, shaking her head.

"Guess he figures we're detectives," Cavanaugh said. "And we can figure it out."

"I don't think anyone will ever figure out Andor," Bonnie said, laughing.

Cavanaugh could only agree to that.

THIRTY-THREE

January 20th, 2019
Seattle, Washington

BONNIE had really enjoyed the flight from Vegas to Seattle in Doc Hill's private jet. Actually, it was very short

flight, especially considering they didn't have to wait at all for security or time to park and get through the airport. Just over three hours from the time Cavanaugh picked her up in front of her building, they landed in Seattle.

They had driven up to a private parking lot in front of what looked like an office building attached to a large plane hangar on one edge of the airport. They had shown their IDs at the gate and then again at a front desk and got escorted to the steward who would be on the plane with them.

Both of them had left their guns at home, but brought their badges. Neither had brought even a change of clothes because their return flight was later in the day, as soon as they got finished. The plane was going to wait for them.

The jet itself was large and decorated in soft brown leather tones and light mahogany. The seats were huge and she had ended up sitting facing Cavanaugh across a small table with more than enough leg room, something on regular commercial flights, she always fought with.

The steward, a nice younger guy named Carlson, seemed amazingly competent and friendly and even laughed at her and Cavanaugh's one-liners. He served them both coffee and a few butter cookies and then answered a few questions about the jet and Doc Hill, before seeming to vanish somewhere into the back.

Doc Hill was married to Lott's daughter. He was also widely known as the best poker player in the world. And he and his partner had built a multi-billion dollar business from Doc's winnings and shrewd investments in real estate and who knew what else. They often helped different people on problems, just as they were helping them today with a quick ride to Seattle.

It was said that Doc and his partner also had a small private force of ex-special service folks at their disposal and that they loved helping the Cold Poker Gang in tough situations.

It had been Doc's men, led by a guy named Mike, who had helped a number of members of the Cold Poker Gang roust out that huge sex ring that had been existing in the tunnels under Vegas for decades.

Bonnie had heard parts of the story at different times and was just amazed. That case had been one of the main reasons she had wanted to join the Cold Poker Gang task force when she retired.

"You know," Cavanaugh said, climbing in behind the wheel of the big Cadillac SUV that they had been given to use in Seattle. "You and I are both pretty well off. But this kind of money I just can't imagine."

Bonnie could only agree to that. When you got rich enough that it was no big deal to loan out one of your private jets and one of your many Cadillac fleet of cars to a couple of detectives just so they could go interview someone, you had real money.

As they left the private hangar, Cavanaugh shook his head. "How can anyone actually live in this city?"

He had turned on the windshield wipers. "Like living in a mold bath."

Bonnie just laughed. "Never been here before. Looks pretty."

"Oh, it is pretty," Cavanaugh said. "Wet, but pretty."

Bonnie mostly just watched the scenery of the lush, green Seattle area as Cavanaugh got them away from the airport and onto the freeway and headed toward Seattle proper.

"You going to want to call your daughter?" Bonnie asked after a short time. "See if she has time for lunch?"

"Let's see how this goes with Myra first," Cavanaugh said. "Hate to hold up Doc's jet and flight crew for longer than we need to."

Bonnie agreed to that. She had no idea what this private jet trip to Seattle had actually cost. Didn't really want to know, actually.

It took thirty minutes of driving before Cavanaugh pulled the big SUV up in front of a nice-looking home in a subdivision. Even though it was the middle of the winter and a gray mist was soaking everything, the house looked well-tended and the yard almost freshly mowed. Everything was so lushly green, coming from the desert and Las Vegas, it seemed almost too green.

On the plane they had worked out a set of questions and how they were going to approach Myra. Bonnie was going to do most of the talking.

From what Jacob had told them, Myra worked from home for some internet company and should be home when they got there.

When Myra answered the front door, Bonnie felt a jolt. She had so expected to find this woman's body, not see her healthy and smiling.

"Yes?" Myra said.

"Hi, my name is Detective Bonnie State, from the Las Vegas Police Department. This is Detective Cavanaugh."

They both showed Myra their badges as the color drained from Myra's face. For a moment Bonnie thought the poor woman was going to pass out.

"Don't worry," Bonnie said. "No one knows we have found you and we don't plan on telling anyone. We would just like to ask a few questions is all."

Myra nodded meekly and indicated they should come in.

The home was exactly as it looked from the outside. Clean, modern furniture, and light and bright, decorated in tones of green and brown. The smell of eggs and bacon still filled the air of the place from breakfast.

"I suppose I was always expecting to be found," she said as she led them into the living room and got them seated on a comfortable and clearly well-loved couch. "But after all these years, not sure why now."

"We're on a task force working to solve cold cases," Bonnie said. "Your missing person's case came up and your clothes being found in an old shuttered hotel led us to the hidden room and tunnel in that old hotel. And that led us to you."

Myra nodded. "I had to leave the clothes I was wearing and my identification and purse and everything I owned in that basement room."

"So we need to ask," Bonnie said. "Why did you run? From who?"

"You don't know?" Myra asked, clearly surprised.

Bonnie shook her head. "That is why we have told no one we found you. We did not want to put you or your family here in danger."

"Doesn't matter," Myra said. "Just by you finding me, my family and I are all as good as dead. And more than likely, you both are as well."

And with that she broke into tears, sobbing into her hands.

THIRTY-FOUR

January 20th, 2019
Seattle, Washington

CAVANAUGH was stunned at Myra's statement. He glanced at Bonnie, who was just looking as confused as he was feeling.

Myra was sobbing and after a moment Bonnie asked her softly, "Can you tell us why you feel that way?"

"Actually," Cavanaugh said softly, "Can you start from the beginning and tell us exactly how you ended up here."

Bonnie nodded to that. "Yes, we need to know what happened."

"Devon and I were planning on being married," Myra said after a few moments of pulling herself together. "We hadn't told anyone."

"Not even your brother?" Bonnie asked.

"Especially not my brother."

Bonnie glanced at Cavanaugh who nodded at the force of that statement, so Bonnie said to Myra, "Go on."

"I went to a shop to order my wedding dress, then stopped by a tux shop to see if Devon's tux was ready. That's all I remember. When I came awake I was in some sort of deep underground tunnels with apartments."

"The August Tux Shop?" Bonnie asked.

Myra nodded, looking puzzled.

Cavanaugh sat back, stunned. Myra had gotten mixed up in that massive sex ring that Sarge and Pickett and Robin had broken open in 2016. Women who were about to be married had been kidnapped by a very large and very well-organized sex traffic ring. Many had been held for years in underground apartments being filmed. Others had been forced to be married by a fake Elvis on camera and then released.

"So what happened next?" Bonnie asked.

"I was kept there for just a day, forced to go through a fake marriage and then I was raped while it was all filmed."

Cavanaugh was impressed that she could even describe that.

With that Myra broke down again and Bonnie moved over and put her arm around her shoulder and held her until the tears stopped.

"So what happened next?"

"They let me go and threatened that if I told anyone what had happened, they would find me and kill me. And I believed them. I called Devon and he made a few calls and got me into an abused woman pipeline to get me out of town."

"He met you later?" Bonnie asked.

Myra nodded, sniffling. "I told him everything and he understood. We moved to Seattle right after that and I went into counseling to get past what had happened."

"You never contacted your brother?" Bonnie asked.

Myra looked horrified and shook her head. "Why would I do that? He was part

---

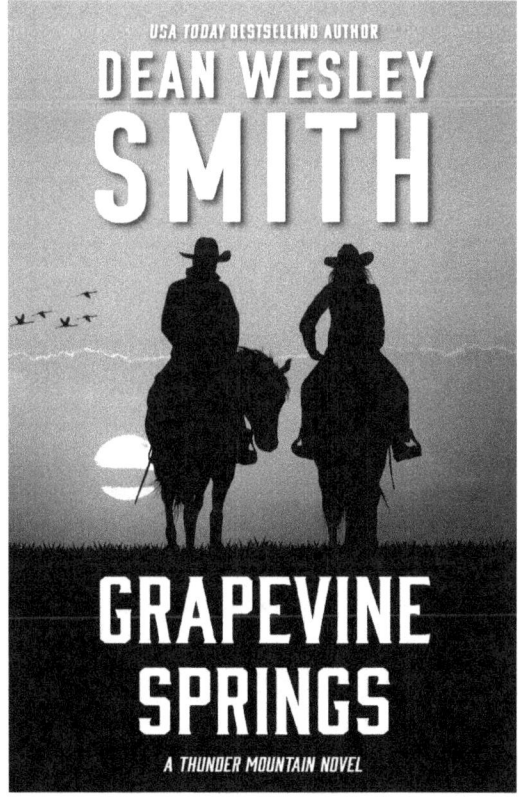

of the people who held me and made me do those unspeakable acts. He thought after they let me go that I would just go back living with him as if nothing had happened."

"Oh, shit," Cavanaugh said, softly. No wonder the bastard was so interested in finding Myra.

Cavanaugh stood and moved quickly to the window. He couldn't see that they had been followed, but that didn't mean they hadn't been. It seemed that nest of scum that Pickett and Sarge and Robin had found had not all been cleaned out when they cleared out the tunnels and apartments.

"He doesn't know, does he?" Myra asked, panic in her voice.

"We did not tell him anything other than we were looking for you." Myra said.

Cavanaugh quickly dialed Andor and said softly, "I think we may be in trouble."

THIRTY-FIVE

January 20th, 2019
Seattle, Washington

BONNIE TRIED to comfort Myra as best as she could, sitting next to her on the couch in the comfortable living room. Bonnie couldn't hear the Seattle rain, but the bright interior of the house at the moment couldn't seem to hold the oppressiveness of the gray away.

In fact, right now, the house seemed more like a tight and dangerous space.

Cavanaugh had gone to the window and did a quick check of the street, then had made a phone call, more than likely to Andor. She had listened as he told

Andor in a very calm explanation of the fact that they had run into a victim of the sex-ring that Sarge and Pickett and Robin had broken a couple years back.

And that there may be parts of that ring left, including Myra's brother.

After that Cavanaugh nodded a few times, then said, "Thanks."

Cavanaugh clicked off his phone and came back over and sat in a recliner facing Myra and Bonnie. He nodded to Bonnie and she knew what he was going to do. He was going to tell Myra everything.

Bonnie nodded in agreement.

"Myra," Cavanaugh said, learning forward, "you need to listen to us for a moment."

Bonnie had a hand on Myra's shoulder and she could feel Myra take a big shuddering breath and let it out, then nod.

"The people who kidnapped and filmed you were captured in 2016 and the entire ring broken up. All of them are in jail."

Her head snapped up. "My brother?"

"It wasn't known that he was a part of it, so no," Bonnie said, softly.

"How do you know he was part of it?" Cavanaugh asked.

"When I was being phony married, it was by a man wearing an Elvis mask. That man was my brother. I knew his voice and shape anywhere. I pleaded for him to stop, or at least I think I tried, but I was pretty drugged."

Bonnie could feel the anger coming back to Myra, which was better. Anger was going to get her through this.

Bonnie also knew that the standard procedure for those disgusting people in that sex ring was to perform a fake marriage with the kidnapped woman, then have the fake husband rape the wife while it was all filmed for sick humans of the world to watch. Often the guy in the Elvis masked watched or took part.

"We are fairly certain your brother did not follow us here," Cavanaugh said. "But we have some para-military coming to set up a parameter around this house and also to keep an eye on your daughter and husband without them knowing they are being guarded.

"You can do that?" Myra asked.

Bonnie was just as surprised to hear that. Clearly Andor had known exactly what to do.

"We can," Cavanaugh said, acting as if he did something like that every day. Bonnie really admired his calmness. She was remaining calm as well on the outside, but inside she was scared to death for Myra and for them. Now she was really questioning why they hadn't brought their guns.

"And we have people making sure your brother is still in Vegas," Cavanaugh said.

Myra seemed to relax a little. Then she asked, "The police caught everyone?"

"We thought so until you told us about your brother being a part of it," Cavanaugh said. "We will tell you the entire story after everything settles."

Bonnie looked at Cavanaugh. "I need to get Jacob on this."

Cavanaugh nodded and Bonnie quickly dialed Jacob's number and told him what they had discovered and what was happening.

"Mike's people will make sure you are safe," Jacob said. "They were the forces that went in with the police and Sarge and Pickett into the tunnels to break all this up in the first place. From what I understand, he has people all over the nation and in different parts of the world."

"You are going to have to explain who this Mike is later," Bonnie said to Jacob, glancing at Cavanaugh who just sort of half shrugged.

"In the meantime," Bonnie said, "could you do a deep dive on Myra's brother. We need to know if he is now alone or is working with another group."

"Won't be admissible or maybe even legal," Jacob said.

"Myra's case is past the statute of limitations," Bonnie said. "I'm more concerned about what that creep can still be doing in that basement to other women."

"Got it," Jacob said. "Stay safe, Mom."

With that he hung up.

And the three of them sat there in silence. Bonnie had no idea what they were going to do next. Not one clue.

And that scared her more than just about anything.

THIRTY-SIX

January 20th, 2019
Seattle, Washington

CAVANAUGH sat silently facing Myra and Bonnie in Myra's suburban living room. He wanted to ask Myra more questions, but felt the time wasn't right just yet. Andor had told him that he would have Mike, the man in control of a security firm in Las Vegas, a very secret and high-end security firm, get people around them and would call Cavanaugh when that was in place.

Cavanaugh had heard of this Mike and his business, mostly concerning working the case in the tunnels. It seemed that before the regular SWAT could go in, Mike and his men had already disarmed without a shot all the guards in the tunnels. There was no doubt it saved lives. Plus they had disarmed a nasty system of bombs that would have killed even more.

Just like the Cold Poker Gang, Mike wanted no credit and had left all the credit to the police, even though everyone knew it was Mike and the Cold Poker Gang task force that had taken down the long-standing sex ring.

Cavanaugh had never met Mike and never had expected to. Of course, they had never expected to uncover more of those slime sex's-traffickers with this case, either. But it sure looked like they might have.

"So now what do we do?" Myra asked after a few moments.

"We wait," Cavanaugh said, "until everyone gets into position and we find out exactly where your brother is at."

Myra nodded.

At that moment Cavanaugh's phone rang and he glanced at it. "Andor."

Cavanaugh clicked on the phone. "You are on speaker with Bonnie and Myra. We are still in Myra's living room."

"Mike's got two of his people covering her house and two more on the daughter and husband. All are safe and no signs of any trouble."

"Oh, thank God," Myra said, letting out a deep breath.

"The brother is in his office," Andor said.

"I got Jacob doing a deep dive on him," Bonnie said.

"Good," Andor said. "Mike and his people are doing the same. He won't sneeze without us knowing about it."

"Thank you," Bonnie said.

Suddenly someone knocked on the back door of the house.

"Mike's people supposed to make contact with us?" Cavanaugh asked.

"No," Andor said.

"Anyone ever come to that door?" Bonnie asked Myra.

"Never," Myra said.

"Andor, we got someone trying to come in the back door," Cavanaugh said.

"Shit," Andor said and hung up.

Bonnie jumped to her feet, pulling Myra up. "Safest place to hide?"

"Closet, back bedroom," Myra said.

"Get there," Bonnie said, shoving her in the direction of the hallway, "and don't open it unless you hear our voices."

"You have a gun in the house?" Cavanaugh asked as the person knocked on the back door again.

"No," Myra said as she went for the back bedroom.

Cavanaugh had figured she wouldn't with a kid in the house, but felt he had to ask.

Bonnie made sure Myra was doing as she was told, then followed Cavanaugh into the kitchen. Both of them stayed low and out of sight of the window over the sink. There was a block of large knives on the counter and he grabbed one and handed it to her, then took one for himself.

He hated knives, but better than nothing.

Then he saw something better.

The back door was through a small mudroom and was solid wood, thankfully. No window. Just inside that room were a couple baseball bats leaning against a wall.

He grabbed one and glanced at Bonnie who nodded she wanted one as well.

They both slid the knives they had onto the counter within easy reach.

Cavanaugh went to the right of the door to the mudroom, Bonnie to the left as something smashed into the door. Sounded to Cavanaugh like a kick.

The door held, but barely.

Another kick and the door smashed open.

The next moment a body hit the floor, coming slightly into the kitchen face down. A pistol with a suppressor attached slid into the kitchen past the man's outstretched hand.

Baseball bats would not have done much good against that.

Cavanaugh could tell the guy was big and strong. The back of his head was bleeding and he was clearly out cold.

"Detectives?" A voice said from the door. "It's clear."

Cavanaugh glanced around at the back door at a thin, short guy standing there. He was smiling. He looked like just about anyone, except for the gun in a holster under his light rain jacket. He was holding a five iron that looked like it had some rust on it from sitting outside.

"I'm Ben, working with Mike. Sorry this guy got so close."

With that Ben came inside and bent down and put some zip-ties on the unconscious guy's hands and then his feet.

Cavanaugh glanced at Bonnie who still had the bat on her shoulder like she was heading for home plate. Then he looked back at the guy on the floor.

Thunder Mountain Series Available...
These novels are available in electronic format or print at your favorite booksellers.

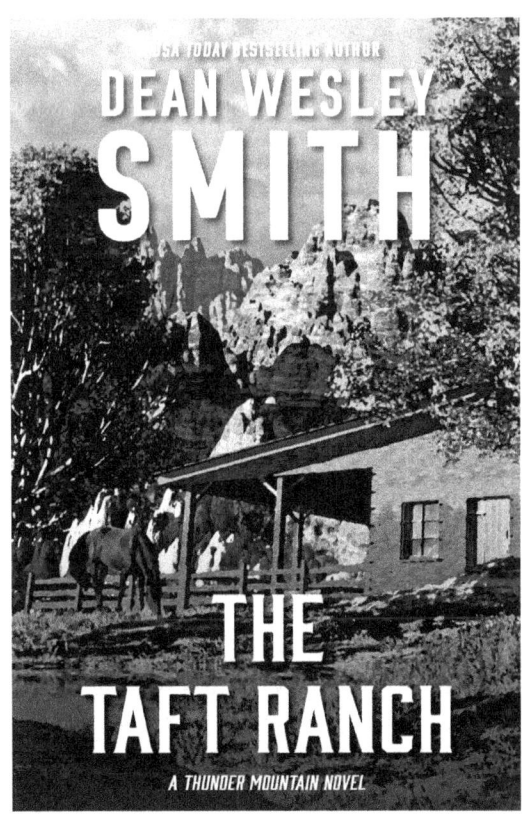

It seemed that whatever hornet's nest they had kicked over, it was bigger than they had imagined.

Far bigger.

THIRTY-SEVEN

January 20th, 2019
Seattle, Washington

FORTY MINUTES LATER the big guy was in the back of a Seattle police car with a bandage on the back of his head. Bonnie, Myra, and Cavanaugh were sitting on the couch facing two Seattle detectives by the name of Hoff and Yardley. Ben stood to one side.

Both men had been wearing raincoats that they had taken off and left by the front door. Under the coats, they both wore jeans, tennis shoes, and dress shirts with holsters under the arms and badges attached to their belts.

Bonnie had a good competent feeling about both of them instantly, even though she had no doubt she would have trouble telling them apart. Both were the same height, weight, and dark brown hair color.

Yardley's nose was bigger and he seemed to smile and talk more than Hoff, but beside that, it was almost creepy how two partners could look so much alike.

Cavanaugh had just finished explaining what they were doing there, and Ben had told him who he worked for and why he was there and in position to hit the big guy breaking in with a golf club.

"The guy who tried to break in," Yardley said, "is Terry Greenburg. He's a known thug for hire in this area and this event should put him away for enough years that he won't matter anymore to anyone."

"So that's how he got here so fast," Bonnie said, nodding.

"I bet my brother called him and somehow traced you two here," Myra said, her voice soft.

"Flight plan," Cavanaugh said. "More than likely your brother got our flight plan and Greenburg tailed us from the airport. He's good, since I didn't spot him."

"And he was already in position and hiding in the backyard when we got here," Ben said. "That would make sense why we didn't spot him coming in."

Yardley nodded. "So you think this was all set up by someone connected to that broken sex video ring out of Vegas?"

Myra started to say something, but Bonnie stopped her. "Myra's brother, an attorney in Vegas, was involved, but Myra was the only one who knew that. He has been obsessed with finding her since she went underground after her attack and vanished."

"Your brother helped those perverts rape you?" Yardley asked, clearly stunned. Hoff looked like he might say something as well, then shut his mouth.

Myra nodded. "He performed the phony marriage wearing an Elvis mask and then watched me get raped. He expected me to come back and live with him after all that, but I got connected to an abuse network that got me hidden and out of town. Since my brother didn't know about my boyfriend at the time, I changed my name and we moved here."

"Well," Yardley said, nodding. "Taking that sex ring down in Vegas helped us take down the parts that were functioning here. Lots of other cities around the nation had the same success."

"Any part of it left functioning?" Cavanaugh asked.

"Always some slime like that," Yardley said, "but locally grown stuff now. Nothing imported as all that was from Sin City."

"So think you can get the guy in the car to tell who hired him?" Bonnie asked.

"Already has," Yardley said, looking at Myra. "It was your brother, as you all thought. The idiot in the car is singing like an opera star, hoping to spend a little less time in jail."

Bonnie glanced at Cavanaugh, who nodded.

"It seems, Detectives," Bonnie said, "that Cavanaugh and I need to get back to Las Vegas. We have some scum to round up."

"Namely my brother," Myra said.

"Top of the list," Cavanaugh said.

Ten minutes later they were headed for the airport. Bonnie knew that Mike's people would keep Myra and her family safe until her brother was locked up nice and deep and the key tossed away.

THIRTY-EIGHT

January 20th, 2019
Las Vegas, Nevada

CAVANAUGH felt the trip back to Vegas had taken forever, but actually from Myra's house to his car at the Las Vegas airport had only taken just under four hours. All the way back they had been in contact with Jacob, Detective Fawn, and Andor.

Fawn had gotten all the warrants needed to go into Danny Stemple's office and home from the information furnished by the Seattle detectives.

And Jacob and Mike's people had found all sorts of interesting and ugly stuff in computer investigations once they had a few warrants. It seemed that Stemple hadn't left the sex video business at all and was still distributing on the dark web. Cavanaugh didn't want to think about what they would find going into that office and the hidden basement.

By the time Cavanaugh got them within a few blocks of the brother's office to meet Fawn and Andor, everything was set for the raid.

Around them the neighborhood looked completely normal. Calm streets, very little traffic, nice remodeled older homes that all now had attorney signs in front of them.

Not at all like there was going to be a major police raid on an attorney's office in just minutes.

The day had turned nice for January and comfortable to be out without even a jacket. Fawn and Andor stood on the sidewalk in front of a large stucco building that housed five law offices as Cavanaugh pulled up.

"Great work, Detectives," Fawn said, as Cavanaugh and Bonnie got out and joined them on the wide sidewalk.

"Scary moment up there?" Andor asked.

"Baseball bats against a guy with a pistol," Bonnie said. "I didn't like our odds."

"Thankfully you got Mike's man to take control just before we had to go to bat," Cavanaugh said.

Bonnie nodded. "Mike's guy swung a mean five iron."

Fawn just shook her head. "Remind me that when I join the task force to not expect it to be easy."

"Oh," Bonnie said, "it's like being a regular detective. It's easy until it isn't."

"But no paperwork," Cavanaugh said.

"Don't remind me," Fawn said.

Both Cavanaugh and Bonnie knew they wouldn't be able to go in with the raid with Fawn and the other active police and detectives. In fact, they had both decided they would be just fine sitting back and watching. Turned out Fawn had other ideas for them, and wanted them close to the house and going in quickly after the first wave cleared everything.

She said she felt, since they had been the closest with everything on this case, there might be something they would see that she would miss.

And Cavanaugh agreed, as did Bonnie. Even though they weren't active, they knew enough to not screw up a crime scene and just might spot something.

"One caution," Cavanaugh said. "From what I remember hearing about the tunnels, these folks like explosives."

"Shit," Fawn said, "you are right."

She stepped away and got on the phone, clearly ordering in a bomb squad to check as they went in.

"Good thinking," Bonnie said, touching his arm.

A moment later Fawn turned back to them. "You three stay here until we give the call that we are going in, then move up and come in after I give the all clear. Maybe ten minutes."

She turned away and climbed into an unmarked sedan and headed down the street toward the office.

Andor took his phone out and as he hit a button, he said to them, "Check with Jacob, make sure he hasn't found anything more. I'm checking with Mike, going to mention the chance of explosives and see if he has any suggestions."

"Besides not going in?" Cavanaugh asked.

"Yeah, besides that," Andor said, then turned away to talk with Mike as Bonnie called Jacob.

"On speaker with Cavanaugh," Bonnie said a moment later to Jacob. "We're a couple blocks away and Detective Fawn and her forces are about to go in. Anything else?"

"Place might be bigger than you would think," Jacob said. "I just found out that one of the minor drainage tunnels runs under the street right next to the office. Empties out just beyond the freeway into the larger system. He could have connected down to that tunnel fairly easily."

"Which way would he go?" Bonnie asked, looking at Cavanaugh.

"Tunnel starts real small up about ten blocks to the east of his office," Jacob said, "with nothing there but drainage grates, so that opening on the other side of the freeway is the only way out of that tunnel. He would go that way."

"Damn it!" Cavanaugh said and moved to Andor. "Tell Mike there is a chance this guy might try to make a run for it in the drainage tunnel that runs under the street next to his office. Bonnie and I will be at the entrance in minutes."

"Go!" Andor said. "I'll tell Fawn that you'll need backup."

With that Cavanaugh and Bonnie scrambled to his car with Jacob still on the phone giving them exact directions to the tunnel exit.

As Bonnie had said, this being retired was easy until it wasn't.

THIRTY-NINE

January 20th, 2019
Las Vegas, Nevada

BONNIE DID a check of her pistol as Cavanaugh drove quickly down Clark Street to get to the other side of the freeway and to the large area there where some of the major drainage tunnels opened.

The vast network of tunnels under Las Vegas drained large parts of the city during the heavy storms that sometimes hit in the winter, but more often in the heat of the summer when the monsoon storms swept up from the south.

Before the tunnels were built, entire areas of town were impassable and flooded in almost any storm.

The homeless often used the network of tunnels to live out of the sun, and the police had regular patrols to warn those living in the tunnels when a storm was coming. No one really had any idea how many were killed by flash floods in those tunnels every year. But Bonnie knew it was a lot. Most of the bodies were never found, buried under feet of sand and dirt miles downstream. And since they were all homeless, very few were even reported missing, sadly.

Cavanaugh pulled up and parked near one of the openings in the chain link fence that surrounded the deep wash where the tunnels opened. This was where the homeless went down into the massive river wash framed on one side by huge concrete rectangular tunnels. The bottom of the wash was covered in concrete and piles of weeds, junk, and trash scattered along the banks from the last flood.

In all her years on the force, she had never been down in one of the tunnels, but she had done her share of climbing down into flood washes to get to bodies, not a part of the job she wanted to repeat now that she was retired.

She called Jacob back as she and Cavanaugh climbed out of the car. When he answered she said, "We're looking at a large opening and a couple smaller ones."

"As you face the openings," Jacob said, "tunnel on the far left. No other place for him to come out if he does have a way into the tunnel near his office."

"Got it," Bonnie said.

"Mike has a guy headed your way and a couple of squad cars are also headed to you, but they are four minutes out at least."

"You linked into the police channel?"

"I am," Jacob said.

"Has Detective Fawn gone in yet?"

"Just did," Jacob said. "No sign of the brother upstairs."

"Call me if they get him," Bonnie said. "Thanks."

"Careful, Mom," Jacob said. "This guy is a piece of work."

With that Jacob hung up.

Cavanaugh handed her a flashlight.

"Oh, joy," she said. "Another tunnel."

"Think all these tunnels on our first case has something to do with my personality?" Cavanaugh asked.

"God, I hope not, since I'm stuck partnering with you and I hate tunnels."

He laughed and held open the chain link fence for her to duck through and down the hard dirt bank of the wash. Thirty steps down they were on a slanted concrete side. Thankfully they both made it to the bottom without either one of them falling. Luckily they had both kept in shape. A fall on that kind of slanted concrete could do damage to a young person, let alone someone their age.

Standing on the bottom of the wash felt like they were in a deep canyon and the sounds of the city had faded to almost nothing. It was impossible to tell that they were in the middle of a large city. It felt like they were out in the desert, actually.

She had seen this same area thirty feet deep in raging, ugly brown water at different times. Flat terrifying to imagine, especially now that she was standing on the bottom of it facing gaping massive concrete tunnels.

They both pulled their guns and headed for the tunnel on the left at a fast walk. She really wanted to get out of the open and to some cover. And the concrete of the tunnel opening would offer some protection.

The tunnel opening wasn't more than ten paces across and about as tall as a single-story house. All four sides of the tunnel were concrete.

Bonnie went to the left, against the concrete holding up the hill and Cavanaugh went right, both of them staying on the outside and hidden from anyone who might be in the tunnel.

The tunnel smelled of mold and rot and there wasn't an ounce of cover or protection once they started in. She really didn't want to go in there if they didn't have to.

Bonnie's phone buzzed.

Jacob.

"We're at the tunnel mouth," Bonnie said.

"They found cameras and explosives set on the basement area," Jacob said. "So they are slowed down, but heat-sensing tells them no one is in the large basement, so they think he's coming toward you."

"How far away is backup?"

"Mike's guy will be there in two, police are close behind."

"Thanks," Bonnie said and clicked off.

"He's likely coming this way," Bonnie said to Cavanaugh across the opening. "Backup is still two minutes out."

"So depends on when he figured out what was happening and what kind of start he got," Cavanaugh said. "I'm betting he got a good start on the raid."

"We stay put right here," she said, indicating their positions, hidden and not in the tunnel.

Thankfully, Cavanaugh nodded.

FORTY

January 20th, 2019
Las Vegas, Nevada

CAVANAUGH MADE sure he didn't hold his breath as he and Bonnie stood ready on both sides of the concrete drainage tunnel. The smell coming from the tunnel was choking. Mold, rot, and clearly something dead. Not counting the background smell of human waste. Cavanaugh was more than glad to stay right where they were. At least here they had some fresh air and they had cover.

Then two things happened at the same time.

The sounds of steps echoed from inside the tunnel. It sounded like more than one person, actually.

And a police cruiser pulled up near where he had parked. Someone coming close to the mouth of the tunnel would be able to see it.

Cavanaugh stepped back out of view of the tunnel and waved at the cruiser, indicating that it should pull back and out of sight. The cop driving understood and quickly pulled the car away far enough to not be seen.

The steps from inside the tunnel were getting closer. On the other side of the tunnel mouth, Bonnie was pushing herself back as far as she could from the edge so that she wouldn't be seen.

He had more room and had moved a step back completely.

From the other side of the deep ravine Cavanaugh saw a man with a rifle take up position, lying on his stomach, so he could see the opening of the tunnel.

Cavanaugh waved at him, more than likely Mike's man.

The guy gave him a thumbs up.

The steps inside the tunnel were now coming closer quickly. And it was very clear there was more than one person.

If they let him and the other person get too far out, he and Bonnie would be in the direct line of fire from each other. So Cavanaugh held up his hand and started a slow countdown from five, listening as the steps got closer and closer.

By the time he reached "Go" the steps were very close.

Both he and Bonnie stepped from cover, guns aimed into the tunnel.

It was Danny Stemple, all right, and he was pulling along a brown-haired short woman in a white wedding dress that had gotten stained along the bottom from the tunnel. Over his other shoulder he was carrying a duffel bag.

He looked out of breath. He wasn't more than twenty paces inside the tunnel. He had on a suit jacket and nice black leather shoes that clearly had gotten dirty in his trek through the tunnel.

"Hands in the air," Bonnie said.

"Drop the bag slowly," Cavanaugh said.

Stemple stood there, staring at them, his hand not letting go of the woman, who looked totally stunned.

Then Stemple dropped the bag.

"Let go of the woman!" Cavanaugh ordered.

"Hands in the air," Bonnie ordered. "Now!

Stemple didn't move, just holding onto the woman firmly with his right hand.

"I would love the chance at putting about six shots into your pathetic body," Bonnie said to Stemple, her voice low and mean. "So if you want to live, let the woman go."

Wow, Cavanaugh was impressed with the power Bonnie had in her voice. Cavanaugh hoped that power would never be directed at him like that. No wonder people had been worried about him when they learned she was his partner.

Stemple glanced behind him.

"Nowhere to run," Cavanaugh said. "They have disarmed your explosives and are coming down the tunnel behind you. So hands in the air."

Stemple finally let go of the woman, who immediately went sideways away from him.

"Move toward us," Bonnie said, low and mean once again.

After a moment Stemple did as told.

As he reached the opening, Cavanaugh held his gun on him while Bonnie patted him down, then said, "On your knees."

Stemple did and Bonnie planted a foot solidly in the middle of his back and shoved him hard, face first onto the concrete.

He went down scraping his face and hands. "Hey!"

"That was for what you did to your sister," Bonnie said. "And move a muscle and I'll show you what I think of what you did to all those other women."

At that moment the woman in the wedding dress walked up to him and kicked him with high heels solidly in the side of the head, rolling Stemple over like a rag doll.

"And that's for what you did to me," the woman said.

Stemple was now out cold and Bonnie moved over to the woman in the wedding dress, getting her back and away.

Cavanaugh just smiled, keeping his gun pointed at the unconscious pervert, doing his best to not add a kick to the guy just for good measure.

Damn, he wanted to.

FORTY-ONE

January 24th, 2019
Las Vegas, Nevada

BONNIE LOOKED around the crowded Main Street Station Buffet, finally spotting Cavanaugh sitting by himself at a table in the back, near a stained-glass window. Wow, that man was handsome. She noticed that more and more with each passing day.

And he was fun to be with as well, something she hadn't expected to find in any man near her age.

He saw her headed his way and waved, a smile lighting up his face and making him even more handsome. She loved how he laughed easily and his sense of humor could match hers.

And he was smart, really smart. No wonder he had had such a great reputation as a detective before he retired.

Now tonight, they were meeting for dinner before heading to the Cold Poker Gang meeting to get their second case. Andor had told her yesterday that he was almost afraid to give them another one after how the first one had blown up on them.

But they both had gotten nice calls from old friends and even the Chief of Police on how well they handled the case.

In the four days since they had arrested Danny Stemple, they had given a dozen interviews, sorted once more through Stemple's papers in Cavanaugh's house, sorting and labeling all of them, and turned them all over to Detective Fawn.

And then leaving at sunrise the next morning, they had driven up to Seattle to talk with Myra and give her the full story of how she was now safe and why.

They had spent a night along the way in Oregon, in separate rooms, enjoying a great dinner and some wine on a log deck overlooking a peaceful river. The motel itself was made entirely of log cabins and each room had a real wood fire going.

It was a wonderful drive and a wonderful dinner and evening. She hadn't enjoyed herself so much in a long time.

They had talked with Myra early the next afternoon, then the two Seattle detectives, then they had had coffee with Cavanaugh's daughter before heading back to the same log cabin motel in Oregon for a late dinner and more wine.

Cavanaugh's daughter seemed wonderful and was surprised and pleased to see Bonnie with her dad. She had given Bonnie a hug as they left and said softly, "Good luck."

On that second night in that wonderful log hotel on the river, Bonnie had really wanted to suggest they just share a room, but she hadn't. They hadn't even known each other for a week yet. They had time.

And she was honestly looking forward to that time ahead of them.

Now they were back in Las Vegas with just enough time to stop by their places, change clothes and get a shower, and get ready for their second Cold Poker Gang meeting. And with the smell of KFC filling that house, there was no chance they were going in there this time hungry.

Cavanaugh stood as she approached the table, always the old-fashioned gentleman. She loved that about him as well. He had changed into new jeans, some expensive running shoes, and had on a silk shirt under a brand new sports coat that actually fit him. He didn't look like he was hiding from anything tonight.

And that made him even more handsome. She shook her head to clear that thought away.

Time.

They had time. But if they waited too long, she was just going to have to jump him.

"Got you an iced tea," he said. "You hungry?"

"Starved," she said. "That lame excuse of a hamburger in Barstow just didn't hold me."

"Oh, that's what that was that I ate," he said, turning toward the buffet. "At least here the food is recognizable."

"And I can't tell you how thankful I am for that," Bonnie said.

He laughed and together they walked toward the buffet, something she hoped they would do for many years to come.

FORTY-TWO

January 24th, 2019
Las Vegas, Nevada

CAVANAUGH WATCHED Bonnie come toward him, trying not to stare at the beautiful woman he had just spent a very adventurous week with. She had changed into jeans and a white silk blouse and had a thin yellow jacket over her gun and badge. She moved with grace through the tables and toward him in the Main Street Station Buffet.

In just a week knowing her he had come to love watching her walk.

And he had been amazed at how much he enjoyed just being with her. Even the long drive in three days to Seattle and back had shown him that he enjoyed her company no matter what they were doing.

Never in his imagination, since the death of his wife, had he thought he could feel like this for another person. Yet here he was, retired, with a new partner, and falling in love. Go figure.

They ate quickly because they didn't want to be too late to the meeting, then she asked as they were leaving if she could leave her car here and just ride with him.

"Feels like that is a natural thing to do this time," she said.

"I would love that," he said, smiling. He had wanted to suggest it, but had been afraid to, actually.

"How about you swing your car back to your garage and I'll pick you up out front," he said. "We got the few extra minutes that would take."

So they did and as she climbed into the front seat beside him, he reached over and touched her arm.

"This has been an amazing and really fun first week, partner," he said. "Thank you."

Her smile lit up her face and filled her eyes and she put her hand on top of his. "I have a suspicion it's only the first of many, many to come."

"Damn, I hope so," he said, turning to start the car. "So can we tell your friends I survived?"

"Oh, my," she said, laughing, "one week and getting confident I see."

"Just proud of myself is all," he said.

And with that she laughed.

Ten minutes later, surrounded by the smell of KFC, they went down the stairs together, arm-in-arm, into the game room of Lott and Julia's house. And as they appeared to the gathered detectives, they got a standing round of applause.

They reached the bottom of the stairs and both stopped and bowed.

And outside of the week before meeting Bonnie, that might have been the best moment of Cavanaugh's life.

Or at least the best moment of the week.

He had a hunch with Bonnie, he had a lot of great moments ahead.

—

Coming in the Next Issue
Hot Springs Meadow
A Thunder Mountain Short Novel

All Issues Are All Still Available

#1...October 2013

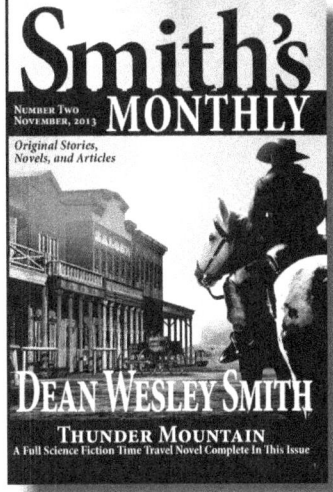

#2...November 2013

#3...December 2013

#4...January 2014

#5...February 2014

#6...March 2014

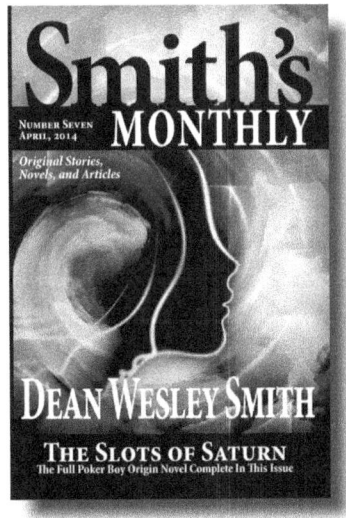

#7...April 2014

#8...May 2014

#9...June 2014

#10...July 2014

#11...August 2014

#12...September 2014

#13...October 2014

#14...November 2014

#15...December 2014

#16...January 2015

#17...February 2015

#18...March 2015

#19...April 2015

#20...May 2015

#21...June 2015

#22...July 2015

#23...August 2015

#24...September 2015

#25...October 2015

#26...November 2015

#27...December 2015

#28....Januaray 2016

#29...February 2016

#30...March 2016

#31...April 2016

#32...May 2016

#33...June 2016

#34...July 2016

#35...August 2013

#36...September 2016

#37...October 2016

#38...November 2016

#39...December 2016

#40...Januaray 2017

#41...February 2017

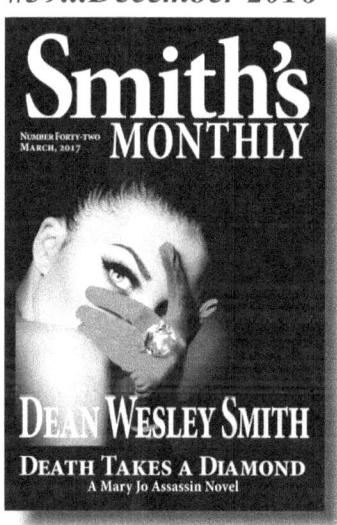

#42...March 2017

#43...April 2017

#44...May 2017

#45...January 2021

www.ingramcontent.com/pod-product-compliance
Lightning Source LLC
Chambersburg PA
CBHW081151170626
46813CB00009B/3151